SUICIDE RUNNERS

SUICIDE RUNNERS

A NOVEL

KEVIN THOMAS

Suicide Runners
© 2024, Kevin Thomas
ISBN: 979-8-9896496-1-7
Library of Congress Control Number: 2024910855

Cover art, "Full Court Run"
© 2024, Danny Voight

First Edition, 2024

Printed in the United States of America

Cover design: Danny Voight
Layout design: Krystle May Statler
Author photograph: Paige McLaughlin

for my mom,
the great artist

Oregon is alive. The trees fight one another for the forty inches of annual rainfall. Towards the end of Fall, when lesser trees wither, when their leafy offspring jump to their independent yellow and burnt orange deaths, the crisp blue sky clings to bare limbs. Follow the Columbia River west from Riverview High School to the Pacific and you can run to the edge of the horizon atop the South Jetty. Jumping from one man-laid boulder to another, shrouded in fog, you can stand in the spray of crashing waves at the tip of the world and watch the fishing ships and starfish fight the unforgiving waters for their daily bread. When God made the Earth, when It laid the framework for this plot of land, It was clumsy. Mountains smash against one another. Rivers intersect at odd angles. Lowland valleys press in amongst high peaks. Cliffs drop without warning to rocky coastlines. When God decided It was done, It demanded rain. And the clouds never knew when to stop. They can only wait for further instruction.

PART ONE

1

There may be a murder at the end of this. Spoiler alert. *Patricide*, to be exact. It's how all father-son relationships end, isn't it? In one way or another. The son must kill the father to blossom into the man he's supposed to be. Isn't that Biblical? Or, at the very least, Oedipal? And what if the father isn't really the boy's father? What if he's a stepfather? Or merely an opaque version of a stepfather? Then what? Then is it just plain old boring murder?

Ever since Father Figure 3.0 fucked everything up a couple of years ago, Greg doesn't have a ton of patience for his half-assed attempts at connecting. Today is October 3rd, 2016, the beginning of basketball season, and Father Figure 3.0 tried to give Greg, who was thickly engrossed in the middle of smearing peanut butter on toast with a knife, a pep talk before Greg left for school. The kind of thing a *real* dad would do. "Listen, um, run hard. Play hard. If you're supposed to make it you'll make it. Like your mom always says, it's in God's hands… or whatever."

Greg raised the knife to his mouth and slowly scraped the remaining extra-crunchy peanut butter off the face of the dull blade with his teeth. "Those are some real invigorating words, Three-point-oh," Greg said. And then he took the butter knife and lopped 3.0's head right off. It fell to the ground, eyes caught in comic surprise as it rolled out of the kitchen, down the hallway, a trail of spongy brains in its wake, towards the bedroom 3.0 shares with Greg's mother, Jasmine, who was just waking up, where 3.0's severed head bumped against the door. Jasmine yelped, "Who's there?" and Greg yelped back, "It's just your sweaty husband and his fat head." Take two. Greg chewed his toast methodically, swallowed, and saluted Father Figure 3.0, whose head was still intact with the rest of his doughy body.

The beige façade of Riverview High School is truly magnificent. A monument to mediocre education. At the center of the windswept courtyard is a flag pole that, if Greg were forced to find a word for it, *soars* toward the gray, cold sky. An extra-large American flag at the top of the pole is whipped by the frigid Columbia Gorge-produced wind. The kind of easterly wind that only the furthest North and Eastern parts of Portland, Oregon, are lucky enough to experience when Fall starts longing for Winter. A group of White students have circled the flagpole, holding hands, heads bowed, petitioning the Lord for a return to a nebulous greatness. The Presidential election is a bit over a month away and Greg, who's White, feels complicit. He panics, drops to a defensive stance, pivots, and heads for a side entrance before any of these prayer warriors from his church recognize him.

Safe within the chaotic blur of students and teachers, Greg meets up with Nassir, his best friend (who is Black) to exchange things (Nassir's Blackness isn't the only defining quality to Greg, but to the outside world, the world beyond the bubble of their friendship, it's pretty much the only thing about Nassir the world cares to notice). Nassir hands Greg a book about *Afropessimism* he finished reading on his walk to school. In return, Greg hands Nassir a PBJ squished inside a clear ziplock bag that Jasmine prepared for Nassir last night. She even tried to write his name on the bag with a Sharpie, but gave up after the first *s* started to smear.

"Nas. My dad had all of Nas's CDs. Tell your mom thank you."

Greg thumbs through the book and reads a line Nassir had underlined: "'Afropessimism is premised on a comprehensive and iconoclastic claim: that Blackness is coterminous with'… there's a lot of words I don't understand in here."

"Good thing I gave you that dictionary last year."

Kids swirl around them. Greg picks up where he left off, "'… Blackness is coterminous with Slaveness: Blackness *is* Social Death: which is to say that there was never a prior meta…' meta… moment?" Nassir looks at the word on the page, and gives Greg a thumbs up, "'… a prior *metamoment* of plentitude, never equilibrium: never a moment of social life.'"

"You're gonna love it."

"How am I supposed to read this with all my school reading?"

"Just 'cause you're in honors and I'm not, Greg, doesn't mean you gotta rub it in my face."

"Come on, you know I—"

Nassir drops his hurt mask and makes his facial muscles do something more like teasing. They laugh and head off in their separate ways. "Thanks for the book!" Greg calls out over his shoulder. Once his focus on the day returns, his stomach drops. Because the real, pressing issue at hand for both Greg and Nassir is: impending basketball tryouts after school at 3:20.

The day's classes dissolve into a fever dream of faces, words, intrapersonal inanities, and an attempt to not think about the only point of the day that matters: the world-ending screech of Coach Day's whistle. If you think about it you've already lost. Total focus on the unthinkable is what's required. Total release of your desire to succeed, "Because," as White Pastor said in church on Sunday, "our desires, our wants, our plans, are nothing but specks of dust in the grand cosmos of God's galaxial-like (sic) concept of time." Or, was that a metaphor for the election? Did it have something to do with masturbation? Everything at church comes back to masturbation. You'd think commandments one through four were about masturbation, given how much White Pastor and his youth leaders talk about it in youth group. Masturbation, abortion, virginity. Don't do any of those things (well, don't *not* be a virgin until you're married) and then you'll get into heaven. Easy. Life's easy as blessed American (*White)* Evangelical Christians, the Church with a capital C says. Just be like us and all will be fine. Oh and sure, love some of your neighbors and all that, but really, just don't touch yourself too much and, if you're of voting age, vote the right side of the ballot. When White Pastor made the galaxy comment, Nassir, who was there in church with Greg because Jasmine insisted that he come, leaned in close to Greg and whispered, "White Pastor has all the answers."

Pay attention. Suddenly, there's only one minute left before school's out. Greg is focused on the clock above Mr. Hatton's balding head. Not a one of Greg's Honors English classmates—his conspicuously White classmates—is listening to Mr. Hatton. Not that Greg has ever questioned, in an official way, the racial makeup of the honors program at the relatively diverse Riverview High School; or even questioned the supposed academic achievements that landed *him* into the Honors program in the first place, and *not* Nassir—who's categorically and state-test-verifiably way, way smarter than Greg—but he has definitely thought about it in a defiant if not protesting way.

Focus. This is the final basketball season. Senior year. Five days of tryouts. An expected 18-20 wins. The last chance for Greg, Nassir, and the rest of the Seniors to make the State playoffs—something Riverview hasn't done since anyone under 65 can remember. The last chance to have their faces immortalized online in the Oregonian. All that clickable fame. It's 3:14 now.

"You've got nothing to be sorry about," Nassir says.

"I feel like it's my fault. You know?"

"Your stepdad's, possibly," Nassir admits. "But, then, how far back do we go to assess and assign blame? Frank Wilderson III believes we've never left the plantation state, so maybe there's no blame needed. Maybe it's all just worked out the way it was designed to have worked out. Even down to these:"

Nassir is wearing Vans. Skater shoes. Not basketball shoes. Greg and Nassir have been best friends since before time; since before the fact that their skin color is different was an issue known to them; since before they knew race would eventually be the central component of their relationship, and, more importantly, the primary tenet exerting a heavy-handed power over Nassir's life. Nassir's dad is Black, his mom is White. You'd think it wouldn't matter anymore, the "mixing." But it's 2016, and for the past eight years, there has been a Black man in that Whitest of houses, so it matters. There was an assembly last week that the whole school was forced to attend, where a White history teacher, Mr. Brian, who happens to be Greg's brother-in-law, tapped the mic and straightened his cardigan and informed the sea of faces that White domestic terrorist groups had experienced an explosion in membership in the years following Obama's election, and, in his words, "Portland is a donut hole of progressive ideals surrounded by a state full of *good ol' country folk*." Mr. Brian's point was, basically, after a series of fairly self-righteous tangents about equality and equity ("equity" said each time as if he was reciting a magic spell), that the power of Whiteness still matters in Portland. Nassir and Greg haven't talked about it, directly, too much. Race. Racism. Responsibility. The three Rs of informal education. They don't fully know what or how to talk about it. So, Nassir gives Greg the books he reads, the books he got from his father, and, for now, they are content with that arrangement. All they know for sure, for now, since Nassir is wearing Vans instead of basketball shoes, is that:

"You can't wear those to tryouts. Coach will kill you."

Vans. The same worn-out black-and-white things Nassir wears every day. They're standing just inside the locker room, contemplating Nassir's shoes at 3:15 p.m.—only five minutes before they are required to be on the court. Nassir shakes the embers out of his eyes and, ultimately, shrugs.

Scraggly kids of all colors and ethnicities, equal in that each of them has no chance of making varsity, and that each of them will barely register a narrative blip in Greg and Nassir's world, burst from the locker room, zipping towards their demise, oblivious to their impending doom. They scream "Hell yea!" and "Let's go!" and "Fuck yea!" They lie to themselves and build up ephemeral self-defenses as they plot their crossovers and stepback moves they saw on TikTok last night. "Nice shoes, Nassir!" Their laughter precedes and accompanies and trails after them.

"I don't know what to do."

Greg can see it in his eyes: the desperation Nassir shows only to Greg in razor-thin slices of authenticity. "We'll figure something out."

Nassir was woken up this morning by the shrieks of his mother before the sun was even up. There were heavy footsteps. Something crashed. Nassir heard the deep bass of his father's voice who, months prior, as demanded by Nassir's mother, was banned from their tiny apartment. Nassir rushed into the living room.

"Monty, stop it!" screamed Nassir's mother, Gloria.

"It's for his own good!" Monty screamed back.

"Dad?"

Monty and Gloria froze, mid-struggle. Monty held Nassir's basketball shoes in his left hand, up and away from Gloria. Monty had scissors in his right hand. Nassir's shoes were in tatters. Someone banged on the front door. The shadow of a man's head trying to look through the thin curtains bobbed in and out of view. "Gloria! You okay in there?" It was Phil, their nosy neighbor. Their neighbor who always lingered at the door when Gloria and Nassir came home. Who always gave Nassir that extra look. A middle-aged White guy with an impressively round belly who is never not wearing his Air Force hat—just in case you questioned whose side he was on. He banged on the window, "You need me to call the cops?" The imperial shadow of his head bobbed left and right. He pressed his hand against the glass, trying to see the unseeable. Trying to be the hero. Answering the primal call of the White woman put in harm's way by the Black man. That age-old struggle White society was built upon.

"Everything's fine!" hollered Gloria. She didn't want the cops to come in with their guns and bullets and fingers that were triggered by faces like Monty's and Nassir's.

The wire that runs vertically inside Monty's neck bulged red against his dark brown skin. Monty calmly placed the scissors and shoes down. He removed a device with a dial on it from his pocket (the same one he's had ever since the operation a couple of years ago). The device connects to a cord that runs from the device directly into Monty's chest and underneath his clavicle. He slowly turned the dial up and smiled, accordingly.

"What'd you do to my shoes?"

Phil banged on the door again. "Gloria! GLORIA!"

"Go away, Phil!" Gloria yelled back. Yelled at him like a lover.

Monty looked at Gloria, his wife of two decades, like she was a stranger. Better yet, like she was a Corinthian column—if not in form, in spirit. Holding up the roof over Monty and Nassir's heads. Threatening collapse. Monty looked at Gloria and realized she'd always represented death at a moment's notice—

"Can you hear that, Son? Hear the history in her voice? Maybe it's in her genes. I don't know if she can help it or not."

"Hear what? It's all in your fucking head!" Gloria wailed, crumpled. "Get out, Monty. Go!"

Phil yanked on the doorknob, "I'm coming in!"

"You've been reading my books, you know what I'm talking about," Monty said to Nassir. "They'll do anything, anything to prove they're human."

Monty was right. Nassir had been reading his books. But, reading the books, knowing the words, the ideas, even feeling the truth, deep down, in his bones, every day, still hadn't given Nassir the words he would need for this scene: Dad falls apart. Dad rips apart shoes. Dad blames unseeable forces.

Monty could see speechlessness envelop Nassir. "He said something about you—"

"Who did?" asked Nassir.

Phil threw his shoulder against the door. Gloria hyperventilated.

"He asked about tryouts, about you and Greg. I thought he was going to do something to you, to your shoes. Because you can never underestimate them, Nassir. You can never underestimate how far they'll go to erase us."

Nassir knew that Monty believed what he was saying, and knew he believed he was protecting him, but as he surveyed the cut shoelaces, the ripped-apart soles, the untethered tongues of his new Nikes scattered around the floor, he didn't know what he was going to tell Coach Day. Gloria whimpered. Phil raged against the door. Nassir shut his eyes.

"Get out of here, Monty!"

Monty took Nassir's shoes and pushed open the door, knocking Phil to the ground. He looked back through the open doorway, the gray morning light washed over his frame, and Monty thought Gloria looked like a wide, sweeping porch, looked like a hot summer sun, looked like a broken cotton gin.

Now, Nassir is on the court wearing Marcel's old, red and black Jordan XIIs. Marcel was headed to the gym, following his pre-basketball ritual of sucking down three consecutive monster hits off the one-hitter he keeps inside the secret compartment he built in his locker, when he saw Greg and Nassir standing there looking like, in Marcel's words, "Someone just murdered your fucking puppy." They told Marcel what happened and he said, simply, "I got you." Seconds later, he was back, shoes in hand. "They might smell a little like the beneficent herb because they've been in my locker, but they're better than nothing."

"Marcel." Nassir was truly touched. "You are my supplier and my savior."

When Greg and Nassir pushed open the gym doors at 3:21, an entire minute late, Coach Day assaulted them with an infinity of curse words. And now the whistle is screaming. The whistle is the enemy. The whistle is pain. The whistle is correction. Greg and Nassir suck at the air around them, chests heaving.

On the track circling above the gym like a quarter-mile halo, cheerleaders watch the sweating basketball pledges below. They kick and stretch and practice their tight-elbowed claps. Jenny Owendale and her auburn hair are up there with Naya and the rest of the cheerleaders. To Greg, Jenny Owendale is perfect in every way.

Last year, Greg dunked on a defender in a game against Madison. The cheerleaders leaped off their feet and the crowd exploded and shouted their approval into Greg. Jenny Ownedale yelled *his* name, ecstatically, and he almost fainted. His dad, the biological one, had said he would try and make it to the game but was nowhere to be found amongst the hollering audience.

But who cares, because Andre the Captain has a forty-one-inch vertical. Marcel a thirty-six-inch vertical. Nassir a twenty-three. Manny, forty when high, thirty-four when un-high. Ben Jones, thirty. Greg, thirty-eight or forty on a good day. Okay, but Manny is *always* high off Marcel's stuff.

The whistle. Turn and run the other way as the whistle commands. No, don't just run, sprint. Sprint like your fucking salvation depends on how fast you can make your body sprint. Knees high. Hands like blades slicing the air. The kid who didn't run all summer is bent over underneath the bleachers throwing up. Everyone can hear him. He has nothing left to give, but he keeps on retching. It sounds like he's attempting to time his heaves with the whistle. Jenny Owendale, and the rest of the cheerleaders, laugh and point.

The whistle blows. It obliterates. Greg is first on the other side. Nassir is a close fourth, a handsome smile spreading across his face. Muscles seize up and collude towards cramps. "Cramps are real fucking common," Coach Day likes to say, "for those who are weak of spirit. Lacking fortitude and such." Water is rationed in Coach Day's practices, because water, too, is a sign of weakness. Water is a reward. Water is only allowed *before* the first whistle and *after* the last whistle of each day of tryouts. "And if anyone's got a problem with it, go ahead and quit right now."

Coach Day needs the team to be better than last year. Even better than the lofty expectations of the Riverview community at large. Actually, he needs them to be demonstrably better than any team that came before this year, regardless of coach. Coach Day is the first Black head coach in the history of the Riverview High School men's basketball team. Certain members of the neighborhood blamed Obama for Coach Day's hiring two years prior. Coach Day felt the judgmental eyes on the back of his head after every crucial foul shot was missed last year in the final regular season game, causing them to miss the playoffs. The game lost *because* of missed free throws. The game lost because Coach Day, obviously, didn't force the team to practice enough free throws like a good coach (see, *White coach*) surely would've. Coach Day, who has yellowing eyes from years of covertly downing brown liquor, will most likely get a pink slip from the community if the team doesn't, at the very least, make the playoffs.

Whistle. Sprint. Whistle. Sprint. Coach Day walks with a limp that appears medical. Nassir hypothesizes, currently, between ragged breaths as they sprint, that the limp in question is, "Probably from his days in 'Nam, the shit, the bush," wheezes Nassir. "When he was an Army Ranger whose detail it was to investigate his own platoon, per the Sarge's orders, to see who or maybe *whom* was bordering on borderline alcohol and slash or substance abuse. 'So don't try and come to my goddamn mother fucking practice high off that weed or or or drunk because you won't last in here! Not on my goddamn watch!' And while Army Ranger Major Coach Day was snooping around his bunkmate's bunk one balmy 'Nam night, he got stabbed in the back," says Nassir. "And rightfuckinglyso! as he was proverbially," Nassir takes a deep breath as the whistle forces them to turn and run the other way. "Proverbially stabbing his whole fucking platoon in the back. Hoo-rah!"

A trio of White wrestlers, running laps around the track, draped in sweat-filled plastic garbage bags, echo Nassir's HOO-RAH. Missing the point.

The whistle graduates to a spiritual death. Greg and Andre are stride for stride down the other side of the court. Their feet are thunder. Their bodies eternal.

Finally, after sixty minutes of torture (and, also, long after Coach Day disappeared but then moments later reappeared in a window above the court on the far end of the track, not once but twice, and just stood there and watched as he sipped a spiked Diet Coke while an insane, make-your-lungs-bleed, 99.99% running "basketball" drill was proctored by Rob the Assistant Coach [incidentally, RAC is the biggest block of a man anyone's ever seen: cut with muscles like an onyx Greek statue, complete with an Arkansas drawl and knees that creak and pop from his days playing D-lineman for the Steelers; the man who broke a backboard, and has the plexiglass shards to prove it, while playing for the University of Arkansas; standing 6'8" and weighing in at 280 pounds, who can curl 100-pound barbells without breaking a sweat; the very same RAC who'd give a kid his XXXL black leather duster off his back in the cold, give rides home when moms or dads don't show, and hugs so tight that rib cages snap-crackle-pop like the flavorless cereal Greg's mom always buys because she likes the way it sounds in the bowl]), Coach Day and RAC now stand, finally, on the sideline watching those attempting to make the Men's Varsity Basketball Team for the Riverview Broncos of Riverview High School in

Portland, Oregon, in GOD DAMN MOTHER FUCKING AMERICA, run a full-court, 5-on-5 scrimmage.

The whistle demolishes eardrums. Blood pours from ear canals as if a spigot in each of their brains has opened. Greg and Nassir are teamed with Andre the Captain and two underclassmen scrubs. Andre passes the ball to one of the amorphous blobs. Every dribble looks like it could be, maybe even *should* be, the scrub's last—like he might just fall over and succumb to whatever is or isn't lying in wait beyond the gym doors holding the real world at bay. Everyone feels it.

But look, there's Monty now. Do you see him up there, on the other side of the huge windows facing the dark courtyard high above the gym's floor? See how he presses his face to the window, searching for Nassir? See Monty scratch at the poorly placed wire in his neck?

And now Scrub-A passes to Scrub-B as Greg ducks around a screen from Andre and pops out behind the three-point arc. The ball's seams are wobbling, indicative of a weak pass. Due to this weak pass, Scrub-B will be sliced open and fed upon, his thin blood bolstering the strong.

Monty raps his knuckles on the window. Louder and louder.

So loud it's all anyone can hear.

Nassir cuts through the key and the ball is already there—a strong pass from Greg. Nassir lays it up easily. He barely pats the backboard. Mostly he just gets his fingers on the protective foam around the bottom of the plexiglass. Andre yells out, "You got your mom's jumping genes!"

This is how the game of basketball is played. This is how you do basketball things on the basketball court. On the basketball court, Greg and Nassir can ignore all that should be but isn't talked about between best friends. Greg and Nassir slap hands nonchalantly. The nonchalantness is key to impressing all spectators (especially when wearing someone else's old basketball shoes). This is easy, the hands say. Life is conquerable and understandable, the smack of hands proclaims. We will live gloriously rich lives free of strife or anguish. The cheerleader, Naya, who Nassir's in love with, stretches her shining brown legs as she watches and smirks and is perfectly perfect with Jenny Owendale suspended in air above the gym. Shoes squeak. Greg and Nassir backpedal, elbows pumping, to get back on defense.

Look, Monty's up there yelling "Nassir! Nassir!" from behind the windows, forehead against the cold glass. His face gets lost in a new fog with every breath.

Manny grabs Nassir by the shoulders and turns him back to the action on the court. He shakes Nassir and tells him to focus, to forget him. Easy for Manny to say, Manny is high as a fucking kite.

Coach Day nods to RAC, who chugs off towards the exit. Nassir has been on antidepressants ever since his parents unofficially split two summers ago. The decision to separate came after Monty accused Gloria's head of being bodiless. Nassir told Greg it makes his mouth dry, the anti-depressants. But look! Greg steals a pass out around the three-point line and is slapping the backboard on the other end with his full palm as loud as he can before Coach Day can even get a half-slurred insult out to Scrub-C. Greg would've dunked it, but his left leg seized as he jumped. Most likely it's God smiting him for masturbating last night, violating Commandments two through four.

And here is Monty, finally, entering through the door that RAC exited from. The cheerleaders abandon their chants. The gym settles into an awkward silence. Nassir looks up and wonders if Naya knows who this large man is who lumbers towards him.

"Nassir! I'm sorry. There was nothing in your shoes. I thought there might be a bomb because he asked about you—."

RAC charges back across the court. A few kids snicker quietly, practice jerseys pulled up over their sweaty mouths. Nassir tries to say something, but can't find the words. This is why he talks the way he does sometimes. Easier to fake the words and emotions than not be able to find the right words. His face flushes hot. Greg puts a reassuring hand on Nassir's shoulder. They watch, everyone watches, as RAC gently corrals Monty to his broad chest, whispering in his ear as he leads him towards the exit. The White kids on the court do that thing where they give a half-knowing glance to each other. A look that says, *Exactly*. Once Monty, whimpering and apologetic, is removed from sight, attention snaps back to Nassir. He explodes. He flies like Superman through the roof and into the deafening silence of space!

The whistle blows. The kid under the bleachers vomits.

In Riverview, Fall nights slap the skin with a freshly chilled hand. Nassir picks at his thumb. The other kids are long gone. The coaches, too. Rob the Assistant Coach offered a ride, as always, but Greg and Nassir said they were good, said a ride was coming, said one of their parents probably wouldn't forget them this time. They're sitting on the curb next to the gym door, knees pulled up to their chests, still waiting.

"My dad said he might buy the Mustang the Niemanns are selling," Nassir says. He stares across the empty parking lot.

"Really?" Greg tries not to sound too disbelieving.

"This morning. When I was leaving for school. After the whole shoe ordeal. After I pushed our neighbor Phil to the ground again on my way out to catch my dad."

Greg blinks. Be heroic. Look heroic. He should ask Nassir how he feels about Monty not only ripping apart his shoes but then showing his face and grotesque neck and beanied head at school. Greg should ask how Nassir feels, deep down, with all this flattening of his family, and how he, as the role of best friend, can help, beyond just being there in the generic sense and reading Nassir's books and playing basketball and video games and housing boxes of Cheez-Its with him. He should, shouldn't he? ask Nassir how he's doing with the whole rise of the White hate groups, the police killings of Black men and boys that look like Nassir; how he, Greg, Greg Hazel (if you include the last name it sounds more significant), can, if need be, fight for Nassir—*when* need be. Greg should, at the very least, ask about what it's been like at home, alone with his mom ever since Monty had the surgery and then was kicked out. But then there's the whole question of guilt-by-association in the matter.

"What'd your mom say? About the Mustang?"

"Not much." Nassir smiles thinly against a frosty breeze.

"The Niemanns are the ones with the twins who go to Jesuit, right?"

"Marcy and Melinda."

"Does it run?"

"Fuck if I know, Gregory."

"Why do parents always give twins names with the same first letter?"

"One of life's great mysteries."

Three Black teenagers, wearing dark hoodies, fingers and eyes aglow with cigarettes, emerge from the darkness and saunter across the parking lot. Greg and Nassir keep their eyes straight ahead as the trio blazes through the night, chuckling at an inside joke between staccato drags. Chuckling at the implication of danger their appearance is supposed to have added to the scene.

"Marcy's the cute one, right?" Greg asks.

"Melinda," Nassir corrects. "Marcy's got the chin thing."

"Oh, yeah. So what, you'd fix it if it didn't run?"

"Her chin?"

"The Mustang."

"I guess."

"You know how?"

Nassir takes and releases a deep, exhausted breath. "He said Mr. Niemann wouldn't properly speak to him. 'Not man to man, you see, Nassir,' he said. 'Men speak plainly and directly to men, no matter what color they are' is what he told me. I don't know. Maybe he's right."

"Mr. Niemann's always been a prick. Maybe your dad'll buy it for Christmas."

"A possibility," says Nassir, as he forms another icy cloud out of nothing. An alchemist.

Nassir, it's me, Greg. Can you hear me?

Yes, Greg, I can hear your thoughts loud and clear.

Nassir, the impending season feels like the rising tide of an ocean sucking at our ankles. The whitewash gripping and pulling us towards cresting waves.

That's poetic. Greg, I don't have words, the right words, to explain the pain.

God didn't give us the words we need. It's a failure of the infallible Bible—

Greg, please get out of my head. My dad already lost his mind.

A car with one headlight winks past; the light's weak beam filtering through the mist.

"Can you imagine though, if it did run? The Mustang," dreams Nassir. "Things would be different."

"You think?"

Nassir blinks into a gust of wind, eyes watering. He zips up his sweatshirt. Greg hopes Nassir's not crying.

They both check their phones.

They both ignore everything.

They both dive into the black hole's glow of the endless scroll.

It pummels them. The everything.

It's never-ending.

It blows in on the wind. It rushes up the vacant lot. It is constant and metallic under your tongue. It is *the everything* that must be ignored in moments like this.

But everything is so clear, so vivid at the beginning of the season.

Everything holds back the edge.

The curtains haven't even been pulled open. They're left to wander backstage, rehearsing rehearsed lines.

Nassir, it's me again, Greg.

Greg, you're coming in loud and clear.

Do you remember last year's game at Hood River?

Vividly.

Do you remember how the White parents blamed Manny and Andre for the loss? I have a confession, no, shh, just listen, I have a confession to make: I started the fight. Manny and Andre were just sticking up for me. They came to my aid. Please, just let me finish: I screamed and hit the other player in the gut with my elbow as hard as I could. But Manny and Andre were given techs. At church, in secret, I hear them talk about America like God destined us, White people, to have it. It's this thing. I don't know how else to explain it yet, Nassir. This big said but unsaid thing. If you really listen, you can hear it in every prayer. Every sermon. Every time they end a sentence with and. I think it's tied together, the techs Manny and Andre got, the way the White ref slammed his hands together in front of their faces, their Black faces. I think it's all on the same spectrum.

But, Greg, I missed the free throws at the end. I had a chance to win it.

Monty wasn't there. How can a kid be expected to perform in a moment like that when his dad's not there? And that's what I'm talking about, it's all on the same spectrum. Spectrum's the wrong word, probably. But the reason Monty wasn't there—it's all part of this big unsaid thing. Maybe they're saying it somewhere, but not in church. Not here. Not in Riverview.

You're right, Greg. His life is nothing but a long flight from others and from himself. He's been alienated even from his own Black body, Greg. His emotional life's been cut in two. He's been reduced to pursuing the impossible dream of universal brotherhood… in a world that rejects him. A White world, Greg.

Nassir, holy shit, that was deep.

Those aren't my words, they're Sartre's. I'm paraphrasing. Oh, look, our ride is here.

2

Tryouts

On the second day, Nassir decreed Marcel a saint for the selfless nature of his soul when Marcel handed Nassir his Jordan XIIs for the rest of tryouts and, "If you need 'em, Nas, the rest of the season." The young men of all colors and creeds in the locker room paused, waiting on Nassir's response. *Be the clown*, their silence demanded.

Nassir's face morphed in minuscule ways, an invisible mask, as he wiped away a fake tear, "From here on out, Marcel's new name is 'Marcel the Supplier'; a saint to be idolized and modeled by all." It was too far, too theoretical, too much for the masses. Morale plummeted. In response, Nassir's face changed again, muscles shifting to mock outrage, "Wait, wait just a minute. What's this? Here you are, treating me like a brother, but…"

There was a deep, unnerving silence. The silence plumbed the depths of awkwardness; rooted around and made a home there in its frantic, unsure energy. Marcel the Supplier looked to Greg for help, but Greg was just as confused as the rest.

"I'm just trying to help."

"A bomb! A fucking nuclear bomb in this shoe! What White man paid you to do this to me?" Nassir pretended to rip the shoe apart and inspect every inch of the Jordans with a tilted grin. He scratched his neck, rubbed his chest, ran trembling hands through his hair, "They're everywhere!"

The locker room is filled with the boys who survived the first day's cuts, who hope their lives will always be bright and clear, and that their gooey brains will never turn their backs on them, like Monty's supposedly did, and that the color of their skin will never be a death sentence, erupted in laughter, *Because you, Nassir, Nassir Chissler, son of the town-crazy, son of Monty the Crazy Black Guy, saved us from complicated thoughts of past and present and future, and now, instead of depression, our laughter will launch us, full of unassailable joy, into the second day of whistles!*

Nassir dropped, exhausted, onto the bench next to Greg.

Tryouts continued and were maniacal. An all-out shart show. A vortex of sweat and shouts. Larger bodies slammed into smaller ones. Hard, pointy elbows crushed soft, breakable ribs. Dehydrated lips spat viscous saliva onto the floor and onto hands; those arthritic hands rubbed the spit onto the soles of Nikes, Adidas, Jordans, Pumas. Spit hung from gaped mouths. Rob the Assistant Coach was officially assigned "Monty Look-out Duty."

Coach Day screamed until his throat bled. Blood splattered onto the court during a tirade that was so glorious, so epic, it became its own day, its own sunrise and sunset, a day that would forever be spoken of with a reverie and joy unthinkable in the moment. Another half were cut after day two. Bodies began to fail on day three. Legs cramped at right angles, chests collapsed. Another half were cut. Day four commenced, sadistically, at five-thirty in the blackness of a frozen morning. Basketballs weren't even touched for the first two hours, let alone taken out of the tattered mesh bag. Instead, the remaining twenty basketballers were instructed to perform defensive slides with their knees bent at ninety-degree angles, zig-zagging up and down the court, monastically chanting "De! Fense!" towards a destination of timed wall-sits with their knobbed spines flush against the

SUICIDE RUNNERS

wall. Everything trembled. Three more were cut.

Now, day five, the remaining seventeen boys, beaten and silent, circle the Bronco logo at half-court and wish death upon Coach Day—and upon their godless bodies—and pray that the man next to them, be him best friend or enemy, White or Black or Brown or Tan, will be one of the last cuts. They have come too far. Coach Day puffs his cheeks full of air, eyes tightening, relishing the moment, and he blows his whistle. Annihilating the present.

After all the build-up, the final day of tryouts ended unceremoniously. Nothing but a curt whistle and a proclamation that the list would be posted on a wall outside a door the following morning. A silent, slumped mass of bodies wandered around the gym because muscles and minds had been pushed to their limits, then past perceived limits, and welcomed to the limit's other side by waves of burning exhaustion and numb robotic movements. Seventeen jaws hung slack, thirty-four eyes bulged. Shooting, dribbling, and defensive drills had drilled into and then *through* the pain.

Pain had become philosophical. A new religion. Greg learned to idolize the pain; worshipped its clear, simple message. He petitioned the pain to allow his body to perform the required basketball tasks. Elbows, knees and fists fought in tight places for inches of advantage. Grunts and guttural heaves were set free inside pain's blur.

Midway through the final day, Nassir appeared to fully submit to pain's demands—keeping one of his eyes closed for nearly the whole ordeal. Andre the Captain chuckled. That exhausted, barely audible kind of chuckle, when he noticed Nassir's pirate eye. He wanted to make a joke, something about Jack Sparrow and Nassir… mixing the names to make it funny, make it "Black Sparrow," but he couldn't muster enough energy to form coherent words.

"Nassir jah prow," is all he managed.

Pain, ultimately, demanded sacrifice and was satiated by a felled Junior during a gladiatorial rebounding drill that pitted two randomly selected boys against each other in a fight for rebounds. The unselected fifteen stood, half-bent, along the baseline and half-watched the two rip and claw for position as RAC intentionally missed shot after shot. Coach Day screamed at the battlers to grab the rebound with two hands, to hold the ball above their heads, elbows out, to do whatever it took to win, and to never let anyone take it from them. "They are coming for you! They're always coming for you!" screamed Coach Day. The White players thought it was a bit much, while the Black players seemed to take it in stride as truth. A knowable, biological truth. Prior to the Junior dropping in a paralytic heap and ending the day, Greg and Nassir were forced to fight each other for the ball's freedom. Coach Day circled their sagging bodies, chewed on his silver whistle, and informed them that friendship meant nothing in the basketball arena. The whistle fucked time and space and RAC began missing shots again. Each ball a live grenade. Greg and Nassir jabbed forearms into each other's stomachs and sternums, hips crashed into groins, legs and feet tangled; their faces a blank canvas inside pain's refuge. Nassir was victorious the first two times, Greg the next four. If there was a metaphor to be found in their struggle, there wasn't enough mental juice left to comprehend anything beyond the ball in the air. Ball hitting rim. Ball in hands. No smiles. No tears. No reactions. Only the whistle. Only the next set of boys made to fight each other's pain. That's when the Junior collapsed to the floor. His head smacked against the wood. A hollow thud. Andre the Captain, the victor, stood over him, chest heaving. If a photographer was present, it would've been a great picture. But there wasn't. Just the rank smell of cold sweat and defeat.

     SUICIDE RUNNERS

4

Nassir wasn't present for the excited huddle outside Coach Day's office the next morning; wasn't an owner of a finger sliding down the list to see if his name was amongst the chosen. Greg and Andre the Captain slapped hands. Marcel the Supplier asked if Greg knew where Nassir was.

"Hold, please."

Nassir, can you hear me? Where are you?

Ten-four, good buddy. Over and out.

"Not sure," Greg reported back.

Manny slurped from a Slurpee as the huddle broke apart. "Is that Cherry?"

"Cherry *Blast*," Manny replied happily, as he sucked up a big enough mouthful of frozen goodness to ice over his brain.

When he was little, Greg hated anything cherry-flavored. The lone exception could be found at the Astoria Ice Cream Company, where he would watch the round man behind the counter dip his vanilla ice cream cone, followed by his half-sister, Shasta's, chocolate cone, into the bubbling vat of cherry syrup. That bright red syrup hardened into an imagination-defying shell. Magic. Physics. God. Angels. Heaven. Ice cream. This was Camping with a capital C. The tradition he never wanted to end. His father, his *real* father, and his half-sister next to him at the counter. His father and his leather belt. Their mom in the car, smoking cigarettes. They felt like a family back then, like the kind of families that school friends talked about. The kind of family that even Nassir had back then. Little Greg would thank the round man like his father instructed as he was handed the cone with the stiff red curl.

"Why'd you let him get such a big cone?" Jasmine asked Greg's father, annoyed, as they climbed back into the car. "It's bigger than his head."

"He wanted it." Simple. Things were simple back then.

Was Jasmine in the backseat? Why would she be? Shasta, seven years older than Greg, old enough to feel the weight of context, looked out the window and bit the curl off her cone.

His father's pale blue eyes strained in the rearview mirror as he put the Buick in reverse. The engine groaned in response. Driving to the coast. To camping at Fort Stevens. The sun blinked behind passing trees. Yellow and green hills gave way to bursts of ocean blue. Greg watched how his father steered with his right hand, left arm resting on the open window. Greg looked back and saw Jasmine's hair blow across her face. He saw his father check her in the mirror. This is how to drive a car. This is how to eat ice cream in a car as your father drives.

We are here. We made it. You can relax. Take a deep breath. It's the first game of the season. A preseason matchup against a lesser school from a lesser division. There was a pep rally at lunch, the band played, cheerleaders tumbled, Jenny Owendale and Naya destroyed worlds, layup lines turned into a dunk contest between Greg and Andre the Captain and Manny (who was super-duper high), and Nassir dribbled and shot with his left hand, his off-hand, the whole time, just because it'd piss off Coach Day. A speech was given by the Athletic Director and his big teeth. And then Coach Day tried to say something but struggled to speak in full sentences without cussing, so he cut it short. It was a whole thing, the pep rally.

Greg, Nassir, and the rest of the team are lined up in the hallway just outside the gymnasium in their green, white and black suits of armor. They bob up and down. They close their eyes. Roll their necks. Shut it out. Let it in. A home game. A holy war. Winter on the horizon. The hands of night progressively reaching further and tighter around the day's neck. Nassir flexes his hands. Greg bends his knees. There's nothing to hear except the waiting crowd's roar.

Nassir, I just wanted to say—

Greg, I can't hear you, it's too loud—

Someone pushes the doors open and a wall of sound hits the team as they take the floor. It's too soon to look at the crowd. To take it all in. What's *it? It* is the mob. The mob's expectations. *It* is what happens when expectations are not met. *It* is the years of practice that led to the arrival of *It* on this public stage. *It* is hiding inside. *It* is waiting to be let out. *It* is a ruiner. A liberator. *It* is watching from above. *It* asks for everything. *It* requires all. *It* is different for Greg and Nassir. For White and Black. Separate and not equal. *It* requires obedience. The skinny White referee spins the ball in his bony hands and mouths rehearsed words to Andre the Captain and the opposing player waiting for the ball to be pushed into the air.

Greg hocks a loogy onto the floor. Rubs his shoe bottoms in the bubbled spit. But he doesn't look around. Doesn't look up. Not too high. Not above the head of Nassir. Not above Nassir's eyes. Look, Nassir's eyes are holes overflowing with magma.

Nassir stares back, smiles vacantly, absently, eyeballs avoiding the windows, the corners, the dark edges of the gym—anywhere that might shelter Monty.

The band blows their horns and beats their drums as the ball sails towards the ceiling. Andre the Captain tips it to Marcel, who passes it to Greg, who is already past his defender, and he catches the ball and pushes it towards the ground with force, a dramatic two-handed dribble, and he slaps the backboard as hard and as loudly as he can, spinning and screaming, bumping chests with Nassir, because they are unleashed, for now, inside the roaring crowd's cocoon of approval.

3
8 October 2008

Day Zero. The day Monty Chissler would see a dead person's leg hanging from the trunk of a black Lincoln Towncar. Monty was in Washington, D.C., waiting at a crosswalk on the corner of U and 14th NW. Northwestern Industrial Solutions Corporation (NISC), Riverview's foremost leader in office & industrial complex solutions, sent Monty, their second-best salesman, to acquire contracts in the nation's capital.

A White Lady in Pink, hunched over next to Monty, mumbled to herself that her pastor said the Y2k conspiracy was hatched by "The Liberals, The Jews and The *Blacks*." And the way she said Blacks (more like *BlaKs*) was reminiscent of the country folk Monty was familiar with just outside of Portland. Monty smirked, not because of her blatant racism, he was after all, at the time, a 40-year-old Black man, so he was used to that, but because Monty was all too familiar with Y2k. He was oddly disappointed when he awoke to the same world that had rolled over the night before on January 1st, 2000. Streetlights still worked. Nuclear power plants hadn't melted down. Planes weren't smashing into each other. The potential to press the reset button on the whole *American* experiment had fizzled away.

His mission in D.C. was simple, though. Monty must finish, just simply finish, the day in which he would see the dead leg (in just one more second) and move on to the next day as if it didn't happen because he promised his wife before he left for the airport that he was done with any and every conspiracy-related thing. No more message boards. No more chat rooms. No more "Deep web shit," as she put it. None of it. Cold turkey.

But, then it happened: a black Lincoln Towncar, with what looked like a dead leg dangling from the trunk, skidded around the far corner. The White Lady in Pink was knocked to the ground as the crush of people jumped back to safety. Monty didn't miss a beat: he clocked the Towncar's license plate before he scrambled to help the woman to her feet. She thanked him. She said he was one of the good ones. Her passive racism flowed right through Monty because he was transfixed. The city swirled about him. Traffic piled up behind him. Monty was scared. No, he was *thrilled*. Alive (again). But no, he told himself, he *must* stay on mission. He *must* keep his promise. But it was too late, it was already in his brain. It buzzed. The what if. The beginning of a new rabbit hole. It itched. He shouldn't itch it, he knew. But he would. He would itch and dig and keep digging.

Monty watched the naked brown leg with the pronounced kneecap, marred by red slashes, bob up and down from the trunk of the Towncar as it disappeared amidst a cacophony of horns, and he knew he wouldn't be able to keep his promise. He took out his notepad and scribbled a hasty note:

H dc crest 99 leg car hairy real? Oct8 9am EST

And it felt so good to do it.

As of this moment, everything about Monty Chissler should be subject to extreme skepticism.

4
October 2016

The application glows on the laptop's screen. Greg's at the kitchen table.

"Where's that application for, honey?" Jasmine's hands and braced wrists work her son's shoulders like she's his corner woman. And isn't that basically what a parent is? "That the George Fox one?"

"U.C.S.B."

"Didn't you see the letter from Coach *Murgle* down there at Fox?"

"…"

"D'you call him back? He called again yesterday. I told you, yeah? Just before you got home from practice. He said he tried your cellphone first. Sounds like a nice guy. Name is a conundrum though, isn't it? Murgle. Mur-gull. Like bugle, or seagull. Sea-gull."

"Bur-gull."

"There you go, burgle's a good one. You see a missed call? We talked for a bit. Coach Burgle and me. I think he's got a good heart. He talked about the way the Lord's been working on the team, how they've really bonded together as men, *an*. Thinks you'd really benefit from the experience." She's folding doilies into perfectly edged half-moons. "Shasta has friends who went there. Said they enjoyed it."

"Then why didn't she go there?"

"Well."

After Jasmine and Greg's father got divorced, a man named Trench showed up, all big smiles and broad shoulders—a man who would greet Greg the same way every time, with a "Whatd'ya say" and a hearty, I'm-a-man kind of slap on the back. Soon after, Shasta moved to *her* biological father's and new stepmom's house on the west side of Portland. Jasmine put up a fight, hoping to convince Shasta to stay. It hurt to watch Shasta go. Packing all her stuff. Leaving behind the unimportant things. The things she wouldn't miss.

When Shasta's father, Matheson, arrived to pick her up, Greg cried and hid behind Jasmine's body. Jasmine held back her sobs until Shasta was out of sight. But she did sob. Greg heard her in the bathroom sucking in great big breaths of sobs.

Jasmine's now telling Greg that last week, in her Women's Bible Study Group, they learned about giving all of our wants and desires to God. Every single one of them. The other Bible Study Ladies practically fought each other to get the last *amen* in after Judy, the outspoken leader of the group, finished the reading.

"Are you doing that?"

"Doing what?"

Jasmine can't stand Judy if she's being honest. But, she goes to the weekly Bible Study because sometimes it's better to make yourself believe in something more powerful than yourself. And, for now, Judy and her minions are palatable. Mostly.

"Giving it all to God?"

"I think so."

"It's called *Kenosis*."

"Okay."

"It's supposed to help."

Jasmine flexes her hands and makes grabbing motions

with her fingers as she rotates her wrists. She's had braces on her wrists for years, ever since she gave birth to Shasta. Her doctor said it was birth-induced carpal tunnel syndrome. She's tried *everything* to fix it. All the doctor-recommended remedies. All the weird-smelling home remedies. Nothing worked until she discovered Tyrell Jones and his workout/dance show on late-night Portland Public Cable Access: *Dancing with Tyrell Jones*. She swears up and down that he's curing her.

Father Figure 3.0 shuffles into the kitchen and rummages through the refrigerator. The yellow glow of the refrigerator's light illuminates half of his extremely punchable face. Outside, it's raining. A mighty thunder should clap. But it doesn't. Instead, Greg grips his pencil like a spear and chucks it at 3.0. It sails right past Jasmine's left ear, through the kitchen, and lodges into 3.0's jugular. Blood sprays inside the refrigerator, covering the milk carton and the orange juice and the purple stuff, too. Father Figure 3.0 drops to his knees, and with his last gurgling, blood-soaked breath, whispers, "You did well, Greg."

Back in reality, Father Figure 3.0 turns on the radio in the kitchen and tunes it to NPR. A man's soft voice crackles to life, asking but trying not to ask for donations. Asking but saying they're doing an anti-fundraising fundraising drive this season. Whatever that means. A woman's nasally voice follows, sharing details about a group of White men and women who stormed a donut shop in Alexandria, Virginia, in an attempt to free the child sex workers that were, according to their online chat rooms, supposedly trafficked from the tiny donut shop's non-existent attic.

Father Figure 3.0 moves behind Jasmine, miming her hand motions as she talks about God's will and how everything that's ever worked out for her, Greg, and Shasta, no matter how it may have looked at first, is because of the unflappable certainty of God's will and His plan for their lives. For everyone's lives. It sounds like she's willing herself to believe it. And now she's laughing at 3.0's lame jokes; now they're tickling each other; now they're in their bedroom where later they'll be fighting. Even later, she'll watch *Dancing with Tyrell Jones*, smiling at the Black, leotarded and shimmering man who is, isn't he? offering her a whole different kind of salvation.

Greg looks down at the page where he's been scribbling half-hearted answers to the essay questions. Question 1: Why do you want to attend UCSB? He wonders how honest they really want these answers to be. He wonders how honest he really wants to be with himself. He closes the laptop.

Later that night, in bed but wide awake, Greg watches the night inch towards sunrise. Trains rumble in the sky. Red eyes plummet toward blinking lights at PDX. Rails of shadows stripe the wall. A new human-shaped shadow moves across the wall. Greg jolts up. Outside the window, Nassir is standing stone-still, looking fully agog. The dark brown of his forehead catches the glint of the bare moon.

What the fuck are you doing out there?

I was looking for my dad. I ended up here.

Maybe actual words are exchanged. But maybe blank stares say more. Say all that needs to be said. Greg grabs a beanie, puts on his basketball shoes, and Nassir silently, excitedly, claps.

Under the glow of the streetlights, below the wispy clouds, Greg blows O-shaped rings. Nassir walks too fast, too slow. Is electric. Frenetic.

Nassir, you okay?

I was out looking for my dad, nightly, as one does. As I do.

Another train blows its hollow horn, screaming past the

upper part of Argay Terrace—Greg's neighborhood, a little over a mile from where Nassir and his mom stay. Wires of blood spike the whites of Nassir's eyes. They pick up speed. Walk with a fiery purpose. When their steps sync into a momentary march, houses tremble.

My mom told me she wished I could just go back to being happy, Greg.

Fuck your mom.

Indeed.

Skeletons, spider webs, witches, and orange and red and purple lights haunt the edges of their directionless path. A coffin over there. A mummy over here. Houses drip with Halloween. A car with darkened windows zips by. The white headlights blind them, leaving them with nothing but rouge dots in the slurry night.

Hey, slow down, Nassir, I don't want to sweat.

Sweat purifies.

A gaping zombie hidden in the shadows of an overgrown front yard moans as they hurry past. Nassir takes a hard right turn up a skinny pathway that slices between two houses, leading to a narrow parkway. These grass and tree-dotted greenspaces criss-cross Argay Terrace. They were a major selling point back when it was a majority-White neighborhood; back when things were supposedly Great. "But we'll see," the worried left-leaning adults in Riverview say, "Hillary'll win," they say; but Greg and Nassir heard from Coach Day that you can't trust these White People with anything. Greg, being White, could've feigned being offended by the comment, but he's not blind. Instead, Nassir mimed being offended on Greg's behalf. Speaking of Nassir, Greg finds him standing behind a tree, holding his body tight to its rough bark. The dark parkway stretches out to their right.

Who are you hiding from?

I told her I'd be happy from here on out. I said, 'Mother, my dearest White Mother! I'll forever smile and laugh and run with elbows out and knees up and everyone'll point, even the White people, Mother. They'll point and say, "Look how happy the Chissler boy is!" They'll say, "See! If he, this Black boy, can be happy, why can't they all be?"' Get closer, Greg, I'm going to whisper to you… the secret is, they want me to be an exception. They love exceptions, these White people do. It makes all the unexceptional so much easier to deal with. I'm telling you this because I can trust you. Can't I?

Maybe words. Maybe just small, puffy plumes of chilled breath. Can words freeze, lose sound and meaning? Greg places a hand on the tree's clammy skin. Here is tree as anchor. Here is tree as buoy. If they both hold on, maybe they won't plummet when the ground gives way. In a large picture window of the only house with a light on, its off-white light soaring out over the greenway, a man stands, backlit. He stares out towards the parkway. Greg and Nassir are fifty yards to the left of the house, just outside the light's edge.

He can't see us, Greg.

We should go.

Nassir's hand slowly moves to Greg's arm. His icy brown fingers flat against Greg's ghostly white wrist. The man's shadow expands across the parkway.

Look, he's sweating, Greg. He feels like a god towering over this trembling terrain, cowering inside the black of his shadow. He is purifying.

Maybe he just works nights? I have to pee, we should go.

No, stay. I'm becoming happy like my White Mother wants. Be witness.

Greg grabs Nassir and makes a move towards home, but he trips on the tree's gnarled roots and crashes to the ground. A sliding door whooshes open.

"Who's out there? I have a gun!" The White man in the window is now the Armed White Man on the back porch; the Armed White Man scanning the parkway; the Armed White Man exerting his 2nd Amendment loudly and proudly. Greg doesn't like the way the man's eyes shift from tree to tree like he's looking for an adventure. A target. The man keeps yelling. Nassir smiles. Eyes joyous.

Here we go, Gregory. The oldest story in the book! He's going to protect his land! Take what's his! Manifest his destiny!

Nassir, let's go!

Greg scrambles to his feet.

"Stop!" the Armed White Man yells, hands braced against the patio's railing.

Words, maybe. Maybe just Nassir stepping into the light, holding his arms out wide, Come and get me, his body says. It's what you want. It's what you need to feel whole. To feel American.

"What the fuck do you think you're doing out there!"

Nassir looks over his shoulder. Greg is still huddled near the tree. Nassir pulls at his shirt with both hands, trying to tear it down the middle.

Nassir! Come on!

Words fail. Memories fail.

Come help me pull apart my shirt! I want to find purity like this bare-chested White man. I need to be happy, says Mother, so I went looking for my father to discover the secret of his happiness. But look, I found this man instead. Now come, Gregory, and help me rip free from this shirt!

He said he has a gun!

They all have guns. Don't you get it? Every single one of them is a gun.

"I'm going to call the cops! You hear me?"

There's death inherent in these movements. Death baked into that word. The threat of the *Boys in Blue* showing up to solve problems. Greg uproots Nassir from his spot and drags him the first few feet before Nassir gives in and laughs—an opaque version of happiness plastered to his face. They jog back down the path to Greg's street.

The pink morning sun creeps up along the eastern edge of the night. How long did they wander? When Greg's house is in sight, Nassir veers off, headed in his own direction.

Tomorrow, at school, at practice, we will continue the fun, Gregory.

Wait. The cops.

(He's right, look: in the sky, like the Bat Signal, the reds and blues swirl against the low clouds. The siren of the righteous. Up and down the streets they go. Searching.)

Greg says it again, *Wait. The cops.*

Nassir tilts his head to the sky and feels the colors press against his skin. *It's just basketball, Greg. That's all I want. I didn't ask for this. Remember Trayvon? Remember his hoodie? Remember his candy? I'm not wearing or holding, Greg. It's just me. My skin. It's my skin they want. Even when I talk like them, like they want me to, even when I lactify my speech, it doesn't matter. All they want is my skin.*

Stay the night. It's not safe out here.

Remember Alton Sterling, Greg? Remember Philando Castile? One day, then the next. Do you remember them, remember this past summer? Does your stepdad know their names? Did your mom talk to you about Alton Sterling? My mom didn't. My White Mom didn't. Did your White Mom? Did she explain it away because of Loose Cigarettes? Because of Illegal CDs? Because of Toy Guns? Because of Cell Phones? Because of Sleeping in a Car? Because of a Sandwich? Because of a Failure to Signal? Did she, Greg? My White Mom did. My White Mom condemns

   SUICIDE RUNNERS

the cops in one breath and then says BUT. And the way she says BUT. She lives on the promise of that BUT.

Let's go. They're getting closer.

There's nowhere to go.

Maybe just a blank look, a shared, blank look. Maybe there are no words. Too many words. Too many sirens metastasized inside these boys.

5
2014 (+/-)

You see, it was an electrical problem all along. That's what was making Monty so… what's the word? So *prone* to vast conspiracy theories. Monty was slumped against a wall in a makeshift waiting room. The overhead lights buzzed. Fresh stitches ran from the crown of his skull to the base of his neck. He didn't notice the wire in his neck, yet. There were four heavily bandaged areas on his newly, but poorly, shaved head: one above each temple and two at the back of the skull. He probed the copious, bloody bandages with a finger.

"Like we've said, *sir*, you're free to leave whenever you feel ready," a White nurse said.

"My son's got a game tonight," Monty remembered. "I promised him I'd be there."

"We understand. You've made yourself *very* clear."

"If I don't make it, he'll think I forgot about him."

"You've already signed the paperwork, sir."

"And what about these stitches? When do they come out? They feel like—"

"Sir, don't! Oh, shit, dammit! He did it again. Someone get me a goddamned rag. Sir! Stop thrashing, sir! Get the doctor! And where's Mr. Peterson? Just let us—stop! Someone stop him!"

"I said I'd be there! I told Nassir I'd be there! Don't you see?

This is all a mistake! Why's the door locked?"

"Restrain him!"

Monty pulled his bloody hands in front of his face and fainted in the White nurse's arms. She couldn't handle his weight, which was at least twice her own, and they collapsed against the wall.

Here's the issue: the Portland DBS Clinic on NE 82nd and Halsey was not equipped, or certified, to handle long-term patient care. So, while the elective procedure Monty elected to undergo was surely an in-patient procedure anywhere else in the world, Monty might remember when his memory realigns that amongst the stacks of waivers he scribbled his signature onto, he waived the right to sue *if* and *when* he felt, post-surgery, rushed out of the door. But really, is *surgery* the correct term? An *electrical fix* is how it was sold to Monty. A simple adjustment.

Greg's stepfather had made grand promises to Monty. "It'll be easy, Monty. We'll fix you right up."

6
Early November 2016

Last night, marooned at the dinner table once again, Greg clenched his jaw shut and tried to grind his teeth into powder. He was seated across from Jasmine and Father Figure 3.0, forced to listen to them wax poetic about the virtues of a "Christ-Centered Education," as heard and repeated by White Pastor. It's not like 3.0 believed any of it, but once a salesman always a salesman.

Jasmine said she prayed that Greg would go to George Fox. She reminded him that George Fox is just far enough south on The 5, "Almost an hour away even," that he'll *feel* like he's *away* at school. "What about Nassir, Mom? What if I want to go to the same school as Nassir, like best friends in the movies and sitcom spin-offs do?" Jasmine looked at him like he said he wanted to dive on a live grenade.

But all *that* will be dealt with later, or never, depending on the outcome of the whole impending patricide thing, because, right this very second, Greg is at the foul line petitioning Jasmine's God, whom he knows isn't technically supposed to care which team wins, for Greg to make the free throw he's about to attempt. There are only thirty seconds left in the game. He finds the grooves in the ball with the pads of the fingers on his right hand. The game's tied. Andre the Captain and Marcel the Supplier are on the block, their arms, elbows and hands groping for position with the opponents because they, apparently, are under the impression that Greg's going to brick the hell out of it. Nassir is behind Greg, toeing the three-point line with the tip of Marcel's old Jordans. Greg can hear the squeak of the shoes as Nassir prepares to dive in for the rebound the moment the ball glances off the rim.

The ruffle of the cheerleaders' pom poms, like a building drum roll, drowns out every other sound in the gym. And if he thinks about Jenny Owendale, forget it.

Greg's heart rate skyrockets. If he misses the free throw, the scout in the stands from the tiny college in Klamath Falls, Oregon, will note the huge fucking miss by the huge fucking waste of talent named Greg Fucking Hazel and word of his enormous failure will be passed around amongst all the scouts from all the schools, like mono at a Christian summer camp, and Greg won't get a scholarship to play at UCSB, or anywhere even fucking close to D-1, and he'll end up at George Fox, just like Jasmine prays for every night before she goes to bed—and but wouldn't that be better? wouldn't that be *God's Will?* and wouldn't him, Greg, accepting it as fate, accepting it as what the Lord wants, be exactly what White Pastor and Shane the Youth Pastor have been talking about, *Kenosis?* emptying himself? because Jasmine most definitely prays more and harder for what she wants for Greg than what he wants for himself. Then again, what does Kenosis or God have to do with why Nassir can't just walk down the fucking street in Riverview without having a cop called on him?—and Greg finally takes a deep breath

A DEEP FUCKING BREATH

and focuses on the spot at the center-back of the rim.

And he releases the ball.

And the crowd is silent.

Unified in their thunderous silence.

The ball leaves his fingertips with a *wick* sound; the net *whaps* as the ball goes through the hoop, echoing through the cavernous gymnasium. Greg and his Riverview teammates run back on defense because the game isn't over—Riverview is merely up by one now.

Greg exhales. All that for a one-point lead.

West Linn calls a timeout. Greg, Nassir and their teammates hustle to the sideline to huddle around Coach Day. Rob the *Massive* Assistant Coach—he's gotten even bigger and stronger somehow since the season started—pats Greg on the back so hard he might've popped a lung out of place. Nassir slings his arm around Greg's shoulders and squeezes him tight. Ben Jones whispers "Good job" to Greg. Ben Jones is the best shooter on the team. Lights-out in practice. Shot after shot after shot hit nothing but the bottom of the net. Ben Jones's career high in an actual game, though, is eight. The crowd groans every time Ben shoots and misses. They want him to be good. The great shooter. The oddity. Black players, racial-historically, are supposed to be athletic, raw, talented—supposed to be "beasts," naturally gifted, with a genetic predisposition towards jumping higher and running faster than Whites. Greg learned about *Eugenics* from Nassir last summer, as they stuffed their mouths full of Cheez-Its and played NBA2k for hours on end. Nassir said, "I don't want to have to teach you about all this shit forever, Greg, but I'll get you started." Back to Ben Jones. Even though the current NBA and the history of the game are full of incredible Black shooters, if a White player can shoot it well, it somehow makes more sense than if a Black player can. But Ben's the thinker. The burdened shooter. Also: Ben's father owns Lucy's Cafe, where Shasta works. Ben Jones shuts his eyes and tries again, "Good job." Greg hears him this time and nods.

Riverview Men's Basketball, currently, has a record of 1-1. The ref blows the whistle. Timeout over. Coach Day can barely watch as the West Linn guard brings the ball up.

The clock ticks down. Tick. Tick. Tick. Greg and Nassir, and their 6'3" frames and long arms, are at the top of the 2-3 zone. They trap the opposing guard. The wings push up and play the passing lanes. The center drops back into the paint.

The crowd is frantic. The older White folks in the audience don't clap, they just stand there, waiting for the final buzzer, for the decision. The Black fans—fans segregated even when cheering for the same team, same result, in the same neighborhood of this "post-racial" city of Portland—implore the crowd to chant "Dee-Fence!"

The older Whites secretly want a loss. It would make firing Coach Day so much less problematic if Riverview were to lose every game. Less racialized, the firing. Their Whiteness, as a people, has never been confronted so clearly as it has been in the last few years thanks to the first Black President of America. They'd prefer their Whiteness to go back to being a non-thing. Or, more likely, to be the *only* thing. But they'll vote soon. They'll show their true colors, soon. Then their Whiteness, if all goes as planned, can retake its rightful center stage.

Greg and Nassir's arms windmill spastically in front of the volcanic pimples on the West Linn Guard's face, a rehearsed orchestra of defensive flailing. Nassir yells "Dog! Dog! Dog!" instead of "ball" like he's been coached to. Greg laughs. Cries. Why's he crying? Greg yells dog now, too.

The Pimple Point Guard screams for help, but his teammates can't get there in time. DOG DOG DOG DOG! Greg and Nassir are rabid. Their White and Black bodies tower over the PPP. The White crowd, sensing blood, finally joins the cheers, releasing that carnal scream they are born with deep inside their bellies. The clock slips down to ten. The PPP tries to pass the ball through the barrage of swinging arms, but Nassir clips the pass. The ball bounces in front of

Greg, who snatches it and takes off. No one in between him and the basket. Destiny.

Nassir should be running to the hoop, filling the lane opposite Greg as the PPP chases them down, just like Coach Day would want. Instead, Nassir filters out beyond the three-point line, and just before the PPP can foul Greg, Greg whips the ball back over his head to Nassir—to the disbelief of every person in the gymnasium, cheerleader to fan to opposing bench to last but not least, Coach Fucking Day—who all scream "Noooo!"

Nassir catches the ball with a grin forming on his face and shoots the three with three seconds left and their team ahead by one. A shot that makes no sense. Not right now. Not at this point in the game. There are too many *what-ifs* if he misses. The ball hangs in the air. Nassir leaves his shooting hand up, a perfect follow-through, giving Coach Day and the crowd exactly what they don't want: time to contemplate.

Swish. The horn. Game over.

Jubilation? Anger? The crowd flushes their separate but equal emotions. Greg and Nassir hug and laugh, ignoring their missing fathers in the stands, eyes briefly connecting.

"With White Jesus as my fucking witness, if you two fuck*een* idiots ever pull that kind of mutha-*fuck*een shit again I will rip the spines right out of your mutha-FUCKEEN. ASS. HOLES. And hang them from the goddamn RIMS! You hear me you mutha-fuckers! Think this is some kind of fucKEEN game out there?! I will never EVER play you two goddamned IDIOTS together AGAIN! You fu-CKEEN understand me?"

Andre the Captain and Marcel the Supplier swallow their laughter as Coach Day sputters to the end of his cardiactic post-game speech. Ben Jones' shoes are off, placed neatly in front of him, and he stretches his toes one at a time. Manny is very high off Marcel's very new drugs. His pupils try to track the words floating from Coach Day's mouth inside cartoon speech bubbles. Each word pops and fizzes.

Rob the Massive Assistant Coach waits for Coach Day to exit stage left. Alone with the team now, he shakes his head and smiles warmly. He tells them that if they keep playing like they played tonight, and if Nassir and Greg stop being quote-unquote fucking idiots—said with his trademark gap-toothed grin, "This could be our year, you hear me? We could win it all. I swear. I know what winning looks like." And they believe him. They believe, at 2-1, that through the trials and tribulations that are sure to come, this team of so-called men will claim victory in the end. They believe it and they want to believe it and they need to believe it. And they will bathe in the blood of their enemies at the end of the season. They leave the building as warriors. Victors. Fates glowing and golden. Lives momentarily beautiful.

7

The Promise Ring Ceremony

The flowers. The birds. The bees. The pollen and the bright, life-giving sun. Is that poetic? Does poetry lead to sex? Does dancing? The boy can put his hands on the girl's hips *but* he must leave room for the Holy Ghost. And how much space, volumetrically speaking, does a ghost that's holy require? Is it different, the size of The Spirit, for Blacks and Whites?

In lieu of their fathers being present and accounted for at the church's annual Promise Ring event—that hormone-bursting time of the year when fathers and sons gather to sign the son up for a life of abstinence until marriage—Greg and Nassir are stuck with Shane the Youth Pastor and his boxy head and swollen red sausage fingers to guide them through the Promise Ring workbook.

"He's gotta pay the bills, Greg, I understand that. No shame in your dad not being here. Gotta work. Gotta pay the bills."

"So, Shane, this'll," Nassir interjects, thumbing through the workbook, "get me into heaven? The Great White Beyond? The most-green other side of the fence?"

"Well, Nassir." Shane does that thing with his hands where he makes a little church out of them (there's even a steeple). "It sure is a step in the right direction."

"My dad says, and by the way," Nassir makes sure his

facial muscles are relaxed, friendly, non-violent, "I appreciate you not asking why *he* isn't here. My dad, I mean. Like all these other young men, here with their papas, squiring their little boys into the sanctity of adulthood. Teaching them the honest and true ways of abstinence."

"I was going to ask about Monty, but—"

"My dad says—

"Nassir." Shane the Youth Pastor searches for the right words. "Hey."

"Hi."

"Hello," Greg says, reasserting his existence.

"I really didn't mean to make you feel, I don't know," he searches for the best wrong word, "*different*. Left out?"

"There ain't a damn thing you could do to help with that, I'm afraid." Nassir opens the workbook, forcefully flipping the cover open. The White fathers and sons, seated at nearby tables, lower their voices to make room for the fatherless void at the teacher's table.

Jasmine thought it would be a good idea for Greg to take part in the Promise Ring conference. The church had bought the workbooks. The rings, en masse, had been shipped. Someone had to be there to promise their virginity to God. Why not he and Nassir? Shane the Youth Pastor showed the rings off during youth group on the previous Wednesday night's gathering. And now it was Saturday afternoon and boys were hearing their dads say words like *dick* and *semen* and *jack-off* for the first and hopefully last time. Shane is trying. He is. But he just prattles on. He runs his finger down the first page of the first chapter, trying to find a foothold. He decides to go off-book and fires scatter-shot thoughts about the purity Jesus exemplified. "He even sat next to a prostitute on the edge of a well and *wasn't* tempted."

"Do you think he made a wish?" Greg wonders aloud.

     SUICIDE RUNNERS

"What'd you mean?" Shane asks, and then immediately regrets that he did.

Nassir's eyes are strained. Contained. Withholding. (They may have, Greg and Nassir, may have, just *might've*, right before walking into the church, swallowed a pill that Marcel the Supplier was handing out after the last game. TBD.)

"I mean, Jesus sat there at the well, as you said, and, you know, the tradition goes that you throw," Greg tosses an imaginary coin into an even more imaginary watering hole—

"Bloop," Nassir narrates.

"—a dime, a quarter, a nickel maybe?"

"The value of currency being proportionately correlative," Nassir inserts, "to the grandness of said wish."

Shane the Youth Pastor can feel the room's eyes glance his way, like, Come on Shane, I'm trying to have a father-son moment here; like, Come on, Shane, have you ever even had sex?; like, Come on, Shane, I need to have this moment with my son where I can explain manhood and the inner sanctity and responsibilities of said manhood and, at the end, Shane, I will clap my son on the back and tell him, and tell myself, that he is doing the right thing, that we are blessed and chosen and White and right, as we so proved in the election just a few days ago, and, Shane, if you haven't even ever had sex, why then should these fatherless boys trust anything you might have to say on the subject of Biblical Relations involving anyone or anything other than their hand?

"Guys, please. Let's just get through this."

"Because," Greg continues, still dwelling on the well-wishing conundrum, "one would have to assume—"

"One would *most certainly* have to assume."

"That Jesus, were he to sit at the well and not be tempted by a woman whose *very job* it is to tempt and seduce, whose very job is the kind of job, no pun intended, that this workbook says I must promise to stay away from until I've secured a wife who will obligingly do the job for me, the point being, that if and when Jesus sat at said well—"

"Not if, *when*," Shane the Youth Pastor clarifies. The fathers around him can at least approve of that, can't they? his strong assertion of the Bible's infallibility? That would, at the very least, explain the Sons of Ham.

"When, as you said, as Paul says—"

"Paul, the apostle formerly known as Saul," Nassir clarifies.

"Correct! As *Paul* who was once *Saul* says: when Jesus sat at the well and his leg, it must've, you know? when his bare leg made contact with the woman's bare leg, the prossy's, the mattress back's thigh, at the well, did he then need to toss a coin into the well to make a wish to withstand the temptation? And would that wish, then, be granted by… *himself?* Would Jesus, STAY WITH ME NOW!, would Jesus, were he to make a wish at a well—"

"Preach, Greg, preach!"

"Would Jesus then grant… his *own* wish?"

"The greatest theological question of all time!" Nassir declares triumphantly.

"Listen," a father at a table nearby blurts out, "I'm trying to have a, I mean, please gentlemen, just can you please keep it down."

Shane the Youth Pastor says, "I'm sorry, Dan."

"We don't have fathers, *Dan!*" Nassir hollers.

"Can't you see, *Dan*, we are without our fathers!" Greg's voice hits a falsetto note.

"I'm not equipped to handle this," Shane the Youth Pastor mumbles to himself.

"Fathers of all the fathered, I apologize for this outburst," Nassir exclaims cheerfully. "But my dad and Greg's dad are not here."

Greg stands. Nassir stands because Greg stands. Shane the Youth Pastor stands because the boys are standing. And the walls quake. The tables eject their legs and shatter against the maroon carpet. Maroon because of the blood of Jesus? Maroon because Jesus turned water into wine? And the father with the bowl-cut, Dan, the father with the bowl-cut and the tie that only reaches down to his belly button, just above the belly button, not even the belly button's equator, *that* father, whose name is Dan, is indignant. (He'll soon learn the trick, re: the tie, from the master of tricks: that wearing a big long red tie covers up all questions of masculinity).

White face full of red-cheeked rage, "This is not how it was supposed to go!" Dan screams.

"What's the *it!*" Nassir screams back.

"Be specific!" Greg encourages.

"Boys!" Shane the Youth Pastor squeals from the shamed depths of his quasi-virgin soul.

"I've had it up to just about here! Okay!" Dan yelps.

"My dad's got four holes in his head!"

"My stepfather, the *father* part being a mere legality, drilled holes into Monty's head!"

"I've had sex before, but, well, only the backward kind," Shane the Youth Pastor quietly admits to the ruckus. Only Nassir heard him.

"I just want my son to be happy," Dan whimpers.

And are Greg and Nassir standing on tables? Are they splitting atoms? Or, do atoms split around them? Are the young and old alike wishing they could go back and do it again? *It.* Re-emerge from the celestial labia?

Ultimately, White Pastor was called in to quell the madness. He shouted and turned anger into holy rage and expelled Greg and Nassir, pointing to the exit. He was especially harsh to Nassir, to no one's surprise. As the fathers clenched their peach fists, Nassir reminded them that, "My dad was once one of you. That's the dirty secret, isn't it? Once a deacon, the only Black deacon. Once a man of the brevitous-tie club. Once a man who held the communion plate for others. A greeter, a parking lot attendant, who observed the Sabbath like all the other Deacony men of America; who squired us home, just as you are squiring your sons here into a life of supposed delayed sexual satisfaction by way of sexual denial. Denying the destructive consequences of denial. AND BUT! Where's my father? Where's the former deacon? What did the masquerade get him?"

"He was given a way out," Greg proclaims. "A pacemaker and a wire and electrodes and now, miraculously, he smiles per the dial's turn!"

"He smiles unseen smiles to faceless alleyways!" Nassir screams, his face a maze of complex angles and lines. "Smiles and grins to his forefathers and, by extension, my forefathers, and to the half of my forefathers, on my mother's side, who whipped and chained and beat the backs of Blacks, and but why! It's true. Look it up. My dad did. He looked it up and now he can no longer look forward, so he smiles to the darkest corners of the web and to those Americans who, dare I say it? dare he thought it? never forgot Tower Seven! As if that ever meant anything. He smiles at those same people who now believe that the man with the orange face will liberate the pedophiled. The *pedophile* who will liberate the *pedophiled!*"

"Blasphemous!" Dan shouts.

If it were the 1980s, Greg and Nassir would've been tossed from the church's doorway and the scene would have frozen with our heroes in mid-flight. Their eyes the size of balloons. Their mouths like zeros.

8
The Jasmine Interlude

Last night, an email was sent to the Bible Study Ladies, by the perma-smiling Judy, reminding the Church Ladies about their Bible Study having been rescheduled to the morning, instead of its usual evening time, because The Deacons were having a "post-election shindig" in the same place, and at the *exact* same time, that the Church Ladies' weekly Bible Study has always been held. "And you know how our men are :) Please be sure to adjust your calendars accordingly."

Don't even get Jasmine started. Regardless, she was up earlier than normal today so she offered to drive Greg to school on her way to church. She packed the coffee thermos and crate of various alternative creamers into the trunk and yelled for Greg. She tightened her wrist braces as she waited for him. She could hear his footsteps coming down the stairs towards the garage. He opened the door. There he was. Her son. She thought, *Don't cry.*

(Sidenote: a phone call was placed to Jasmine a day after the Promise Rings were left unclaimed and Greg and Nassir's virginity/salvation was, as a result, left up for grabs. A word of warning was offered: "Greg may be going through a *trying* time, the evil one pressing in on all sides," the phone call said. "Greg may benefit from some one-on-one time with an elder, you know, one of the God-fearing men from the church, and," the phone call said. When Jasmine asked about Nassir, and whether he, too, could get in on this sacred one-on-one time, the person on the other end of the call almost choked on their trepidation and managed to mumble something about needing to find someone who'd be a *good fit* for Nassir. She thanked "the church" for their concern and hung up.)

As they backed out of the driveway, Jasmine and Greg nearly hit their neighbor's empty garbage can that had rolled into their driveway. Its lid was flipped open. Greg said, "Look, Mom, the garbage can has emptied itself." And they both laughed. Jasmine's laughter was poorly concealed by a half-hearted, "You can't say that."

Greg has practice after school. It will end at 5:30. Jasmine said she'll be there to pick him up. Greg said, "Are you worried about me or something?" Quite frankly, yes, she wanted to say. She wanted to say, Don't be like Nassir, or, I don't know, like Monty? But she didn't, because maybe it's her fault, too? *She* married the man who put the electric things, or whatever, on Monty's brain. So she makes PB&Js for Nassir and makes Greg invite him to church. Although, now that it's pretty clear most of the church voted for quite possibly the closest thing to an anti-Christ that's ever been on the ballot, Jasmine's not sure she'll be forcing Nassir to attend anymore.

It was still dark out as they drove to Riverview, and it'll be dark again when she picks him up. She wants to apologize to Greg for Trench, or, The Man Named Trench, as Greg refers to him, and she wants to ask Greg if he remembers much about that time, pre-Father Figure 3.0. Which, really, is a silly thought because it wasn't that long ago. Jasmine doesn't know how or if or when to bring it up, so she wrote a letter to Greg that she has yet to give him. One day, soon, she will.

Her own mother never apologized to Jasmine. She doesn't want to be like her mother.

Jasmine *has* apologized to Shasta, in person, about Trench. Mother to daughter. But when she did, Shasta told her she had nothing to apologize for because, "Well, Mom, I don't know." Shasta moved to Matheson's the moment Trench showed up. So, Lord forgive me, but maybe Shasta should be the one apologizing for leaving her and Greg with him. But again, Shasta was young, and Trench was a tight-knuckled fist of anger. He's probably dressed in MAGA gear and waving Trump flags along the waterfront these days. Anyway, she presses the little lever thing for the right blinker and turns down 122nd after a semi-truck careens past them. She looks over to Greg, out of the corner of her eyes, to make sure he is still there; make sure he hasn't evaporated.

Jasmine has doubts about the church, of course, but that's allowed, isn't it? The doubts? The doubts are a known quantity, an aspect of the agreed-upon faith she wants to agree with, *and*. But really, for The Church Ladies it's more like an *an* she's noticed… not an *and* with the d at the end. An. They drop the d and pick up Salvation. Pick up meekness. Pick up modesty. Pick up membership, an.

These are all things to think about when taking your kid to school. When you're taking your son to school it's okay to have doubts, isn't it? She thinks it is. Her husband, her third but kind of fourth, only wants to talk about the work he and Dr. Whoever are doing; how what they're doing at the DBS clinic is revolutionary, and how it'll change the way people look at mental disorders and genetic disorders and, "Maybe even change the way people pray for healing, Jasmine. Can you imagine?" When she asks him about Monty, the only thing her newish husband can do is grip the table until his knuckles turn white and say something about it being

Monty's fault. "Okay? For the last time, it's his fault, Jazz." And only he can make Jazz sound flat.

These are all things that happen and things to think about when your youngest child is walking away from the car toward another day at Riverview High School. She hugged him before he exited, as much as he'd allowed, and whispered to herself, *Don't cry*, and she didn't, because she's a big girl and not worried about Greg. Right? And there he goes. Off to another day.

A group of Asian, Mexican, and Black kids ambles past her, in front of her car, and she smiles, does that thing White ladies do: smile at Non-White people like, *I'm okay, you're okay, we're okay, aren't we?* She hates that smile, hates herself for allowing her mouth to do it. Look, Greg's shoes are untied. She prays that Greg isn't doing drugs (as she assumes Nassir is) (because the call from the church assumed both Nassir *and* Greg most positively were, that they must've been on something). Every night she prays that Greg'll be okay. Just okay.

She's on her way to church now. The sidewalk ends just past the school, beyond the baseball fields and the cracked tennis courts. The curbed cement giving way to ruddy grass that creep out from the bottom of unpainted fences. She passes the Niemann's Mustang, with the red for-sale sign in the driver-side window. She turns left on 102nd and the drive from Idaho to Oregon was a two-night trip that she could've done in one full day when she left home for good at eighteen, but she didn't get out of the house until a little past noon because her mother didn't want her to go. A story retold to herself so often and in so many Bible Studies that the words have become rote. The words and the memory are a constant slipstream. Jasmine stayed in a roadside motel built for truckers and sex workers. Her mother's last words were: "Then go. God won't forgive you." Jasmine said, "I love you, Mom." But the woman who brought her into the world was wearing a blue nightie with yellow socks rolled at the ankles and was anchored to the couch, smoking, watching Matlock reruns. It was a Sunday. But these are just things, AN.

She thinks she wants Greg to be a man of God. To know His love. She demands that God answer her prayers. Jasmine kneels beside her bed every morning, first thing after waking up, and prays for Greg and Nassir, for their increasingly outsized outbursts, and for Monty about whom her husband said, "I don't know, Jazz, okay? Maybe something went wrong because Monty's not responding like all the rest of my patients." He said, "We used the same fucking wires and electrodes, but don't worry, legally speaking, because it's most likely Monty's fault."

The rear parking lot of the squat brown church is already full of modest four-door sedans. And look, there is suddenly a peppering of brand-new MAGA stickers on a few bumpers. Stickers that weren't there until the day *after* the election. Jasmine checks her reflection in the mirror and sees her mother's lips. It's early in the morning, so no one will be wearing makeup, she hopes, because she isn't, because she was rushing to get ready to go on time, and it was her second husband, Anthony, Greg's father, who took Jasmine to church for the first time as a grownup, as a twenty-eight-year-old. Anthony was going to church then, was renewed and revived and committed to clean living, and he took her to his uncle's church in St. Johns, in North Portland, the one with upside down V for a roof, out there where Portland ends, and Anthony introduced Jasmine to his family before the service, forever ago, two lifetimes ago, or three? and Anthony's mom hugged her and pulled her close and said, "I think I like this one, honey."

These are all just *things* because the Bible tells us God will make believer's paths smooth and straight, and all we have to do is trust in Him and empty ourselves because everything happens for a reason, an. And sure, she doesn't think the liar racist pedophile human garbage who grabs women by their private parts should be the president, but, and, *an.* She doesn't have to tell anyone who she voted for, does she?

"Hello, Mary; hello, Sue; hello, Juanita. I am *so* glad to see you, too. I love your hair. Oh, I just woke up, too, and yes, I *too* thought the reading was just really good this week; I think Job was such an interesting man of God. It just goes to show that God can use anyone and that no matter how bleak things appear, God's still in control, doesn't it? Isn't he? And, oh, I don't know, Judy, I don't know about that, I think we could've done better, don't you think? Because, I mean, he was not even that good of a business person, was he? And. *An.* Amen." And don't they all kind of look at her like she's an outsider when she forgets to say *and* without the d?

Jasmine Booker then Matheson then Hazel then Trench (unofficially) then and now Peterson. How many times can a last name be changed, legally? Jasmine just wants to blend in, sink into the monotone fabric of the Bible Study Ladies. Even the non-White ladies seem to *act* White in church. Whatever that means. First, it was her name, Jasmine. *Jasmine?* Yes. *Well, isn't that an interesting name?* It isn't vanilla. It can't be found on the grayscale of accepted White lower-middle-class names. *Is it a family name?* Not that I'm aware. *Was she a stripper?*

Jasmine pretends to work out, like the rest of them; shops at WinCo on NE 102nd for food, and the Fred Meyer across the street from Winco for everything else, just like the rest of them; recycles plastics and papers in separate bins, and even has a small compost next to the sink, like the rest of them; AND, she watches *Dancing with Tyrell Jones* every night after the local news, just like they all do, except, unlike the rest of them, she swears up and down that he, Tyrell Jones, is curing the carpal-tunnel that she's battled ever since Shasta was born. Unlike the rest of them, she didn't turn the channel in disgust when Tyrell Jones melted down on stage last week, in the middle of helping an older White woman touch her toes for the first time since she had breast cancer, and he looked off-camera and must've seen a monitor or something because he absolutely, Jasmine admits, lost his cool because, apparently, the new curtain hanging behind the set—the dark blue curtain Tyrell Jones told the audience the week before to expect, and to furthermore expect it to look a lot like Jimmy Fallon's curtain, because, and to not be weirded-out, but, he admitted, also on-air the week before, that he, Tyrell Jones, was slightly, you could say, *obsessed* with Fallon and thought that were he given a chance he could be the next Fallon but, obviously, Black and gay and, also, an aerobics instructor, and so, maybe, Tyrell Jones said, "Come to think of it, maybe I'm more of a blend between Fallon and Richard Simmons, but, obviously, Black,"—so when he looked at the monitor off-camera, Jasmine assumed, and saw how dark the curtain was behind him, darker than Fallon's curtain by a shade or two at least, he lost it, threw a fit on stage, right there on-air, and even seemed to curse the color of his own skin while cursing the darkness of the curtain, and Jasmine assumed she'd never understand what he was really flipping out about, but that she'd try, she promised herself, try to understand, and really, the main thing is: as long as her carpal tunnel was feeling better, she would stick with Tyrell Jones.

But yes, Jasmine has had three or four-ish husbands and has, from the outside looking in, kind of drifted from one life and one man to the next, seemingly without much confidence in herself or her ability to be a strong, independent woman, which she knows is all the rage now, but what they all don't know, all those women judging her, is that when given no solid foundation from which to build upon, no love, no support from any mother or father figure of her own, she thinks, as The Bible Study Ladies release each other's hands, murmuring *Amens* in different octaves at the end of Judy's peppy prayer, Jasmine thinks they can all go fuck themselves, if she's being brutally honest because they don't know the half of what it's like growing up next to a lake that doesn't even lap with a mother who entered her into beauty contests at eight so the town could get a good look at her pretty daughter. A town full of not-so-secret White Supremacists. It being Coeur d'Alene, Idaho, and all. *Be pretty, Jasmine. Be pretty for us. Redeem us with your prettiness, Jasmine.* AND.

So every time it's her turn to bring coffee to the Bible Study, like it was this week, she makes sure the coffee is extra hot. Hotter than the week before when Juanita brought it (and Juanita has to make sure her coffee is super-duper hot for the obvious *Where is she really from?* type of reasons), because if it's lukewarm, if it isn't extra-hot, they'll look at Jasmine like they looked at Juanita and say, "It's okay," and their heads' half-tilts will collectively say, "We understand, Jasmine, we're just glad you're here, and we know how hard it is *every day* for you to JUST make it through the day because you've had three-or-so husbands, and obviously that means something is inherently wrong with you, and we're JUST thankful that you came, and, you know what, Jasmine, the coffee could be cold and we'd STILL love you because you've been married so so so many times, and who knows what or whom you *did* before the first marriage and in between the following two, before you found this church and re-rededicated your life to

Christ and started talking and thinking in terms of Jesus and his plan, again, and isn't the love of Christ JUST so GOD damn FREEING?" So. The coffee is hot. Like burn-your-fucking-tongue hot.

Amen.

Jasmine Booker → Matheson → Hazel → *Trench* → Peterson.

9
8 November 2016

Even Andre the Captain is doubled over, hands on sweaty knees, lungs hemorrhaging. Nassir stands up straight and flexes his back—his chest cries out for air. Greg tries to say, "It's okay, you got it," but he can't. He can only manage a groan. Coach Day couldn't be happier with himself. Look at him. A sadist. He's probably even got a sadistic boner behind those sweats. His whistle hangs from his mouth, saliva glistening on his chin. Nassir didn't make it, for the fourth time in a row. He didn't make the time. The time is 23 seconds for Guards and 25 for Bigs, and Nassir came in at 24. Rob the Massive Assistant Coach verified it, begrudgingly. Everyone has to run it again.

It is a suicide.

The whistle explodes. Shoes resume their tiny progression of shrieks. Fingers swipe at the foul line extended, back to the baseline, then the half-court line, back to the baseline, then the far end's foul line extended, baseline again, then a full sprint to the far baseline and back, and it's already at 16 and Coach Day's laughing again, the whistle bobbing up and down in his mouth, as shoes and fingers push off from the far baseline. At 23 seconds, every Guard is in safely, even the notoriously slow Ben Jones the Double Outsider (who runs with his head tipped up and back). Every guard except Nassir: eyes wide and panicked, the skin around his temples stretched tight, fear of the impossible suicide growing in impossibility. His shoes (Marcel's old Jordans) slap the floor, echoing against the rafters. The cheerleaders, mid-practice, are watching him fail from their perch on the track above the court. Even Naya. And they just had sex last night for the first time. And Naya said it hurt. He thought it'd be different, better, thought he'd be able to find inside of her whatever it is he knows he's missing.

And, in that tender moment after sex, the first time for both of them, when they couldn't think of anything else to say, when they didn't know if she'd be pregnant or not, she pressed her head into his shoulder and asked, "Why do you talk so funny sometimes, Nassir?" and he said, "Like how?" and she said, "Like you're on a stage," and he said, "I'm using the master's language to be free of the field."

24 seconds. Coach Day laughs *through* the whistle. Nassir comes to a dead stop at the free-throw line and falls to his knees. The whistle screams. "Back on the line! If even one can't do it, y'all gotta do it again."

Nassir would give his soul to Greg's mom's White God if it meant he never had to run another suicide. Marcel the Supplier pats him on the shoulder. They're trying to be there for him, a team united against suicides, a Suicide Prevention Hotline personified, and that only makes it worse.

Here's what's really going on: it's not that Nassir isn't physically fast enough to run a suicide in 23 seconds, it's that when Nassir sauntered into English 401 this morning, one hundred and eighty seconds late, which typically elicits a snide remark from Mr. Hatton about athletes and entitlement, and by athletes he always means *Black* athletes, and by entitlement he always means, *You're not smart enough*. But, with Monty frantically scribbling away on the whiteboard— diagrams buttressed by phrases like "foundational truths" and "irreversible knowledge" and "past AS present" and "1619!" and "BUILDING 7?" and "Plantation state" and shaky lines and arrows connecting everything—Mr. Hatton simply stood by the door and watched, waiting for security as Nassir entered.

Mr. Hatton said, "Your father's here, Nassir," and moved out of the way so Nassir could fully appreciate Monty's degenerating glory.

Monty tried to set the red marker down on the thin metal tray at the bottom of the whiteboard. His hand trembled under the concentrated effort. The marker slipped off the tray and tumbled to the ground. Nassir stared at his father. How did it come to this? What was the real cause? The area of dark brown skin hiding the wire under Monty's neck looked like it was on the verge of bleeding. Nassir wanted to help, badly; his heart almost stopped beating, his breath seized, but the kids in class were watching. Everyone had their phones out, recording, posting, and sharing Nassir's moment of shame with eternity. For posterity. To distance themselves from *crazy*. To mark the boundaries between *us* and *them*. Monty tried to speak, but someone snickered under their breath as the rolling marker came to a stop against Marcel's Jordans. Nassir turned to the laughter: Jenny Owendale covered her mouth and looked away.

"What're you doing, Dad?"

"Nassir, look, I was just explaining—"

"The apple doesn't grow too far from the tree, I guess," Jenny Owendale blurted out, showcasing her remedial understanding of basically everything.

"Jenny," said a now bored Mr. Hatton.

Nassir couldn't take his eyes off the red marker at his feet. "Just go, Dad. Please." None of the books Nassir had been devouring could help him feel better about what was happening. He knew the colonizer had won. He knew Monty's *allostatic load* was too much, that the stress of a lifetime of racism was, seemingly, ripping his father apart one brain cell at a time, but none of that helped right now. None of it made it any easier.

Monty reached into his pocket and took out the pacemaker-ish device. Nassir's hands shook, "Just go!"

"This is why I prefer honors classes," Mr. Hatton informed his non-honors class, which was *very* diverse. An array of skin colors and ethnicities and geo-political histories blinked back at him and cussed him under their collective, bankrupt American Dream breaths.

Just before security showed up and rushed Monty away, Nassir grabbed the eraser and scrubbed as much of the gibberish off the whiteboard as possible. He completely lost his cool, went fucking wild, as his classmates would later attest to the principal (and as videos on glowing screens would prove).

"Go, Dad. Please. Fucking go!"

"I don't think I'm imagining it, Nassir. I've gotten too close to the answers, to the right questions. Wait, hold on, if I just turn this up, Mr. Peterson said it'll make me think *clearer*. It'll make me smile—"

Monty wrenched the dial on his pacemaker-ish device to the right. It fizzled. His left eye quivered, jammed shut, spasmed. He grabbed at the wire in his neck and fell to one knee.

24 seconds. Again. Coach Day relents. On his way out of the gym, Coach Day tells Nassir that if he can't run a 23 next practice, Nassir won't be in the startling lineup for the upcoming game. Coach Day acts outright flabbergasted. The team knows he loves it, loves that Nassir couldn't make

a 23. And yes, of course, Coach Day knows about Monty showing up at school. Word spread through the well-worn avenues of handshakes, half-hugs and nods to the fellow Black employees and teachers and coaches at Riverview, that, "Yeah, Monty showed up again." Even more reason Nassir should run a 23, Coach Day's probably thinking: Monty is making it harder for *him* to keep his job.

So. There was a meeting with the White principal and the White, loving counselor, Mrs. Schuster, shortly after the incident in English 401. Nassir was barely present for the intervention. Nassir asked if he was suspended, and when they said, "No, it's not your fault, Nassir," he nodded and said, "That's very kind of you," and checked out. Mrs. Schuster frowned and made notes. Copious notes. Reams of notes. Multiple pens ran out of ink. Nassir waited for her to finish. He began to fear he was just a part of their story.

Nassir can hear the semi-trucks growling against the night from inside his tiny room. The windows shake when they roll by. Nassir can't fall asleep because the screen on the window rattles every time the semis rumble over the bump in the road in front of the motel. Nassir has examined it. The bump. He stood in the middle of the busy street in the middle of a cold, sun-blistered day, and examined the offending bump. Everyone honked and flipped him off. His mother ran to him, screaming, crying, and pulled him back to safety. Pulled him past Phil and his look of disgust back into the safety of their motel room. His medication was upped. 10mg to 20mg. Twice daily, taken with water. The doctor said it would help even him out. Squeeze the lid on both sides, press down, twist to the left. Earlier in the day, Marcel the Supplier said, "Fuck the doctors. I'll help clear things up."

Nassir's White mom said Monty had lost his mind long before Mr. Peterson put four holes in his head. What does she know? She also said she thought the White President they voted in would make a good leader, despite all the historical facts that gave evidence that the polar opposite was true. "We just need a leader that speaks his mind," she and every other White apologist told Nassir. As for Monty losing his mind, Nassir thought the pacemaker-ish device was supposed to solve that. Recalibrate the flow of electricity to his brain. "It's just an electrical problem, then?" "Exactly, that's right, Son."

When Nassir was in eighth grade he woke up one morning to find Monty asleep on the couch in the living room. Nassir was at the kitchen table, purposefully making more noise than necessary to eat a bowl of cereal. He scraped his spoon along the bottom of the bowl, over and over. Monty snorted awake, looked caught, startled. Nassir watched as Monty remembered where he was.

"Morning."

"Doing good, Nassir?"

In Nassir's freshman year, Monty was fired from his job at N.I.S.C. Nassir was unable to parse specifics from the undialogued yelling backstage between his parents in the master bedroom about what happened. What went down in Washington, D.C. What started the downfall. But Monty emerged from the wings, face flared, eyes bulged, and could only manage a blank look at Nassir.

During Nassir and Greg's sophomore year, Nassir traveled with Greg's family to Canada for an extended weekend getaway. They were in Mr. Peterson's spaceship-esque minivan. Their bikes were locked to the roof, out there with the wind, speeding north on The 5, mountains and waterfalls zipping past. They pulled over for burgers and shakes, where Mr. Peterson tried to play the paternal part. "It's on me, boys.

Young studs like you gotta eat." Mr. Peterson put a hand on Nassir's shoulder and squeezed. Nassir wanted to hit him, as a thank you for the then-fresh holes in Monty's head.

There was a swimming pool at the hotel in Canada. Pale blue chlorinated water rippled underneath an endless sky. Greg and Nassir were swimming, when Mr. Peterson suddenly appeared on the balcony and barraged them with water balloons. Mr. Peterson cackled, balloons in mid-flight. A big blob of yellow smacked Nassir in the face. The next thing Nassir knew, he was trying to drown Greg. Both hands were on Greg's head, pushing him down, brown hair between Nassir's brown fingers. He watched air bubbles escape from Greg's mouth, amoebas under the surface; watched his best friend struggle, green eyes dissolving into the blue; felt the watery weight of Greg's arms and could hear Mr. Peterson yell, "Hey, stop that!" Nassir cried, unsure of what or why he was doing what he was doing. Greg came up for air and punched Nassir in the chest.

Nassir's grades cratered during junior year. While he wasn't paying attention in class, Nassir consumed books by Frank Wilderson III, Saidiya Hartman, Frantz Fanon, Nell Irvin Painter, Richard Wright, Alex Haley; articles by Ta-Nehisi Coates; anything but what they were teaching him in school. Anything and everything he found in Monty's boxes of books. Finally, the four holes in Monty's head were blamed by the White teachers and administrators who were unable to think past the present. So, when senior year rolled around and Greg was applying for college, with that easy certainty that White kids have about college and, in general, their future, Nassir didn't want to think about filling out applications with their questions that demanded simple answers. He began one application online, but stopped when he was faced with:

Address: "In a state of constant flux."

Parents' highest level of education: "IN QUESTION"

Recruiters from small colleges all over the Northwest called Nassir. "Nassir Chissler, we need you as our two-guard." Recruiters who most likely didn't know about Monty and his make-happy device. Small schools in Nowheresville, USA. Nassir used to be the son of the man with a dependable job at N.I.S.C. The son of the tee-ball coach. Of the rec-league basketball coach. The man whose voice boomed and filled gymnasiums. Nassir used to be the son of Mr. & Mrs. Monty Chissler. He is forcibly becoming someone else.

The whistle blows. Nassir sprints. Heart rate soaring past 200 bpm. His teammates are lined up along the sidelines. Are we here again? Did we ever leave? Practice jerseys are strewn about the floor. Bodies contorted in various shapes of exhaustion. Nassir touches the free-throw line.

Coach Day stands with arms across his sunken chest in front of his squadron. Nassir touches half-court. 10 seconds. "He runs flat-footed, that's his problem," Marcel the Supplier whispers to Andre the Captain. "He needs to straighten his hands out," Andre whispers back, "make himself more aerodynamic." The soles of Marcel's worn-out Jordans slap the court.

24 seconds.

"Fuck it," Coach Day says. And that's the worst. Failing so many times even the belligerent Coach gives up. Nassir collapses on the baseline.

Greg's hands wrap around Nassir's ribcage, helping him to his feet. "I tried," Nassir says. The team gathers around and says things like, "Fuck coach, Nas," and, "You okay, bud?" and, "Let's go fucking smoke the Beneficent Herb." Marcel the Supplier says, "Forget that. I have something new that'll clear this all up."

10
Three Days Later

Shane the Youth Pastor is on stage teasing out the merits of abstinence (again) to an audience of teenagers who are hornier than monks nearing the end of their regretfully celibate lives. Greg and Nassir, both massaging their aching muscles from Friday night's game, are seated near the back of the church's beta sanctuary in the annex, down the street from the main church.

"You see the boxscore on the Oregonian?" Greg asks.

Nassir opens his eyes wide, "We're without the world's widest web. Mom and Phil rely on Tucker Carlson for all their knowledge now."

"They got our stats wrong." Every time Greg or Nassir talk, the kids sitting in front of them do that thing where they turn their heads and half-look, giving the half-sign to fully shut the hell up. No matter how many times Greg or Nassir apologize, their heads continue to half-whip.

Shane: By the grace of God, Jesus was nailed to the cross to deliver us from ourselves—

Greg: Only had fifteen points for you, not sixteen. Sorry. And—

Shane: (takes a deep breath) For even, the Bible says, lusting after a woman is akin to cheating—

Nassir: It's okay. Sorr—yyy.

Greg: They had me for eight boards. Pretty sure I got nine.

Shane: How do we stop this? It's human nature, right? Right!?

Greg, Nassir, and The Head Turners: Right!

Nassir: You know the cheerleader with the long braids? My apologies!

Shane: And by emptying ourselves, ridding ourselves of everything we desire—

Greg: Naya?

Nassir: She's in history with me—

Greg: Who's your teacher? Watch your hair, Cindy! You're half-whipping it so fast! Mrs. Lake? Or, my brother-in-law, Mr. Brian?

Nassir: Mrs. Lake. Naya sits next to me and she handed me her number a few weeks back. I called. Sorry, Cindy! Listening now!

Shane: His desires, his plans, his needs, not ours. Amen?

Greg, Nassir, and The Head Turners: Amen.

Shane: Kenosis. (Letting the word hang there). Kenosis. (Eyes misting now). Kenosis... We all fall short. We all fall short...

Cindy the Head Turner: Forgive me, God!

Nassir: You're forgiven, Cindy!

Greg: Mrs. Lake is hot. I heard her husband cheats on her.

Nassir: A tragedy of Biblical proportions.

Shane: Let's bow our heads. Lord, we come to you, broken, sinners, in need of—

Greg: Andre told me.

Nassir: When? You're right, Cindy! My eyes are closed! Praying.

Greg: After the game on Friday, she was in the hallway on the way to her car—

Shane: Amen.

Greg, Nassir, and The Head Turners: Amen.

Nassir: Naya and I fornicated.

Greg: And now?

Nassir: And now I know her Biblically.

Greg: After the game, in the hallway, Mrs. Lake smiled at us and said 'Good game', and Andre told me his aunt is fucking Mrs. Lake's husband. Ow, Cindy! Right in my eyes!

Shane: Remember, it's not our will, but His. Only in Him and through Him can we ever be truly free.

Random White Boy in Audience: Freedom! Trump! MAGA!

Cindy the Head Turner: Free me!

Nassir: Damn. She is hot though.

Greg: Who? Naya? Shh! Cindy! I'm talking!

Nassir: Mrs. Lake. If only I had the Niemann's Mustang, I wouldn't be afraid of losing Naya. Cindy, you're an angel.

Greg and Nassir follow the herd of pimple- and hormone-bursting-teens through the backdoor, headed for that angry late-November air. Cindy flips them off and jogs ahead, wanting to be the first to the real church service in the main building. The flat sun in the cloudless, windswept sky is blinding. Terrifying.

Jasmine made Greg invite Nassir to church, again. She was worried, since Coach Day didn't let him start the last game, that Nassir would drift too far afield if she didn't intervene. To her credit, she was quick to note the precipitous decline of Nassir's personality last year. She told Greg she was worried about Nassir long before anyone at school took official notice of his mood swings and increasing theatricality. "To be honest," she said, "I think it's a bit racist they didn't notice beforehand." Greg said, "That's very woke of you, Mom."

So, they picked up Nassir from the motel and drove to church like one big fucked-up family that ABC would love to make a sitcom about—*You're telling me there's a half-black kid as the main actor, but we'll hardly talk about real race issues?! SOLD!* Jasmine told Greg, before they picked Nassir up, that she hoped Nassir's recent dosage increase would "do the trick." Greg wasn't sure how she knew about Nassir's antidepressants. In a whisper, in the backseat, as both Father Figure 3.0 and Jasmine watched them in the rearview mirror, Greg asked Nassir if he'd told her, or left the bottle in the bathroom by accident one day. Nassir told him he didn't need his pills like that, "Enough to carry them with me, the bottle in my basketball shorts' pockets or whatever. It's more like a once-a-day thing, for as long as I live, for infinity to the end of the universe and all that, into perpetuity, legally speaking," Nassir whispered back.

Shane the Youth Pastor catches up to Greg and Nassir on the way to the main church and extends a congratulations about the quote-unquote big win on Friday in the form of a meaty, hearty handshake. Shane's head is tilted out of shape, possibly mangled by a rock or crowbar when he was young and skull-malleable. His eyes are warm but needy, creased at the sides, with heavy bags on this shallow Sunday morning. "Guys, good game on Friday. I don't know if you saw me but I was up there in the stands," Shane says, his excitement a tick past eleven. "You played well, Nassir. Even though you came off the bench. You seemed *really* focused out there?"

"Did I? It must be the Lord's omniscient hand of guidance."

"You joke, I get it. But it just may've been God's hand. How else can we explain your ability to be so laser-focused with *everything* going on around you?"

The question drops to the ground like a dead opossum. Nassir and Greg examine it, then:

"Zoloft!" Nassir blurts out joyously. "And wouldn't you know it, the psych prescribed the wonder pill to me for, get this, PTSD, and not, as we all seemingly assumed, the big D! Not dick, Shane. *Depression.*"

"Really?" Shane is clearly surprised and weirdly relieved.

Hey, Nassir, it's me.

Not right now, Greg.

They ascend the old, stone church's stairs. Green ivy covers its exterior walls. The church was built during a time when houses of worship were intended to inspire the sensation of feeling small, helpless, and, most importantly, in desperate need of a savior (to whom you'd tithe). On the balcony of the main sanctuary, Greg and Nassir find two empty seats next to a White man named Gilliam. Gilliam wears tinted glasses and a short-sleeved button-up with a dark brown tie because he has big dreams of being a deacon. He's trying to fast-track it, he once confessed to Greg in unasked-for confidence inside the echo of the men's bathroom—hence the unofficial Deacon uniform. He punctuated his urinal speech with a hard slam of the metal flush handle.

Gilliam vigorously shakes hands with everyone around him when White Pastor instructs the congregation to stand up and say hi to someone they don't recognize. "Press flesh" is the well-worn pastoral punchline. Nassir dodges Gilliam's eyes and shrinks from his spectral hand when Gilliam reaches across Greg to shake Nassir's hand. Nassir notices a small "Q" pin on Gilliam's dirt brown tie.

"Nassir, good to see you *again*. How's Monty? I haven't seen him around for a while."

If time could stop and crystallize, it would here for Nassir. He clears his throat, "Just a sec," clears it once more, then mimes that he's choking, "Too much phlegm!" and excuses himself.

Greg turns back from shaking someone's clammy hand just in time to see Nassir sprinting towards the back stairs.

"Like father like son," Gilliam shrugs, plops into his seat, and straightens his short sleeves.

Greg sits, "Something like that."

Across the way, seated at the other end of the U-shaped balcony, Greg sees Jasmine lean against Father Figure 3.0. She's wiping tears away. And 3.0 just pats her on the thigh, like she's a child. Why's she crying? What'd he say to her? Jasmine once told Greg that she sometimes refuses communion, but only on those occasions when she doesn't feel like she deserves it. *But, Mom, isn't that kind of the whole point?*

White Pastor takes his place behind the pulpit, "Let's pray. Lord, we come to you today, on this beautiful Portland morning, to thank you for ensuring that *your* candidate won, even though it wasn't a fair election—"

"Amen!" the congregation shouts. "Hallelujah!"

"—and that, no matter who would've won, we can be sure your will was *surely* carried out. Amen-amen, an."

Gilliam whispers to Greg, "Things are in motion. Just ask your friend, Nassir. His dad couldn't handle the truths."

The look on Gilliam's face makes Greg's stomach do somersaults.

After Greg fled the balcony, after he found Nassir hiding in the bowels of the church, down in the basement where the basketball court is, in a gym the size of a thimble, a gym with dark brown wood slats for walls, walls that raise up two stories, like something out of that old movie *Hoosiers* that White men swear is the best basketball movie in the history of Cinematic Basketball, because the good 'ol White Boys from the Country pulled themselves up by the bootstraps (which is physically impossible, if anyone's counting) and beat the Black Inner-City Boys, and after Greg told Nassir that on his way out of the sanctuary he heard White Pastor say that "If Ben Carson the *brain* surgeon!" is a fan of the new White President, the White President can't be all that bad, and after Nassir said, without taking his eyes off the lines of the gym floor, "Ben Carson is striving for *lactification*, as Fanon said," and after Greg said, "You mean, he's… lactating?" and after Nassir ran his eyes from the baseline to the freethrow line and back again and said, "Nah, man, he's trying to Whiten himself, trying be closer to human, in *their* eyes, you know what I mean?", and after Greg couldn't remember which of the books that Nassir had given him to read were by Fanon, and after Nassir sprinted his eyes from the baseline to the half-court line, the whites of his pupils in his light brown face looking even more white and sparkly under the old sodium lights, and after Greg put his arm around Nassir and said, "You alright? You want to go to 7-11 and get a slurpee?", and after Nassir said, "Do you think I could do a suicide here? In *this* gym? It's shorter, you know, the gym is, by like twenty feet, so maybe I'd make the twenty-three?", and after they did go to 7-11 and they did get slurpees and they did suck them down, pressed against the cold wall, there at 7-11, outside in the rain, because the gray flat clouds had moved in, because it's Portland, and after they both smiled at each other with big open mouths, revealing their blue- and green-colored tongues, respectively, and after they laughed, and after they didn't talk about Gilliam, and after they didn't talk about Monty, because it would lead to nothing but more of everything, and after they both pulled their hoodies up over their heads and slowly walked back to the big stone church, and after Nassir thought to himself, *I'm wearing a hoodie and have a pocket full of candy*, and after they met up with Jasmine who was, per usual, parading Father Figure 3.0 around the crowded foyer after service had let out, jawing on and on about 3.0's latest client at the clinic and just how well everything is going, even though she didn't really believe it, is in fact only willing herself to believe it, to believe the marriage is good, is okay, is fine, and after Father Figure 3.0 ran his hand along the side of a potential customer's neck, showing them where the wire would be inserted if they were to partner together and do God's work and, "Just go ahead and give me a call and we'll set-up a consultation and what's that? Oh, of course the consultation is free," and after a cluster of old, White churchgoers with brittle teeth and skin-spots cornered Greg and Nassir and asked about the team, "Are *we* going to make the playoffs?" and "*We* don't know about that Coach Day, ya'know?"—and their look implied the color of Coach Day's skin, his Blackness, being their main point of contention, and after all the White people smiled at Nassir, every single one of them, smiled and nodded and looked at him like they were doing him a favor by smiling at him, like he needed their smile in order for his life to mean something, and after they piled back into Father Figure 3.0's minivan not long after he had disseminated a handful of business cards to potential clients, and after everyone buckled up because Father Figure 3.0 said, "There're a lot of crazies out there today," and maybe intentionally or maybe accidentally glanced at Nassir in the rearview mirror as he said *crazy*, and after they passed the Denny's on NE 122nd and Jasmine wondered aloud why anyone would still go to Denny's when Lucy's Cafe is owned by Ben Jones' father, and also, not to mention, is where Shasta works, and after there was a brief theological discussion about why God, being the loving God that He is, allows some restaurants to fail and others to succeed, and after restaurant-theology was equated to the Problem of Evil and why God allows evil and Free Will if He is Omni-Everything all the Omni-Time, and there was a little passive Manifest Destiny sprinkled in there by Father Figure 3.0, and after all that, Nassir, looking like he is about to fucking scream, finally informs Greg that he knows Gilliam, like he knows-knows him. He's sure of it: "I know Gilliam. I'm sure of it," Nassir whispers to Greg. "He's the bomb maker."

9
12 November 2016

Shasta needs to pee. She wakes up and blinks into the morning sun—and Brian is right there. Millimeters from her face. Noses nearly touching.

"Shit! Brian!"

Brian smiles like a freshly peeled orange. She's pregnant. That's why he's right there—so close she can smell his stale breath. Because she's pregnant, and he, for one, could not be happier.

"Almost scared the piss out of me."

Brian kisses her on the forehead. "I didn't sleep all night."

"That was dumb."

"I just kept thinking about the baby and—wait, where're you going?"

"To pee."

"If you need anything while you're in there—"

"What could I possibly need?" She closes the bathroom door behind her.

Brian, from the other side of the door now: "My mom can't wait to see you, *us*. I talked to her yesterday during lunch break, did I tell you that already?" He doesn't wait for an answer. "When I told her about the baby, she screamed and dropped the phone and called for my dad."

Shasta's sitting on the toilet, rubbing her temples, working the maze of the tile floor with her eyes as Brian rambles about his mother's impending grandmotherly delight. His parents wondered why Shasta hadn't told Brian about the baby until nearly ten weeks. He explained their worries away, just as Shasta had explained his worries away yesterday when she finally broke the news to Brian: "My mom had two miscarriages before I was born. Both at eight weeks, so I guess… I wanted to wait to tell you until I was sure."

Jasmine didn't have a miscarriage. Not one or two. Jasmine *did* have postpartum depression and pregnancy-induced carpal tunnel syndrome. When Shasta was little, she could never tell if Jasmine forgave her for being born, or, later, for moving to her father's, Matheson's house, when the man named Trench became their new reality. Matheson told Shasta he used to catch Jasmine standing above the crib, months after Shasta was born, hands clenched at her sides and crying (the same hands that throbbed through the long days and nights when Jasmine [Shasta learned later] rubbed Icy Hot on her hands and then picked Baby Shasta up, accidentally smearing Icy Hot in baby Shasta's baby eyes, and Matheson ran into the newly decorated baby room and took baby Shasta away from the crying, shuddering and horrified Jasmine and her Icy-but-still-somehow-Hot hands, and Matheson screamed, "What are you doing to *my* baby!"). Is that why Matheson left? Well, first cheated, then left? And is that why Shasta fights against her feelings of preordained doom? How far can a person distance themselves from the oppressive need to be just like their parents?

"Greg and Nassir's counselor came to me today," Brian says from behind the closed door.

This again.

"Babe?"

"Yeah," Shasta finally answers. "Can this wait until I'm out of the bathroom?"

She's recently found herself sitting on the toilet for prolonged amounts of time, waiting for the pee she knows must be there because she can feel it every moment of the day. If not piss, then what? Initially, she worried something was wrong with her because of the constant pressure on her bladder. But, after numerous calls, at all hours, to the 24/7 nurse hotline, during which she was assured it, the nearly unbearable pressure, was normal, Shasta now loves the excuse to get away from Brian and his rabbit trail stories and his never-ending tales of being a history teacher at Riverview. Don't even get him started on the latest election. He can talk nonstop, reciting the latest Guardian articles' *headlines* verbatim, about cyclical American ignorance and things of a systemic nature.

There's green mold between the tiles and the base of the tub. She asked Brian to clean the bathroom last week. Does he consider this clean? And all this concern about Greg and Nassir. As if Brian's concern is going to bring Shasta closer to Greg (which Brian thinks would be helpful to Greg)(to be honest, they're not very close, and Shasta knows it could be better, their relationship, but that's between her and Greg) and, ultimately, she knows Brian secretly hopes: draw Shasta closer to Jasmine, as well. Or, is the end game for Brian the student of his that Greg has a crush on, Jenny Owendale? The student Brian finds ways to bring up far too often.

"Gonna make eggs." Brian again.

"..."

"Babe?"

"Great."

She doubles back, trying to lose herself inside the deep grout separating the tiles, making right and left turns through the slightly raised ceramic and grime. Ceramic? She's not sure. Her father would know. Matheson knows most things. Or, at least he speaks like he does. He doesn't talk to you, he tells you. Instructs. Matheson is the exact opposite of Brian... and isn't that kind of the point? The tiles are adorned with light blue flowers. If they could have afforded to replace them when they moved in two years ago, they would have. If it were up to Shasta.

"Mom asked us to come over this weekend." Brian shuffles closer to the door. She can hear him holding his ear against it, listening. She holds her breath and tightens her butt cheeks to stop the pee that was just about to break free. "You're off Sunday, right?"

She hesitates, but says, "My dad told me he's going to buy us a house."

Brian doesn't answer. She knows he can't answer. She hears him move away from the door.

"Sunday's fine," she says quietly.

The whoosh of urine flows like a damn has been topped, overpowering his plaintive response. She's beginning to show. Her belly-non-belly is magnetic. It bumps into tables at Lucy's Café during her shifts. It is quickly becoming the focal point of every conversation. Her legs have fallen asleep. So. She finishes up and washes her hands. Shasta imagines her knuckles' tunnels and carpals throbbing, burning. But it's just her imagination. Isn't it? Her eyebrows are dark and thick. At least Greg didn't get the thick eyebrows of Matheson. Her brown hair is pulled back in a bun and pinned loosely to the top of her head. Steam fluffs against the bottom of the mirror from the scalding hot water. Her lips are thin but slightly puffed like mosquitoes bit each lip. She pushes a damp finger against the bump on the bridge of her nose, a gift from Jasmine's side of things.

"Bacon too, hun?" Pots and pans bang together. The click-click-click of gas igniting.

"Sure," Shasta says to the mirror.

Her ex-boyfriend, Gerald, used to kiss her on that little bump when he was inside her, as far as he could go. Gerald was, and still is, a listless man who sells pills to highschoolers—with no chin and shapeless eyes fixed on their own axis—but they made love with the smell of joints dying on the ground by the bed in his family's houseboat on the Columbia River. He'd plunge inside her as she gripped the cheap bed frame, feeling the house rock as her body shook. Every time she smells the skunk of a cheap joint, she remembers Gerald and the feeling of a never-ending horizon. Which was either incredibly lonely or weirdly comforting, depending on how high she was.

But that was college. Or, just after college. Or, just before she got serious with Brian. Just before she got pregnant, at the *very* latest. It was just a thing, a phase. Fucking Gerald was. Possibly cheating on Brian was. A time she'll never go back to, again. Shasta made Gerald promise that he'd tell her if Greg ever tried to buy stuff from him. She's not sure Greg even knows what drugs are considering their mom has him inside the church as much as spiritually possible.

When Shasta finally emerges from the bathroom, Brian is watching the news, sitting on the edge of the bed wearing black socks with an orange rim around the tops and boxers that sag in the butt. "They're closing the border. They're railing against Socialism. Well, Socialism in Brown countries."

"Eggs aren't ready?"

"Thought you'd never come out of there, I didn't want them to get cold." Brian gets up and trudges back to the kitchen. He turns the gas on. After a few quiet seconds, the eggs and bacon sizzle back to life.

Brian has never had Greg as a student in one of his classes. He often laments to Shasta that Riverview students don't show real concern for what's happening in the world. What's happening *to* them. "Do you think Nassir and Greg, for instance, even know what's happening besides basketball stuff? The NBA or whatever?" Brian's asked before.

Shasta wanted to say that she's not even sure they know *that* much. But she just blinked. Shasta is at the window. The pale light filters through the hem of her nightshirt.

"Shasta, you okay?"

"I'm listening," she replies and turns a smile to him.

Brian chuckles. Jovial. A new daddy. Nothing can stop him. Nothing can fucking stop him and his black socks! He turns the gas off again, jaunts over to her, and takes her by the waist. He presses his mushy middles against her flat bottom. She tilts her head back and they mirror each other's smile: her's feeling more like an urging to herself (like how it used to feel when she stood next to her mother in church, years after Jasmine and Matheson got divorced, singing hymns from those stiff red hymnals, wishing it would feel real, the worship, and watching Jasmine close her eyes when the pastor prayed over the congregation, watching Jasmine receive the prayer like she *needed* the prayer). She kisses Brian. Presses her lips into his. On the news, behind them, the newscaster narrates as people are shown using six-foot tall ladders to simply climb over the impotent border fence.

"So, what's this about Greg's counselor?"

"Mrs. Schuster."

"Sure."

"Mrs. Schuster's been his counselor, and Nassir's, for all four years I think."

"Okay."

"She asked me if I thought they were taking drugs. Doing drugs. Whatever."

"What kind of drugs? Weed? Molly? Or, are we talking about meth, ketamine, crack, you know, hard stuff? What I

wouldn't give to climb deep into a K-hole right about now."
Shasta walks over to the kitchen table and plunks herself
down.

"You think it's silly for me to worry?"

"Silly? No, Brian… You're right. What else did she say? I
mean, what are you asking me? Do you want me to call Mrs.
Schumann or something?"

"*Schuster*. Look, he's missing classes, you know, for the first
time, really. And Nassir's dad, you know, kept showing up
to school looking for Nassir. And when Monty couldn't find
him, like after he searched the school, ran from janitors and
whatnot, he tried to find Greg."

"I just."

"It's tough, Shasta, being a teacher and having my brother-
in-law having all these issues. It's not a good look."

"…" Shasta is beyond words. She takes a deep breath. Puts
her hands on her belly-non-belly. A reflex. A salve against
reality. A future promise.

Brian pulls another frying pan out of the bottom drawer. A
multitude of blackened pans cascade onto the kitchen floor.

"Crap."

"My dad's going to buy us that house in North Portland."

"I think this place is fine."

There isn't much Brian can say, is there? No matter how
much it makes a man feel like less of a man to have a father-
in-law buy a house (even if the man in question, Brian,
considers himself to be the *new* kind of man, the Modern
Man, a man not caught up with iconoclastic manly things)
(but, along with the house, there's also the implication
that said man is not "man enough" to support his wife, his
increasingly pregnant wife) the man would be an idiot to
reject the house. Reject the equity. The solid future. The
things White people pass on to other White people. So,
the house will be. It will exist. Matheson will speak it into

existence. Shasta knows there is, in fact, nothing Brian can say to change the future. She's not asking. She's telling. She's telling him and he has no choice but to listen.

"I thought you never wanted to go back to North Portland?" Brian asks, attempting a different angle.

That's where they were living when Trench showed up and ruined everything. North Portland. As if geography can hold pain. Shasta runs her hands through her hair and shakes out the bun. "It'll be different."

Then there's eggs and bacon and hash browns on plates in front of them. There were long minutes of silence before. Now there's this thing called breakfast, at least.

"So, I mean, have you talked to Greg recently?"

"A week ago." Shasta scrapes that gross gelatinous liquid from the top of her eggs.

"I'm not saying Mrs. Schuster is right, but, it's not just her, I guess, that's worried, you know? About him and Nassir. When I saw them yesterday at school, they didn't look too… *engaged.* I even tried to ask Nassir for a book recommendation. He just looked at me and said, 'The wretched of the earth, Brian, the wretched of the earth.'"

"They're in high school. I don't think they're supposed to be too *engaged.* I know I wasn't." She hates the filmy stuff on top of her eggs that Brian never fully cooks out. No matter how many times she's asked him to. "Were you engaged in high school?"

"Actually, yes, I was."

"Of course."

"Regardless. They've missed a bunch of classes. I've heard from the other teachers. I thought maybe you should, could, check up on him. Frankly, they're afraid, well, afraid Greg might go the way of Nassir."

"What's that supposed to mean? How racist is that? Riverview, for such a diverse school, really needs to figure its shit out. And, anyway, I always thought Nassir was being dragged down by Greg, if I'm being honest."

"I'm just the messenger."

"I only know what he tells me. But I'll call him if that'll make you happy." She pushes the eggs away.

"Everyone's concerned, Shasta. That's all. And then there's the basketball part of it, you know. But since, well, I'm his brother-in-law, it kind of makes me look bad, too."

Shasta scoffs. She splits the yolk and watches yellow drool slime across the plate. "I'm sorry my family is tarnishing your sparkling reputation."

"I didn't mean anything by it." Brian squeezes her hands between his. "Maybe we could invite him, or them, over for dinner?"

"Isn't there an attendance monitor or something? If he's missing so much school wouldn't they call home, call my mom, suspend him? Something?" At least the bacon is crispy.

"The Athletic Director handles that."

"So?" With just the right amount of fat lining the edges.

"*So*, the team needs Greg and Nassir to be eligible to play."

"That happens? They let kids get by because they're on the team? They aren't even that good, are they?" She looks at the soupy eggs again, makes another go at them (aren't eggs supposed to be cooked hard when you're pregnant? Don't soupy eggs cause birth defects?)

"Riverview needs a win, babe. It's not right, but, I guess, I get it. And, you should know, they're both good. Really good."

"Brian."

"Greg gets seventeen points a game and a bunch of rebounds. Seven, eight maybe? And Nassir gets about fifteen a game, three assists, and two steals. Even when the coach makes him come off the bench. So."

There's a way people talk about sports, about stats, about

the players and how they play during the game, a way that makes every player and every number heroic. And maybe they are. Maybe they're superhuman, if only for the time being. If only in a collective imagination.

Shasta is not impressed.

"I'm just saying," Brian says. "I get it, in this case."

"Do you? Does that make *you* look better in their eyes?"

"Forget it." Brian swallows a large bite of eggs.

Later that night, when Shasta pauses in the middle of the dining room at Lucy's Cafe to momentarily take stock of what her life is becoming, has become—the crush of the dinner rush swirling around her; the busboys careening past her; Mr. Jones sipping a drink while leaning on the end of the bar; servers saying/shouting "behind" as they slip past her with trays of full martini glasses held high above their heads, drinks sloshing to the rims; the expos clattering around her with plates of hot food lining their arms; the chef with the tattoos and the red beard shouting orders in Spanglish to the Mexican line cooks in the auditory distance; clips of dialogue from White guests at tables as they lie to themselves about the *real* reasons they voted for a return to a Jim Crow'd America (as they sit in a Black man's restaurant); the sounds and textures of it all bubbling around her, encasing her like a cocoon; the dining room full of shiny faces stuffing their maws, chewing with mouths agape, punching food in, choking large chunks of steak down engorged necks, sweat rolling down their wide and runny noses—she can feel the edges of her chosen reality starting to crack. And, surprisingly, in that moment, she decides that she *does* love Brian. Not so much a decision as an admission. Not so much an admission as an acceptance. She wasn't even sure it was a question. But, who does Brian think he is, questioning her about Greg? She wants to call Greg and tell him to run. Run as far away as he can. Run directly into the sun.

SUICIDE RUNNERS

12
29 November 2016

Greg attempts to block out Nassir's fake hiccups. To focus on the moment ahead, *after* the final buzzer. *HICK-up.* Win or lose. They are currently seated in the utility room within the women's locker room of St. Helens High School, where visiting teams are made to do their pregame activities. As if this miniature emasculation will help St. Helens on the court. Greg tugs at his shorts. *HICK-up.* Nassir apologizes, quietly, with eyes closed, for the fake hiccup. Coach Day's voice and gameplan and curses and belittlings sift in and out of consciousness, is now just Muzak to Greg, Nassir, and the rest of the team waiting to be set free on the court. Greg tugs at his shorts again. He's wearing boxers instead of boxer briefs—as he normally would for games—and he knows it's an undeniably bad omen for the team. The boxers are. He was distracted as he dressed for school. Father Figure 3.0 kept yelling at his mom. Explaining to Jasmine that he's not to blame. Telling her, with sharply violent tones, that Monty's the only one to blame because it was Monty's choice in the first place. Jasmine said something back, something Greg couldn't make out, causing Father Figure 3.0 to blurt out, "It has nothing to do with him being Black!"

HICK-up! "Sorry."

Not long after the argument, when Greg entered the kitchen, Jasmine was at the stove, preparing eggs, stoic, robotic, numb. Her eyes were underlined with the red evidence of tears. She said, "Good morning, honey," and hugged and kissed him on the cheek.

So here he is, Greg, wearing loose-fitting boxers instead of snug boxer briefs. He tugs at his shorts again. He doesn't want to interrupt Coach Day to tell the team about their impending loss, the inevitable slaughter they are destined to endure because of his boxers, but he knows it'd be the honorable thing to do. He ate the eggs and toast his mom made. She barely ate her own. They both just sat there, too removed to say anything; and she forced a hint of a smile and told him it'd be okay; and it, the second round of yelling that followed the eggs and toast, has been a singular, unshakeable point of focus for Greg ever since.

Nassir is slumped next to Greg. He smells sour, like he hasn't showered for a few days. Nassir interrupts Coach Day's defensive portion of the gameplan with a mighty *HICK-UP.* A sink, somewhere within the depths of the locker room, drips. Greg wants to kill whoever's responsible for the incessant dripping. He can feel the drip form on the faucet. Feel it gain weight. Feel it being pulled down. The drips consume all sound in their wake. The Washington twins of St. Helens, who consume the bulk of Coach Day's defensive concern, are big, ugly, and sport haircuts a weed whacker would be ashamed of. The last time Riverview played St. Helens, there were three technical fouls called and forty foul shots taken—mostly because of the big White twins getting away with murder.

Greg can still hear the words that Father Figure 3.0 used this morning to tell Jasmine exactly how she should be feeling about "the whole fucking Monty thing." They play and rewind themselves between every drip. They went something like: "Don't you *drip* dare question my *drip* judgment." He slammed the bedroom door and stomped into the kitchen, where Greg was, and with a crooked grin, 3.0 said, "Morning. Good *drip* luck tonight, Gregory." And who THE FUCK gave him the right to call him *drip* Gregory? He's just barely okay with Nassir's use of his so-called Christian name.

Nassir isn't starting because he couldn't make the suicidal 23 in yesterday's practice. He hasn't even tied Marcel's Jordans yet. Andre the Captain got his hair done today. He skipped the last period and got the high fade at the barber shop over on Sandy behind the International House of Pancakes. He said, "Nassir, let me have my man fix that hair for you." Nassir said, "I'm growing it out, Dre. My White mom wants me to keep it short. Her new White boyfriend, Phil, told me I look *respectable* with short hair. Told me I look less like a Black Lives Matter protestor." Ben Jones is wearing his lucky socks, the ones that hug each individual toe, and he keeps whispering to himself that he's the Double Outsider. Marcel the Supplier reminds everyone that he has a new drug for them. But then asks in a whisper, "I can't remember, have we already taken it? Shit. Let's swallow another just in case."

Coach Day screams, "We're going to double the Washington Twins every time they get the ball in the post and force the other players to make some fucking shots for fuck's sake!"

There's a KNOCK-KNOCK on the door. Game time. Tip-off in ten. Greg's last chance to address the team, to fall on his boxer-shaped sword. He stands, slowly, stiffly. Nassir pushes him by the butt to help him up. Greg readjusts his shorts again.

"Men, I hate to tell you that, even though I'm confident we, all things being equal, all things being as they should be, could win this game, we won't. Why? Because God has some form of unpaid retribution to exact upon our sinful heads? Because I looked at porn last night? Because I joined in with my brother-in-law, Brian the Teacher of History, in lusting after Jenny Owendale and her spectacular kneecaps during lunch? Because Nassir is having pre-marital sex with Naya? Because Marcel the Supplier has been smoking and selling The Beneficent Herb, sic, for the last three years and has and is now offering us a new remedy for our hazy vision? A new way to blot out the world? Because Ben the Double Outsider is gay but hasn't come out yet for fear that he'll be rejected? And but then who are we to judge his fear? Does he not find himself in a double bind of being Black *and* gay in a community where both are passively frowned upon? Because I lied on my college application essays when I said I hoped to be accepted to UCSB because I thought it would provide me with the best education I could imagine when all I want to do is get as far away as I can from this place, physically and mentally and maybe even spiritually speaking. And is it just me, men, or is there an ever-heightening sense of dread as the season wears on, as we plummet towards matriculation? Graduation. Life beyond. A life in a world where, for you, my Black and Brown teammates, where *you* are a threat and not me, despite all the evidence. Is that why we'll lose tonight?

"Or, is it because of our *collective* unpaid debts; the sins of our fathers and their fathers and their fathers before them, and so on and so forth, pushing up through time like a sliver in a thumb left untreated? Left to fester. To rot. The stench of the American Dream. A dream that was and is often a nightmare for anyone who doesn't look like me? Or, is it because St. Helens has more believers on the team than we do? Is it because Coach Day is drunk, right now, as he scribbles illegible words on the whiteboard? Is it because we, the Whites on our team, come from family lines who've never repented, never righted the wrongs of their slash our imperialistic sins? Come *from* Natchez, but never *went* Natchez way?

"I'm afraid not, men. I *wish* it were that simple. The truth is: I wore boxers today instead of boxer briefs. We will be crucified out there because of my undergarments. And, for that, I am infinitely apologetic. It is the Lord's Will, though, just as White Pastor said the results of the election were the Lord Almighty's Will. We must accept it and move on, White Pastor said. We must accept our fate and move on, because His desires—Jesus's I mean; Yahweh, Jehova, the Triunal Man of Mystery—not my desires, or your desires, are the only desires that matter. I have tried to empty myself—I'm in a constant state of attempted emptying, and, men, I cannot for the life of me seem to come to grips with this emptiness. Marcel the Supplier's pills have made this emptiness all too clear. I am now faced with unanswerable questions. Questions the books Nassir gave me to read provide truthful answers to. But, it's there, maybe, inside the answers to the previously unanswerable and, possibly, even unaskable questions, that I'll find my salvation. *Our* salvation. And by salvation I mean wins. I mean playoffs. I mean destiny. Alas, there are no answers to some questions. And, tonight, we're faced with another unanswerable query: Why did I choose boxers instead of boxer briefs? Why did Nassir's dad lose his mind—if we agree he lost it before Three-point-oh drilled holes into his head? Why did my half-sister contemplate having an abortion and, more importantly, why did she decide to tell me, and only me, this precious fact when, last week, she invited Nassir and me to dinner at their new house in, ironically, our old neighborhood of N. Portland—which she vowed never to return to after she exited stage left when The Man Named Trench became an unblockable fist? The Man Named Trench who's back at Riverview swimming through chlorine, waiting for us. For me. Spitting water out of the side of his mouth when he surfaces for air.

"These are all questions that life, in all its glory and chaos, cannot answer. Why, men, brothers of all colors, did I choose boxers instead of boxer briefs? Tell me! You can't. Only God knows. And the Bible tells us that we must be childlike in our faith. Men, let's go out there and meet our maker."

Greg, can you hear me?

Loud and clear.

That was quite the speech you gave in there. Really got on your White Man's soapbox and laid it all out there.

I do my best, Nassir. But look, the game's in full swing and—

Defensive stance, Greg! Like they taught us when we were kids, when we were innocent, still worthy of being taught things: knees bent at ninety degrees, on the balls of your feet, arms out, hands extended, eyes focused on your opponent's midsection.

This is how you properly guard the opposition, Nassir! You slide your feet, never crossing them, side-to-side. When the opposition attempts a shot, you raise an arm and place your hand in front of his face to obscure his vision. You yell, "Shot!"

Listen, Greg, listen, this is how you box out: you place your butt against the opposition, you hold your arms out behind you, you shield the player, you get between player and hoop, you watch the trajectory of the ball, you anticipate where it will bounce off the rim, you jump and grab the ball with both hands and you keep the ball held high above your head. You swing the ball left to right, elbows out, to clear the defenders away from the ball. Elbows out! Like Rasheed Wallace! Elbows out, Greg!

Nassir, when you check in, when Coach lets you in, when he forgives you for being, *this is how you shoot a jumper: when you're shooting a jumper and the defender doesn't closeout fast enough, giving you too much room to attempt said jumper, you tell that fucking defender as you shoot, "Too much room!" and you make the shot, and you call him a bitch. This is not an option. This is mandatory. Because we are destroyers, Nassir, destroyers of worlds. You'll see, Nassir.*

There are fans cheering for each team, Greg. You must be aware and must be prepared for this. The fans of the St. Helens will boo you when your name is called for starting lineups. Their White faces will contort into shapes of anger and malice, and the veins on their necks will swell when they scream—even at you, Greg! You! A White boy! *The fans will inform you that your mother is ugly. They'll tell you how worthless you are. They'll tell you that every shot you make, every breath you take, is done so only by luck. They'll wish death upon you. And for this, you must kill them. And boy o' boy, Greg, just wait until I get in there.*

I'll pray to my mom's God that we will be forgiven for our thoughts of death and destruction, Nassir—but we must try and kill them, the fans, spiritually, with our play on the court. The opposing fans should forgive us for trying to kill them. They should know that if we were there at Golgotha like they must've been, if the blood from His speared side sprayed onto our faces and turned our eyes black, if we felt the ground shake, if we saw the heavens part, that if we were at Golgotha like they were when Jesus the Christ was crucified, we would be a much better person and, logically, as a result, a more gracious, loving enemy. St. Helens has 'saint' in the name of the city but these fans, these White demonic-faced screaming saints, are wishing that we and our whole diverse team were at Golgotha so that we would be better humans. And they boo you, Nassir, they boo you and Andre; they boo Marcel; they boo Manny; they boo us all, but when they boo our Black teammates, they boo with a righteous venom on their breath.

White faces, Greg. A sea of agony. A tide of fear. Armageddon is here. They voted to bring it, to win it, to end it, to restore it— to Make America White Again. Open your arms. Lift them to the sky and open your arms to what is to come. Because my dad found a truth he couldn't live with.

The White man in the parkway, who called the cops on us? Nassir, he never sleeps. I've seen him walking the streets at night too many times to count.

They all *walk the streets at night, every night, every street. Every White man is looking for me, Greg. You'll get it, someday. Or, maybe you won't. Maybe you'll remember back on the days you had a Black BFF and you'll wear it like a badge of honor and tell all your coworkers later in life that you aren't racist because you once had a Black best friend, Greg! But pay attention, Greg! You just stole the ball from a pudgy kid in a tight jersey and you called him a bitch and you dribbled three times towards our hoop and you can hear him wheezing behind you and, look, you just jumped with two legs and you're soaring towards the hoop, and you feel his meaty hand on your back, and you put the ball off the backboard, and there's a whistle, and you watch as the ball goes through the hoop with your head tilted back, and as you fall to the ground you look to the blur of black and white stripes and see that he's making the sign with his arms that the basket's good and that the pudgy kid was called for a foul, and the White home crowd is frantic because they believe from the bottom of their righteous souls that* you *fouled* their *player first, and so you turn to the opposing crowd, with their twisted demonic faces, and you make your own demonic face, because you can do that, Greg, you have that inside you! And look, you fire a carnal yell right back at them and it shatters the lights and splits the floor and everyone gets goosebumps and you look right into the black eyes of an old White man who is cussing at you and you know, we know, that he* wasn't *at Golgotha either, and we see a crown of thorns on the man's balding head and blood runs down his face and now you're shooting a free-throw to complete the and-one, and Andre the Captain yells "Fuck yea, niggas!" to all the White players on the St. Helens team. And the St. Helens crowd breaks into a chant of "MA-GA, MA-GA," for no reason, for all the reasons, for the only reason.*

It's finally time, Nassir. Coach tells you to check into the game. And as soon as you stand up, the cluster of Riverview fans cheer wildly. They're ecstatic, Nassir. On the verge of tears. All of them. They cheer to cheer you up. Cheer to save your life. Cheer because Monty isn't here to cheer anymore. And Andre's mother shouts, "Let's go, baby, you got this! We love you!"

Riverview won by twenty.

13
Monty's Rabbit Hole

What do you want to know? What will make you feel better? It'd be easier, for you, if Monty's decline had nothing to do with race. Wouldn't it? Be honest. The truth is, after the black Lincoln Towncar rushed around the corner on that cold morning long ago in Washington, D.C., the Towncar with the dead leg dangling from the trunk—if you're to believe Monty—he *did* go about the rest of the day like it was any other day. Not *Day Zero*, but Day 365 x his age + the days already lived during that calendar year. A big number. Days added to more days, all the same day for Monty—until that day. No, stop it, that day *was* just like any one of the thousands of normal days he'd lived. He made it on time to the big meeting; a meeting in one of those faceless government buildings that line DC streets like colonizing soldiers at attention. The meeting went as expected. The White men in the conference room did a double-take when Monty entered and was so clearly not White. Check. Normal. The White women smiled at him with that smile that looked like they thought he won something or stole something, he could never tell. Double-check. His presentation about how much money they would save per quarter, and the incentive-laden contract he presented after the main portion of the presentation, were all received as he expected they would be. A White man in a suit that was just a bit too tight around his neck complimented Monty on such an *eloquent* presentation. CHECK PLEASE. NORMAL. Contracts were signed. Meaty hands were shaken. One White woman curtsied to him, and then admitted that she hadn't curtsied to anyone since she was twelve and in debutante class in Alabama. And, when she said Alabama, she looked at Monty with an apologetic look, as if she'd said KKK or something similar on accident. He took a cab to DCA, got on a flight that laid over in DIA, and landed back in PDX just as the sun was setting. And not once on the way back, did he think about the dead leg—which, come to think of it, *had* to be real, as in from a living person, or formerly of a living person, because what kind of fake leg, from a mannequin or what have you, would have leg hair and bruises and scrapes? None that Monty could think of. But, beyond that, he didn't think about it. He ordered two glasses of red wine on each leg of the flight and by the time he was back home in Riverview, where his White wife was outside smoking a cigarillo—because it reminded her of high school (whatever that meant)—and their son was already in bed—reading, most likely—Monty was properly buzzed and feeling wine-drunk and ready to fucking explode if he didn't itch the itch that'd he been wanting to fucking itch since he and the racist White lady were almost plowed under by the Lincoln Towncar with the dead leg—the most definitely *real* dead leg—and so he kissed his wife on the mouth, and she tasted like trash, sorry, *ash*, and he put his things away in the closet and he splashed water on his face and he peeked in Nassir's room and sure enough, Nassir was reading, and he asked Nassir what he was reading, and Nassir said, "The Autobiography of Malcolm X. I got it from your bookcase," and then Nassir admitted, "I don't understand much of it, to be honest, but I think he's pretty cool," and Monty said,

"He was pretty cool; don't worry, you'll understand it more later, when you're not ten," and then Monty kissed Nassir on the forehead and went to the kitchen and poured himself a glass of cognac and swirled it around and took a big sniff and then he went down the stairwell into the basement and sat in front of his computer and turned it on and the monitor lit up his face and he felt warm and happy—partly because of the cognac, partly because of what he was about to do—and he opened up a web browser and logged into his favorite message board and immediately created a new post:

TITLE: License plate request + missing person report

MESSAGE: ISOI on DC Plate # H(dc crest)99; also for brown-skin man (most likely) reported MIA in the last three days in the DC area.

Monty's finger hovered over the mouse. He briefly contemplated not posting the message, fearing that he'd find exactly what he was looking for, an answer. An answer that would lead to more rabbit holes. The internet had the power to make conspiracies interactive. His finger quivered. He was ready to interact. He pressed POST.

14
Greg Hazel's Clear and Conscious Public Prayer that Led to a Winning Streak

1. What then shall we do in lieu of remaining pure, virginal, and childlike in the practice of our faith? 2. Standing before the fire-breathing gargoyle, the scorching blaze an infernal substitute for the life-giving waters one expects to receive, how are we, then, to behave? 3. To believe? 4. He asks for more. 5. Is He blind? one finds oneself thinking in the face of such a request. 6. Is the requisite emptiness inside not properly radiating, broadcasting the severe, barren state of the wasteland formerly known as the soul of the abject individual? 7. Is the copious amount of sweat, the pained strain of the face, the heave of the chest, not evidence enough? 8. More, the gargoyle demands. 9. More. 10. One can always give more. 11. And when we fall to our knees under the weight of the required, unattainable, emptiness; when we finally give ourselves fully to the demands of the one who stands before us, it is then, and only then, that one is granted the merciful feeling of being fulfilled. 12. One only needs to bend one's knees, hold one's arms out to the side, and, in unison with one's brethren, who if one were to look from left to right, all project the very same desired look of surrender, slide one's feet, left then right, left then right, left then right, left then right, while never crossing one's feet, in complete defensive acceptance of what is demanded by He who stands before us. 13. That, my brothers, is how we prove our worthiness, in accordance with His wishes. 14. Can I get an amen?

15

Portland Cable Access, Channel 22

Tight on a White hand, a fist. A blue light pulses. One finger straightens up from the fist. Then a second, a third, a fourth, and now all five. The lens widens and the studio lights come up.

CUT TO:

Tight on a sliding button as it's pushed to MAX on a sound mixer, and then BOOM, bathed in light, we see one leg bouncing, knee flexing, his back to the camera. A beautiful silhouette. His arms, fully extended, rise to the heavens. His body fills the screens of all those who stay up to watch Cable Access at one a.m. every weeknight.

CUT TO:

Camera B, as Tyrell Jones spins to the camera. He's magnificent, wearing yellow spandex and a loose-fitting red workout shirt around his already glistening mahogany shoulders. As the camera pushes in around his face, Tyrell's smile erupts:

"Good evening, and welcome to the Tyrell Jones Show!"

Jasmine is in bed, her face aglow in the hollow light beaming from the TV hung from the wall. She sits up straighter against the headboard. Her husband, aka Mr. Peterson aka Father Figure 3.0 aka 3.0, is fast asleep next to her. Jasmine presses a button twice on the controller. The volume notches up accordingly.

"Welcome, welcome, welcome to the Tyrell Jones show, family, friends."

Her husband grumbles and turns over, the back of his hairy neck slick with night sweats. She turns the volume down one click. She's not worried about waking him up, she's worried about *him* disturbing *her* nightly ritual. About having to acknowledge his presence.

Tyrell looks straight into the camera and invites his audience to be with him, sit with him, dance with him, to find love with him, every night, for fifty commercial-free minutes. And not one, but *two* phone numbers scroll across the bottom of the screen. He encourages those in need of encouragement, in need of healing, in need of love, to call him whenever they feel the need. His phone rings at all hours of day and night, he says. He says his callers say: You're all I have, Tyrell. You're the only thing I have to look forward to, Tyrell. My husband beats me, Tyrell. My wife doesn't do it for me anymore, Tyrell. My partner lies, Tyrell. My son doesn't love me anymore, Tyrell. I quit smoking six weeks ago, and the cravings are so strong, too fucking strong, Tyrell. My wife is sleeping with another man, Tyrell. You're an answer to my prayer, Tyrell. No, you're *the* answer, Tyrell. You cured my carpal tunnel, Tyrell, praise Jesus, *an*. My so-called husband wanders the streets at night with holes in his head, Tyrell. Help me, Tyrell. God doesn't listen to me anymore, Tyrell. I'm afraid that God has never listened to me, Tyrell.

"Everyone and every *body* up! Let's do some light kicking and some light punching as we meditate on our solution. Everyone up! We can only do this together."

Jasmine pulls her shoulders back, pushes the blanket down to her thighs, and punches, each arm extending a small, balled fist. Each fist cuts through and deflects the light against her smiling face. Only the whoosh of her arms. Only the certainty of these fifty minutes alone with Tyrell.

Tyrell Jones's dual numbers scroll across the bottom of the screen every three minutes. The studio call-in number is followed by his cellphone number for post-show personal problems. He repeats, every three minutes, that he hopes whoever needs to see the numbers sees them and writes them down, if not for now, for later.

Jasmine looks at her phone. She knows what her husband would think. Knows Judy and the Bible Study Ladies would say, "Hmm, really?" were she to call, to tell them she called. Admit she *has* called. Needs to call again. And she knows that the most recent call she received, this afternoon, from Greg's high school counselor, Mrs. Schuster, shouldn't, couldn't, cannot be spoken of to anyone but Tyrell because who else is there to blame but herself? Mrs. Schuster wondered, *innocently*, she assured Jasmine, "An innocent query, nothing to worry about, probably," but Mrs. Schuster called because she was worried about Greg and a possible, "but not *probable*, use of drugs." And was Jasmine aware of his changing behavior? Was Jasmine aware that the powers-that-be at Riverview, including Mr. Brian, her son-in-law, are worried that Greg may be following the path of Nassir? "And, as you know better than all of us, Jasmine, the potential Greg has, you see. You know." And the silence that followed screamed: You are to blame, Jasmine!

"They've been winning?" Jasmine asked, abruptly. Surprising even herself.

"Excuse me?" Mrs. Schuster sounded deeply offended.

"The team, my son and Nassir's team, they've been winning a lot recently, haven't they? Five, or is it six games in a row now?" Jasmine had answered the phone call in the living room, but by that point in the escalating conversation, she found herself out on the back patio, in the cold, pulling dead weeds from long-dormant garden boxes. "You there, Miss Schuster?"

"*Mrs.* Schuster, actually. And yes, they've had quite a run of late. But I don't see how—"

"I appreciate the call, MRS. Schuster, really I do. What I don't appreciate is the insinuation that Nassir is in some way bringing my son down. Tell me, Mrs. Schuster—"

Click.

But that was earlier today. This is Tyrell time. Back to Tyrell time.

"And punching, driving all that negativity away!" Tyrell. Oh, Tyrell. Thank you, Tyrell. "One, two. One, two. One, two! Yes! Good! Good!"

Only the whoosh of her arms. The force of her fists against the air.

16
25 December 2016

Marcy and Melinda Niemann, wearing matching pink with white polka dot pajamas, are seated on a loveseat in front of a brightly lit Christmas tree cluttered with gaudy decorations. A joyous fire burns in the red brick fireplace. The twins smile; it's Christmas. Melinda smiles just a tiny bit less because of the annoyingly apparent chin thing.

Mr. and Mrs. Niemann sip from their steaming mugs and tell their twin daughters to each pick out one gift from underneath the tree, and the Mr. and Mrs. sip in unison from their cups of Yuban coffee. But Melinda, always the one not focusing on what she should be focused on—because of the chin thing—looks out the window and says, "Dad, look. Look, Dad! That Chissler kid is out there standing by your Mustang. Again."

Mrs. Niemann fixes her hair and says, "See, honey, I told you you should've kept it in the garage. After Monty and all. They just. They're just not right. The whole family. Well, Gloria's fine, that poor woman. We all warned her when she said she was gonna marry Monty."

"Because he's Black," Melinda states.

"Melinda!"

"I would've been glad to keep it in the garage," Mr. Niemann says, "but you've got all that Tupperware and all those leggings that you're *supposed* to be selling in there, honey, so, an. Now, come on now, what is he doing? No, stay here girls. Marcy, make sure Melinda stays put. I'll go outside and see what he wants."

"He wants a new dad, is what he wants."

"Marcy."

"Sorry."

"He wants a new dad."

"Melinda."

"Sorry."

Nassir's hands, purple from the cold, come to rest on the frost-covered hood of the red Mustang. A red and white "For Sale" sign is tucked into the seam of the driver-side window. *$2500 obo.* Even though it's below freezing, Nassir is sweating. T-shirt and bones and jeans and Marcel the Supplier's untied Jordans on his feet. Tucked into the back of his pants, like a pistol, is the latest book he's reading, *The History of White People*. A large, white-covered brick of a book. Dark clouds hang low overhead. His breath comes fast and hot, billowing from an ajar mouth. A door closes. Heavy footsteps crunch across the frozen grass.

"Now, Son, I told your dad to stop coming around, okay? And now you. I don't want to have to call the police—"

"Why won't you sell him the car, Mr. Niemann?"

"You have to quit coming by here. Do you hear me? You all are having a fine season, I hear, top of the conference, an, and we don't want you to get in any trouble now."

Nassir moves his right hand behind his back. Mr. Niemann flinches, his body tensing, as if preparing to get shot; as if Nassir is going to shoot him; as if the generational, biological fear of Black teenagers like Nassir has finally come to life in Mr. Niemann's very own front yard, just like he always knew it would.

Nassir pulls the book from behind his back and thumps it against the Mustang's hood. Mr. Niemann is visibly relieved.

"Where are you from, Mr. Niemann?"

"What do you mean? I'm from here. Portland. The beautiful state of Or—"

"Yeah, but where're you *really* from? Your family? Way back. How did your family get here?" Nassir thumps the book against the hood again. A little harder this time.

"Well, my mom's side is—"

"Let me guess, Mr. Niemann, you're Anglo-Saxon? Of 'good English stock' as they, you, White people like to say."

"Why are you looking at me like that?"

Nassir's head is tilted to the side, with a look in his eyes like he knows something Mr. Niemann doesn't know. "This look?"

"Yes, Nassir."

"I'm trying to look at you like Denzel Washington looks at White people. I used to watch his movies with my dad. He'd always point out the way Denzel looks at White people."

"It's getting cold. I'm shivering."

"Me too. Denzel looks at White people like he knows a secret."

"I don't see what this has to do with the Mustang."

"There's a part in *Deja Vu* when he walks into the police department and the detectives give him shit. You know how White detectives are always giving people shit in movies."

"I guess—"

"Sure you do. And Denzel looks at them with this smile. This look. Here, see what I'm doing… this. This look. A look that says: I know you think you're better than me, and I know you think I think I'm better than you, but I also know that you know that I know that I am better than you and that the only reason you're there and I'm here, in this position of me needing you, or being underneath you, is because I'm Black. You see, Mr. Niemann? But the look goes deeper. The deeper level of the Denzel Look says: I know that I have to play this part, like I'm underneath you so that you forget that I know that you know that I'm a shooting star, I'm owning this scene, and not just on film, on the big screen, but here, on set, in the real world. Denzel eats them up, Mr. Niemann. He eats these White men up with this look, both on screen in his roles and on set in real life."

"My wife doesn't like Denzel, she says he's too arrogant."

"Why won't you sell my dad the Mustang? It's not even that nice. I just want to get inside and feel what it's like to sit in the driver's seat. Let me get inside, Mr. Niemann. It doesn't even run, what's the big deal?"

"It does run, I fixed it up. Which is why I'm asking twenty-five now instead of two thousand. Okay? And, well, Monty just doesn't have the money for it. I don't want to be mean about it, but, well—"

"Be mean about it. I read somewhere in this book," he aims the brick of a book at Mr. Niemann, "that White people used to be really mean, in public, about everyone else. About Black people. It was okay, back then, to be mean in public. And, well, I guess it is again, isn't it? White people love other White people who are mean in public. Look at who just won the election. Am I right?"

Mr. Niemann, shocked into silence, rubs his hands together. Nassir doesn't move, except for the slow tilt of his head to the other side of his shoulders, and a slow, soft smile, spreading across his face. The Denzel Look.

"It's cold out here, why don't you go home?" Mr. Niemann asks but doesn't really ask. It's more of a statement. A demand. "My wife'll call the police if—"

"You mean the Runaway Slave Patrol."

"What? I. No! Not at all."

"I'm just kidding. That's just history, you get it. But be mean about it, Mr. Niemann. Say what you wanna say. No one says what they want to say around me anymore. Even when I speak in full sentences and enunciate correctly. Even when I contort my face to make it look harmless, to please your people. Your cops. But I can't get it right… What's that? You're right, I am cold. Freezing, to be exact. No, don't go back inside. Be clear about it. Don't you get it, Mr. Niemann, White people don't say what they mean anymore, to me, to *me,* Mr. Niemann! They speak to my skin. My White mother clearly wants to say that she hates my dad and that she believes it's his fault that her life's fucking hell, but she doesn't."

"Look, I've got no problem with *African-American* people, okay? My wife, though, will call the cops. And we don't want that, do we? We don't need this."

"I like talking to you, Mr. Niemann. You're honest. You tell me what will happen. I read a book this past summer that said, *Black people and non-Black people do not exist in the same universe or paradigm of violence, any more than fish and birds exist in the same region of the world.*"

"Did you memorize that?"

Nassir doesn't like Mr. Niemann's *impressed* tone of voice.

"Well. I don't know what to tell you, Nassir. You seem smart, really smart, but—"

"Am I *Human* to you, Mr. Niemann?"

Sirens in the distance. Mr. Niemann looks up when he hears the familiar whirring sound of the police. He thinks, *Saviors.* Nassir sighs. Deeply. Mr. Niemann peers over his shoulder: his wife and two daughters' faces are framed in the window. Watching. Worrying.

"Do you think I'm crazy? Do you think my dad's crazy? In this book, I read about how White people ended up becoming White. Do you know *how* you're White? Do you even know what White means?"

"Nassir."

"My coach thinks my dad's crazy, but he won't say it. He plops me on the bench as some kind of revenge for my dad disrupting his practices at the beginning of the season. I think he thinks he's an embarrassment. I think Coach hates that he's being the exception, my dad is, stay with me, but the wrong kind of exception, you know? Not like an Obama-type exception. The ideal exception. More like… more like… Qyntel Woods. Remember him? Sure you do, Mr. Niemann. He's a deep cut, but I see that Trail Blazer's flag in your attic window up there. Qyntel Woods. A Trail Blazer. And a real embarrassment to the city. And White people never forget Qyntel Woods, do they? They never forget the Jail Blazers, do they? Nevermind that every Major League Baseball player was juiced beyond the max at the same exact time—beautiful, White Americans like Mark McGwire and Jason Giambi and Brady Anderson, making a complete disgrace of the sport—their heads ballooning to comic proportions, and still no one cared. Why? Mr. Niemann? Why didn't they care? And why did they care so much that the Blazers smoked weed? You know the answer. Deep down inside, you know it. Qyntel Woods is not so much an exception to them as Obama is, he's more of a rule. The rule that proves he, and everyone like him, is disgusting. You get it, Mr. Niemann. No, wait, don't go. But we get it, you and I, don't we? Maybe I'll end up being part of The Rule for all you White people, like another Qyntel Woods."

"Look, I'm going to go back in and—"

"Wait, just one more thing. It seems history and facts don't matter much anymore to White folk. How else do we explain the new President? You voted for him, didn't you? It's okay, don't answer that. Funny though, how there are more MAGA signs in front yards now than before the election? Like, all the underground Whites were waiting to be set free. Maybe it never mattered though, you know?

History and facts, I mean. I read somewhere, in one of my dad's books, that most of the White people around during Jim Crow time—which, by the way, Mr. Niemann, was just an American word for *apartheid*—didn't think life for Black Americans was all that bad. Kinda makes sense, doesn't it? Why y'all voted for our new President? Anyway. I think I'd like to get inside this Mustang. Did you know he's not the only one? My dad, I mean. There's a whole army of men and women in Riverview with holes in their heads, electrodes re-tuning their brains. Pacemakers and whatnot. They're mostly people of color, of course. Had to make sure to get the tech right before White people went under the knife. Anyway, did you know he used to tell me that all he needed to do was turn the dial and everything would go back to normal? Back to the way we always were. Back before he knew too much. That's what he said Mr. Peterson told him would happen. I don't think the surgery worked. Now, when he turns the dial, all that happens is that he looks like he's having a seizure."

"It's Christmas, Nassir."

"I understand."

The heat is on full blast, all the way past the red-blue, full on into the only-red, and there was a CD in the CD player when Nassir fired the Mustang up and it's playing loud, causing the speakers to screech and strain with each spike of treble. Mariah Carey belts *Joy to the World* in that incredibly high falsetto that only she can hit.

Nassir is tearing ass down Shaver Street. The Mustang charges through the low fog. When he blew through the first stop sign, he thought that he'd probably end up blowing past all the rest of the stop signs, too, because it's Christmas morning and everyone is safely inside their homes, opening their impeccably-wrapped presents. And he tries to hit the falsetto note like Mariah, but his voice cracks.

When Mr. Niemann came back outside, from what Nassir

was led to believe was Mr. Niemann jogging inside to call the cops, to make sure the sirens would come to save him and his women, Mr. Niemann was holding the keys to the Mustang in his hand and he said, "I'm moving the car inside now. You don't have to be like Monty, Nassir." Nassir pushed Mr. Niemann to the ground and ripped the keys from his hand and now here he is just really hauling ass down Shaver, towards the major intersection at 122nd and he hasn't made up his mind yet if he's going to stop at the red light or if, instead, he's going to blow through it just like he did all the previous red and sharply octagonal signs.

As he sped away from the Niemann's house, in the rearview mirror Nassir saw Melinda and Marcy trot out into the front yard, in their stupid polka-dot pajamas, to help their dad up but they both slipped on the icy grass and ate shit and Melinda, the one with the chin thing, flipped the bird to Nassir. Joy to the world. *Sing it, Mariah, like only you can!* The light at 122nd is green and thank Greg's mom's White God because Nassir had definitely made up his mind to run the red light and he slams on the gas pedal and the engine roars back and growls its murderous American-made approval and the muffler opens its mouth and vomits exhaust and now Nassir's flying past the dead farms on his right and he sees someone large and beanied lumbering through the middle of the hibernating crops heading towards Fremont and he's pretty sure it's his dad and Mariah Carey keeps hitting high note after high note and Nassir laughs and tries to hit that fucking note but his voice breaks and squeaks and he laughs and does it again and again.

Greg, Greg Hazel, come in. Can you hear me?
Loud and clear, Nassir. Merry Christmas!
I'm coming, Greg! I can't be stopped, Greg! Get the nog ready!
And the heat is on full blast, like way past red.

     SUICIDE RUNNERS

PART TWO

17
January 2017

Greg's hands fidget under the table as Brian finishes the prayer for *supper*, as he called it, with a meek amen. So impressively meek it almost goes unheard. Nassir's eyes remain closed. Greg clears his throat, attempting to bring Nassir back from the nether regions of the supplicatory séance. Tree branches scrape against the new windows. So new there are still traces of sticky residue from those yellow stickers crammed with too many words that every new window comes with. A half-ass wind blows against the double-paned glass. A hum emanates from somewhere, and it may be coming from Nassir, but then again it may be from the new Kenmore 4000 Dual-Door High Capacity Refrigerator in the adjacent kitchen with the bay window and a dining nook, humming away in all its sparkling, fresh-out-of-the-plastic-wrapping newness. Nassir slowly opens his eyes and, a minute late, says, "Aw-men." Greg and Nassir, a tableau of mystery, sit across from Shasta and Brian, a tableau of Manifest Destiny. Man. Woman. House. Baby on the way. Greg and Nassir's pupils are the size of flying saucers. Faces pale. Waxy.

Food is passed around the table and Brian and Shasta form pleasant-sounding words with their mouths and throw them into the void: "Looks good" and "Smells great" and "We're lucky" and "Room for the family to grow."

Shasta brought out the gold-rimmed goblets, the gold-rimmed plates and the gold-plated silverware that her grandmother, Matheson's mother, gave her as a wedding gift. "I only bring it out on special occasions," she says. "I know it's a little much, but sometimes it's just nice to have pretty things." She wouldn't dare have the plates out when Jasmine comes over.

Shasta leans towards Nassir (who has barely muttered a word) to pass him the steaming mashed potatoes, and her belly bumps against the table. The goblets tremble. Water sloshes from the top of Brian's cup.

"Babe, watch the belly!"

"Sorry. It's just like at work. Last night I spilled some lady's red wine doing the same thing."

"It's fine," Brian says while looking at Greg. "Hey, you two feeling okay?" Brain unfolds his new cloth napkin and places it across his lap. "You're being kind of quiet."

"Just swell, Brian," Greg says.

Nassir robotically scoops a helping of mashed potatoes onto his plate and passes the porcelain bowl—with a matching gravy boat—to Greg. Steam wafts from the creamy, round edges of the buttery potatoes on Nassir's plate. He tilts his face into the warmth.

"So, Nassir. How was your winter break?" Brian asks, doing that thing where he looks but kind of doesn't look to see if Nassir knows what he *really* means. Shasta squeezes Brian's hand under the table. Brian squeezes right back.

Greg clears his throat. Nassir chuckles. "It's okay, Greg. They've got the right to ask. I am a minor after all," Nassir says and punches a spoonful of mash into the grinning mouth below his dark eyes. "Just like they told me at the psych ward where I was watched like an alien specimen for twenty-four full hours, 'You're a minor, Nassir Chissler, a

minor who only has the right NOT to kill himself,' they told
me. They stressed the word *not*."

"He doesn't mean to pry. *Do you*, Brian?" Shasta asks, but
more so instructs.

"I don't. Really. I'm sorry." Brain almost leaves it there,
but, "It's just, the stealing of the car and all. The police?
Sounds like a big ordeal."

"The biggest!" yelps Nassir.

"Quite large," Greg says as he shoves a fork full of potatoes
into his speaking device. Silence hangs dead in the air.

Nassir chokes on a bone. "Excuse me. My winter break
was exhilarating, Mr. Brian."

"You can just call me Brian, we're not at school, after all."

"So it seems we're not, *Brian*. Here in this lovely little
home, reportedly purchased for you and your wife by Shasta's
benevolent father, I hear?" Nassir takes a moment to assess
his surroundings, possibly for the first time. "It's a wonder
what generational wealth will do for you, isn't it? My mom,
the White half of me, blames my dad for her own parents
not giving a shit about her—in a financial way. They have
money, apparently, but think Monty should've been able to
provide like a man is supposed to, they said. But, now that
she's with a White man, a White man who loathes me, by the
way, maybe they'll shell out for that all-expenses-paid trip to
Cancun she's always dreamed of?"

"We can only hope, Nassir," Greg says, each word dripping
with sarcasm.

Brian tries to find the magic words that will fix everything.
"That sounds—"

"Anyway, I'm a minor, did I say that already? I'm seventeen
and won't be eighteen until *after* I graduate high school and
so and hence, as it turns out, *Brian*, I'm not allowed, legally
speaking, to do much of anything of my own volition until

said, appointed time—me turning eighteen—at which, *whence* and such, I assume it'd be perfectly okay, *legally speaking*, for me to kill myself. More potatoes please, these're simply delicious. And just look at that damn gravy boat! It's HUGE!"

"Quite, QUITE large!"

"Greg. Nassir." Shasta is at a loss for words. Just saying their names, plus the apocalyptic look on her face, says enough.

Nassir takes a tiny bite of potatoes. "I'm sorry, Shasta. I'll just answer Brian's question. Yes, I stole the Niemann's Mustang. And yes, I drove it fast—"

"Super fast," Greg adds.

"That's right, super fast, to your mom, stepdad, and Greg's house on Christmas."

"Tell 'em about the cops."

"Oh, yeah, you'll love this. The cops came, to Greg's house I mean, right after I parked in the driveway. And seconds after Portland's finest arrived, who shows up?"

"You'll never guess," Greg blurts out.

"Your dad?" Brian says, prompting an immediate squeeze of the hand from Shasta. Brian winces.

"My dad. That's right! See, Brian, I knew you were one of the good ones. White people I mean. That's why I talk like I do sometimes, for the good ones like you, Brian." Nassir, eyes welling with tears, points his fork at Brian. Greg chuckles to himself.

"I don't know what you mean, Nassir," Brian says, attempting to cover his fear with an underwhelming wave of empathy.

"So anyway, I get handcuffed, right there on the sidewalk in front of your mom's house, Shasta; and Greg, Greg flips his shit, as you know Greg's wont to do, and charges the police!"

"Greg!" Shasta is nearly in tears.

"It's okay, Shasta, look, I'm alive."

"And White."

"Ah yes, Nassir, *and White*. And trust me, the look in the cops' eyes when they saw me coming, wearing my Riverview Basketball Jersey and all, they just kept yelling at me, telling me to calm down and go back inside. One of them even called me son."

"And there I was, picture it guys, there I was handcuffed and seated peacefully on the curb, and the moment I said something, the White cop, well, they were both White at heart, them being cops and all, but the White cop tased me!"

"Then I really lost it."

"I mean Greg went absolutely ape shit!"

"Language."

"Oh, right, Mr. Brian, sorry."

"I mean, I hate to ask…" Shasta really does hate to ask it.

"Just ask," Nassir says, angling his fork her way.

"Well, what'd you say to the cops? I mean, to piss them off…?"

"There it is," Greg says.

"My skin, Shasta, my skin said all that needed to be said. So anyway, Mr. Peterson, your stepdad, Shasta, made a deal with the police, White man to White man, and instead of jail, they threw me in a psych ward situation where I was watched and told I couldn't kill myself. Although to be honest, it hadn't crossed my mind. You have to be human to be able to think about ending your human life, and I'm not sure if they, the police, you White people, even see me as human—according to Frank Wilderson the Third. Have you heard of him, Mr. Brian? You being a history teacher and all? Someone interested in social things."

"You're human to me, Nassir," Greg says. "You're my human best friend."

Brian and Shasta are silent. Until—

"Nassir, I'm sorry," Brian says, "but I wasn't trying to—"

"Pry? Pry away!" Greg says. "Pry until there's no more prying to be done, brother of mine by law; until the knees of your jeans have holes from all the prying you've done!"

"Pry because if you don't pry," Nassir adds, "then who, or *whom*? is there to pry for me?"

"Don't pry for me, Argentina!" Greg sings.

"Well," Brian tries, "you see, we're all just worried, all of us at school I mean, the teachers and counselors, that you're taking the *stuff* happening with your father, well, hard, very hard, as evidenced by the car and all. And we'd like you to know we're here, *there*, at school for you, anytime you feel like talking."

"The *stuff*," Nassir repeats. He allows the word to roll around inside his mouth. To take form. To take up space.

Shasta kicks Brian under the table. Greg chokes down a large swallow of half-chewed pork chop he slathered with buttery potatoes. He works it down his throat with his hands, kneading it with patient fingers.

There is silence. Silence echoes across the table. It whispers to the wind blowing rain from the dark, cloud-filled sky. There are trees swaying out there. Swaying and waiting for spring when their leaves will resurrect. Greg can't muster the strength to move his massive pupils, his leaden green marbles, to Nassir. "Can we talk about something else?" Greg asks.

Greg and Nassir look spent, on the verge of exhaustion, total collapse. Their eyeballs swim in the oceans of their pupils.

"Sure. How're you feeling about the season?" Shasta says, her hand on the cusp of her belly. "Brian said you had a good game on Tuesday."

"Ah, yes. I was in the zone," Greg declares.

"The zone?"

"The zoooooooone," Nassir sings, eyes widening, gaining strength.

"What's the zone?" Shasta asks but fears the answer.

"What's the zone… what IS the zone… what is the zone what is the zone what IS THE ZONE the zone the zone."

"Tell them," Nassir demands. "Tell them what the zone is."

Greg places his silverware on the table and wipes his hands on the new, luxurious, cloth napkins (which will have to be washed in the new washing machine). He blinks intently, slowly, "The zone, capital *z* and *t*: The Zone, is where everything ceases to matter. Where all you can hear is your own breathing. Feel the ball's every groove and dimple. Your body extends in every direction, filling all empty space inside the gym, filling every wrong move, every wrong thought, every wrong action with perfection."

"The zooooone," Nassir sings in a higher key.

"It's where I want to live."

Shasta and Brian share a worried look.

"It's where the world ends, is blotted out, and the only thing left in its place is the basket and the ball. There is no room for absent fathers in the stands. No coaches on the sideline. No race. No politics. No religion. No, that's not true. There *is* race. But, in The Zone, capital z and t, the realities of our different skin colors are acknowledged and accepted as truth. The preferential treatment I receive in all areas of life over Nassir is there in The Zone, capital z and t, for all to see and know and feel and to die for. In The Zone, I am not just an ally but an *accomplice*, a co-conspirator. Everything is present and constant. Not even the defender is a real, tangible being. In the Zone, capital z and t, the defender is your puppet. The defender is a lifeless being who can only suck from the life-giving teat of your basketball godliness."

"The zoooooo—nnneeee," Nassir hums.

Shasta and Brian shift in their chairs.

"In The Zone—"

"Capital z AND t," Nassir interjects.

"The flick of the wrist is akin to a wink from the almighty Maker and Destroyer Himself. In The Zone, I can feel the perfectly rotating ball cut through each and every molecule of air floating between my hand and the rim and the net's bottom, with celestial ease. In The Zone, I can feel the waiting tingle of the nylon net. Everything is preordained in The Zone. I am exactly who I need to be and want to be and am supposed to be in The Zone with a capital z and t. I can feel the need, the want of the rim for the ball to come through the net. I can feel the orgasm, or what I assume a non-hand-aided orgasm *would* and maybe someday *will* feel like, of the net and its millions of embryonic fibers, overflowing with the gushing, the—"

"Orgassssssmmmmmic!" Nassir stands and thrusts both hands to the heavens.

"Yes, Nassir, yes! The orgasmic exultation as the net receives the full girth of the ball through its twiney fingers."

"Greg!" Shasta is apoplectic. "Please."

"That's about enough, Greg," says Brian. "Now, let's just—"

"In The Zone, half-sister! In The Zone, there is no right and wrong. In The Zone, there is no identity or obsessive need to find one's identity, as our mother believes she has within the church, or within her third husband, Shasta, my third father figure, Shasta! An identity that requires a giving of, a releasing of all personal desire. Do you not see? In The Zone, there is true freedom. In The Zone, Shasta, there is only *now*. But only the now *of* The Zone. There is no new White President. There are no police killings of men and boys and women and girls with skin a few shades darker than ours, Shasta! In the Zone, Shasta Matheson—"

"Harris," Brian corrects.

"Shasta *Harris*, the daughter of the man who left our mother for another, who by leaving opened the door for my mother to be fucked by my father, which resulted in yours truly, and then allowed for a space in time for her to be left *again*—or did *she* then do the leaving? Who and how could we ever know? Are you following me, Shasta? It was *your* White father leaving who led to *my* White father being replaced by The Man Named Trench who swims and cusses and stomps on any chance of moving on, who was then replaced by *another* White man, the great Father Figure 3.0, who, two summers yore, drilled holes into *Nassir's* Black father's head and placed faulty electrodes on *his* pink brain in hopes of granting a humanistic salvation of the mental and psychic kind, because in The Zone, Shasta! Brian! there one finds euphoria, instantaneous and continuous and mercifully unabated!"

"That's just not fair, Greg," Shasta pleads. Holds back tears. Holds her stomach tighter.

"Tell them how to find The Zone with a capital z and t!" Nassir exclaims, head back, eyes rolling white and bloodshot because the pill that promised a thrice-powered clarity has taken effect and has proven their teammate, Marcel the Supplier, correct.

Greg doesn't look at Nassir, but instead, he stares straight ahead at the alarmed and non-dilated pupils of Brian and Shasta. "The Zone cannot be found."

"Then, but, how?" Nassir screams, a delightful screaming demand.

"The Zone… finds you."

Greg and Nassir whip their heads to the window, where a streak of blinding lightning and rolling thunder should punctuate the end of the speech. But, alas, just the wind and rain. Nassir sits down, dripping with sweat, hands trembling, and says, "The Zone is an elusive bitch."

18
When Jasmine Became a Matheson

Jasmine is forty-eight years old. She was born in 1969. She is White. She never thought too much about it, her Whiteness, until Greg and Nassir became best friends as kids. Then, to ignore her Whiteness felt wrong. She couldn't put a finger on it back then, what Whiteness looked like and moved like. In Coeur d'Alene, Idaho, where she grew up, the whole world was White. White men. White women. White kids. White teachers. White church. White police. These are all things. After Trench, a few years back, Jasmine went looking for answers at church, and she's been trying to attend weekly Bible Study ever since. Greg is eighteen and on the verge of… something. Her daughter is pregnant and showing a genuine interest in having a relationship with Jasmine for the first time since Shasta left her and Greg for Matheson's more stable house when Jasmine let Trench into their lives. When Jasmine prays, she asks for forgiveness for the dark thoughts muttering to themselves in the rumblings of her past. Her life has splintered along so many different paths since she left Coeur d'Alene that it's hard to know when she was who and who she was when before she became the *wife* and *mother* version of Jasmine. She planned on driving to the Oregon coast, to a town called Seaside, when she left home at eighteen. She had overheard kids from school talking about Seaside when they would return from Spring Break with their wind-chapped lips, stories of arcades, endless boardwalks, and, most importantly to Jasmine, big crashing waves. The waves of Lake Coeur d'Alene lapped. She wanted waves that rolled and crashed. Waves that formed way out past the break line; humps in the deep blue. Waves with an undertow that sucked the sand from under your feet when they receded. She wanted to count to seven, waiting for the big one, for the one that would cascade, curl and BOOM as its lip kissed the sand. She wanted to check tide timetables. She wanted to know what a tide timetable was. She wanted to brace against the wind. They called it "the coast" in Oregon. So she would call it the coast, too. Like a real local. She wanted to be a local. She wanted to be anything but Jasmine Booker from Who Cares Where, Idaho. She wanted neighbors who waved (not neighbors who whispered when she walked by, or neighbors who peeked out from behind their curtains, or neighbors who knocked on the back door because, "We're just checking on you, there was quite a bit of screaming, and are you positive, Jasmine, that you, that everything's okay?" "You're just so pretty, Jasmine, it's such a shame."), and she wanted friends who'd come over for cards when the wind and rain battered the beach—*the coast*—and the coastline was so done in with fog that you couldn't even see the revolving light from the lighthouse, only hear its low braying horn. 463 miles. Eight-to-ten hours. Lake to ocean. You could do it one day. But she didn't leave until the sun was setting. And now, as the Bible Study Ladies seated around her are saying, "Amen and thank you, Jesus," and, "Yes, mmm-hmmm, thank you, Lord, teach us, Lord, an," and "Be with us, Lord, an," she remembers the tomato-red sunset and the fire in the clouds as she headed west. At some point in the night, she stopped at a motel in the high desert plains of Eastern Oregon. And the Bible Study Ladies are opening their Bibles, the best-seller of all best-sellers, as the Pastor (or, as she knows Nassir and Greg call him, White Pastor) joked during last week's sermon, and they are turning to Job because, "We are moving on from Kenosis to our study of Job, and hold onto your seats," he, White Pastor, said with a smirk, like he and Job were best friends, like he and Job had been together through the stripping of all that Job cared about. And the dark motel room in Eastern Oregon smelled like years of moldy things and people had lived there. Jasmine checked out of the trucker motel the following morning before the sun rose. She wanted— *needed*—to get on the road before flames of doubt could be fanned by the long day's tremble of a rising and falling sun. And Jasmine was at the grocery store off 122nd last night and a lady who goes to the same church, but whom Jasmine's never talked to, was in line behind her and thought it was her place to ask, "Your son, how's he doing, Jasmine? How's his college stuff coming along, Jasmine? We heard about Nassir stealing, well, *whatever* he did with that Mustang, and, well, Greg, he wasn't, was he, involved?" And Jasmine didn't have enough paper money so she had to use her credit card. And so they had to stand there and not say anything to each other while Jasmine tried to pull her card out of the plastic sheath thing with her shaking thumb and index finger, the woman asked about Shasta, "I hear she's pregnant? How exciting. A grandma soon." And Jasmine wanted to cry or scream or evaporate but she smiled and paid and left. Jasmine prays for forgiveness whenever she thinks of Shasta. She prays that Shasta won't end up like her: the three husbands (plus Trench); the however many different lives. She heard from Greg that Shasta's having a boy. And why didn't Jasmine have the same problems she experienced after Shasta's birth when Greg was born? The Postpartum Depression? The carpal-tunnel? And when Jasmine was eighteen and all of this—THIS—ALL THESE THINGS—was in front of her, and "Oh yes, AMEN ladies, AMEN to that," there was a destination, *Seaside*, but there wasn't a reason. There was hope, but no plan. A foggy idea of living on the edge of a cliff that overlooked the crashing blue and gray. How quickly you forget. And Judy says to the Bible Study Ladies, "Job was given everything. He was loyal. He did everything right. Everything was taken away. Praise be to God, and. An." And this is how the Bible Study goes. Someone says something, and the others amen it. As Job's life is destroyed, they amen it. As lives are taken, they amen it. As Black men are killed by police, they vote for the Angry White Man and amen it. Because it all happens for a reason. Amen. And, finally, the Bible Study is ending. Jasmine is just about to burst. She isn't finding what she was looking for here, is she? She's about to explode—but Judy and her crimped hair that's dyed blonde at the dark roots, with bangs like rainbows, bangs like the '80s, places her hand on Jasmine's elbow and says quietly, but also intentionally loud enough for others to hear, "I heard it turns out that your husband botched Monty's procedure pretty bad, an?"

"It's hard to tell, Judy. Monty isn't doing himself any favors."

"We heard about Christmas, an."

"Monty didn't follow protocol."

"We heard about Nassir, an. You know."

"Judy, please."

"Well. I mean. Is it true?"

"Please."

"We just, you know, want you to know that we care, Jasmine, an. You know, an…"

"AND everything is fine, thank you for your concern."

Six months after she made it to Seaside, had slept in cheap then cheaper motels, watched waves crash against endless beaches, and found irregular work at a place called Seaside Mart ("Home of the Freshest Bait in Town!"), Jasmine met Rick Matheson. The man who would become Shasta's father. He was on a fishing trip, in Seaside from Portland for the weekend, and in need of bait.

"We've got the freshest bait in Seaside. So. You're in luck," Jasmine deadpanned from behind the register.

"That's what I hear."

Rick Matheson was, and still is, a tall, square-jawed missile of a White man. He placed both hands on the countertop when he spoke to her. He leaned in and scanned the whole of her body with his dark brown eyes. He had an imperial nose and eyebrows that were too far apart. When he talked, she felt like she was being told something. She was just nineteen—she'd had a small birthday party with her new "friends," friends who smelled like the sea and partied with meth—and was working at a mart selling bait. So, Jasmine left Seaside when Matheson did. With him.

And Judy is walking, or attempting to walk, with Jasmine out to their cars in the cold, hazy mist, and Judy quickens her pace as Jasmine quickens hers and Jasmine says, "Judy, like I said, I just, well, I just don't know what to tell you, but I can assure you that Greg's doing the best he can, you know, he just, an, I mean and, he just really wants to do well in basketball, you know, and well, boys'll be boys, you know, and. *An.*" But Judy keeps pressing. Keeps insisting with a rising tone that Greg and Nassir are somehow, with their somewhat-public breakage, giving Riverview a bad name.

"Especially since, you know, they pretty much grew up in the church and all, well, ever since y'all moved to Riverview I guess, an."

"I'm not sure our church has much moral authority, Judy, since it's pretty clear who everyone voted for? Don't you think? *Judy?*"

And Matheson lived downtown in the Alphabet District on the front steps of the West Hills in a two-bedroom condo with big huge windows. He drove a 1983 Mercedes Benz 380SL. Mint condition. V-8. What color? Champagne? No, *Champayne*. It was a convertible. Hardtop. "Watch how it folds back on its own." He was thirty-three, worked at Boeing in R&D, or was it Sales?—she could never remember when her new cardboard friends asked her at the new salon she learned to frequent back then—and Matheson was fully insured: Health and Dental and Vision and Life and a 401 and an IRA and Stock Options that were fully vested. And she never thought about her mother or father. Or tried not to. Matheson took her to Boeing dinner parties and Boeing cocktail parties where cocktail attire was required. "But, honey, I don't have any cocktail attire?" So they went shopping every weekend. She modeled cocktail dresses in the mirrors of Macy's and Nordstrom, and Matheson nodded his approval in the reflections. The saleswomen with their hands flopped over and their tilted heads would say, "Doesn't she just, *wow*, just rock this dress?"

"She does."

And Jasmine never thought about her mom or dad or the lake back in Idaho.

"It's not too expensive, *honey?*" She had never before called anyone honey. She never thought that she would be that kind of woman: the kind to pander, to look at Matheson with sparkles in her eyes and portray the need that she knew he wanted from her. But there she was, she pandered and twirled in a black cocktail dress that hugged her slight curves, hugged the ass Matheson placed two hands on when they made love, and she liked it. She learned to embrace that woman (at nineteen). Honey. Sweetie. AND SHE NEVER THOUGHT ABOUT HER PARENTS. And they were married and Jasmine Booker became Jasmine Matheson because the girl takes the boy's last name. It felt to Jasmine like all of Boeing was there at the wedding. All *his* friends. *His* co-workers. She was the jewel. All the Boeing wives were jealous. They looked at her and her svelte frame, her effortless body, her perfect jawline, and her mysterious past from where was it again, Idaho of all places? and they fucking hated her. She knew they hated her and it made her so happy. Cake smashed into mouths. Jasmine didn't invite anyone from her past. From the lake that didn't lap, where mosquitoes festered inside still nights. Her mother and father were not notified. Rice and bouquets were tossed, garter belts in teeth, and people hooted and hollered and whistled and cheeks blushed. The first dance was to a Phil Collins song because Matheson loved Phil Collins. Then the song ended and the lights went down. Blackness engulfed the room. A hush washed over the crowd and a purple laser pierced the void and played on the ceiling, danced along the floor, splintered across the ballroom, accompanied by thunderous applause, and *Purple Rain* shattered the speakers, and Mr. and Mrs. Rick Matheson were at the center of the dance floor, alone in their cosmic bliss, with big, huge, smiles and were nose-to-nose, and Prince serenaded the Grand Ballroom and everyone watched, and Jasmine knew everyone was watching. She pictured all the women at the tables that orbited the dance floor thinking about her ass, and they danced all eight-plus minutes of Purple Rain and kissed full mouth and they finished with a deep, dangerous dip, and there was an eternity together in their oral embrace, and their astrological sex symbols fused. And Jasmine and

Matheson shook everyone's hands and thanked them for coming. And if someone said, "Your parents must be so proud," she smiled and moved on to the next handshake. Thresholds were crossed. Room keys tossed aside, rose petals on beds, naked bodies pressed against each other. And in the end, there were cigars on a patio and the deep heat of an August night. And she hated the smell of his cigar.

Now Jasmine is back in her car, finally, watching Judy fiddle with a loose strand of badly dyed hair as she hurries back to the safety of her own car and Jasmine hopes that Judy's kids grow up and try drugs like Greg and Nassir possibly are and let's see how Judy does or doesn't deal with it and how all the Bible Study Ladies do or don't fake like they're worried and concerned but really they'll only be glad that it's not their kids because it makes them look like better mothers. And Judy said, before she scampered away, "See you at the next game!" And Jasmine yelled back, "My son will be the one starting!" And she fired a double-edged smile at Judy, whose son is one of the nameless, faceless, bench players.

When Jasmine was twenty and told Matheson that she was pregnant, that *they* were pregnant, "Can you believe it, honey, sweetie, can you believe it?" Matheson was surprised and surprisingly nonplussed. She waited for him to burst into the uncontrollable laughter and tears and happiness of the baby-announcement moment. Matheson did eventually cry and hold her tight, pulled her body to his, pressed her so close to his Boeing-puffed chest that she couldn't see his face; but, before that, there was a brief but unmissable pause, an expanded moment of hesitation, where all color drained from Matheson's square face. Matheson held her away from him and told her he was taking a new job with a civil engineering company and he would be traveling abroad six to eight months out of the year. "But…" She held her stomach. It's something mothers do. She was only two months pregnant and hadn't even begun to show, but she placed both hands on her stomach and, for the first time since she was a little girl, she prayed. Mothers do that.

Jasmine waits for Judy to drive away. And when she presses on the gas and pulls up to the terminus of the parking lot and has to decide which way to go, Jasmine turns left instead of right, instead of going to pick up Greg from basketball practice—like she said she would—because she doesn't want to look him in his eyes. She turns left and waits for the wave to crash.

19
Hood River

On the bus, the wheels go 'round and 'round and all are created equal in its misery. The sun has gone down. The Riverview bus trudges through the winter night. Black skies form against the ever-present gray, pressing against the choppy river that curves along the highway's edge. The snores were tremendous, escaping from muddy bowels. They shook the walls of Rob the Massive Assistant Coach's apartment in the early morning hours. He thought a train was charging through his apartment, blasting its warning horn. But it was Coach Day, asleep in RMAC's living room, passed out on the couch in a Dewar's-assisted slumber. When RMAC pulled into the parking lot of the Alibi in North Portland, where Coach Day had called him from at four in the morning, Coach Day was standing next to his car. The car was kissing a light pole. Smoke hissed in sarcastic sputters from its mangled hood. Under the streetlights. Under the skies. Under the heavens. Under the canopy of cold.

But the wheels go 'round and 'round, and the Riverview Broncos Men's Basketball team is scheduled for an away game against Hood River. So everyone is here, inside this yellow vessel, headed east along the river. Coins in their mouths. They are midway through the conference schedule, barely holding onto second place after a recent losing skid, and that's when, that's why, that's who, that's what Coach

Day tried to gargle: the nerves of the upcoming game with a gallon's worth of Dewars. His elbows grew heavier on the Alibi's bartop with each drink. At the back of the cherry-paneled bar, a temptress sang from a karaoke stage—sang Whitney and Aretha in her broken English, her eyes fixed on Coach Day. She probed deep into his empty orbs. The purple and pinks of the lights danced across her eyelashes with every note. What was he supposed to do? He's always been a sucker for a lady who could sing. They all could sing at the pink bar near the base in Da Nang. The pink tassels and pink thongs and pink smoke from pink fields burned pink dreams in pink skies as they smoked pink joints and ate pink mushrooms and dropped pink squares onto pink tongues and had pink nightmares of pink skulls sinking into pink swamps. Coach Day climbed into RMAC's Expedition in the blue-dark of the morning and thanked him for coming to his assistance, "Again. Our little secret."

It's freezing cold inside the bus because the windows don't seal correctly. The bus creaks and pops atop old axles spinning bald tires. Varsity in the back, JV in the front. JV2 was left behind because nobody cares enough to travel forty miles east of Riverview, through the howling rain and wind, to see them play a road game.

RMAC counts the heads. Everyone is present and accounted for. They are a single organism. The man holding the steering wheel is a pale, White, greasy mound of unsanctified humanity that goes by the name of *Spider*. And when it's his turn to go 'round, Spider says, "We makin' a stop at Mac-Donald's, right coach?" Spider is the tried and true kind of Portlander that says *alluhboard* when he pulls the handle that swings the eternal doors shut. He revs the knee-knocked engine of the black-smoke-sputtering bus and merges onto I-84, headed east to Hood River.

"Bus drivers don't get free burgers at McDonald's, Spider," Coach Day forces from dehydrated lips. "I keep telling you that."

"Like hell they don't, Coach. Least they used to, *back when*."

Ah, the Great Back When.

The kids on the bus laugh. They hold their bellies and laugh. "This Spider," they say. *What a guy, this Spider*, they think. *Did he end up storming the capital?* they'll wonder. "Of course he did," they'll scream. For free burgers, he did! Oh, Spider! Future fodder for the stammering and slurring over beers and steaks in the bright and shiny futures that await them beyond the gates of Riverview.

And the wheels keep spinning. They never stop. From the window in the back, pounded by malevolent rain, the Columbia River swims ghost-like between clumps of passing trees and trucks and concrete highway dividers. Whitecaps crest in the wind. Nassir nods off. An unnatural nod. A supplied nod. What's the name of the drug they're taking? Marcel the Supplier, in the face of all name-related questions, only smiled and said, "It doesn't need a scientific name because it, the pill, promises clarity. Take it my brothers, and we will all be clarified."

Greg watches the pined ridges of Washington, north of the river, rise and fall in the waning light as Spider guides the bus towards the burning towers of Hood River. Marcel is blissed out. Andre the Captain laughs at Marcel's high. Ben Jones the Double Outsider is doing college-level math homework in his lap. The numbers grow faces and cackle and vomit more numbers. Greg prays his pre-game prayers, his ritual, his heavenly appeasement, forehead pressed to the cold glass.

Dear Heavenly Father.

Greg, it's me.

God?
No, it's me, Nassir.
Nassir, I'm trying to pray, so that we'll win tonight.
I don't think He's listening.
Maybe the pills will help connect us to Him.
Good idea, Greg. I'll take another.

There is no going back. There will be a game and there will be a result. The game is just a game and nothing more.

They pass Multnomah Falls and everyone cranes their necks in an attempt to see the whitewash cascade from the broken earth, but it's too dark already. Barely lucid conversations redirect from the nothingness attached to the ripped brown seat backs in front of them to whenever the last time they went to the falls was with their family or friends or lovers or never, and how far up the trail they hiked, or how far up her shirt their hands went, or how they scaled the actual face of the waterfall. And they all laugh. Jaws unhinged. Because it's high school and reputations are built on half-lies. His dick is that big. His mom slapped him that hard. I saw it with my own huge-pupil eyes. He punched his dad right in the face. We climbed Mt. Hood in the summer with no ropes. We streaked the stadium downtown. We fucked cheerleaders in the dugout and those rich motherfuckers watched from the balcony of the MAC Club out over the right field wall. And they probably had their dicks in their hands. We did it. All of it. Stories flood the bus. A yellow cylinder of hurtling adolescent dreams. And the wheels charge forward. Spider presses the gas and jerks the steering wheel and Marcel the Supplier is super-fucking blasted. His high has graduated from a simple head high to a full-body high. His face is in his stomach. He looks across the aisle to Greg, with glazed dark brown eyes, and all Marcel can do is laugh. "We are all here!" Marcel screams.

Greg nudges Nassir. Nassir's head bobs up and down. Drool stalactites to the floor from his mouth. Marcel giggles. The wind howls. "It's all becoming incredibly clear, isn't it!" Marcel shouts. "We are clarifying."

The Hood River Valley Vikings. Hood River away games come complete with Hood(ed) River-appointed referees. How much Dewars is the required amount to ignore facts?

And they are full speed.

There are no brakes.

They are crashing into the game—

At center court, Greg shakes the hand of the Hood River guard who was announced after Greg during starting lineups. Greg is booed (but not as loudly or violently as what is about to ensue). The HR-Guard is cheered wildly. Cheered as a hero; a White soldier fighting against the visiting Black team. Greg looks to the stands, where he finds Father Figure 3.0 and Jasmine in the corner.

Plug your ears, because the roar of boos is venomous and roof-rattling and fills the air as Marcel the Supplier then Andre the Captain then Manny then RMAC then Coach Day are introduced. Introduced as Black invaders of the White promised land. Black faces in a strictly White hell. Black faces who fill the nightmares of the Hood River parents. "We had eight years of Black!" they scream. "Wasn't that enough?!"

Nassir is coming off the bench tonight, not because he couldn't suicide it fast enough, but because Coach Day didn't think he looked right. And Coach Day was right. Nassir doesn't feel completely equated. The velocity is too much. Before the game, inside the visitor's locker room, Greg asked Nassir, "Are you alright?"

"I think... so?"

But the wheels on the bus go 'round and 'round and, from

somewhere in the ether, Nassir hears his name being called by Coach Day. But look, there are yellow and blue pompoms that sparkle and shake in the hands of the White Hood River cheerleaders. Fake tans. Bangs. All these fucking bangs! Stage makeup that can be seen from Hubble. Nassir enters the game and the desired effect of Marcel's drug has finally taken place—everything crystallizes, becomes incredibly clear, much too clear, and suddenly Nassir has the ball and he can feel each and every pore of the orange leather. His chest burns. Black and gold spots dance at the edge of his vision, and his periphery is majestic and limitless and—

Greg, is this The Zone?

Nassir!

—Nassir's sweat feels like ice veining down his back, icicling into wings, cutting through his jersey, and the coach, Coach Day, that fucking coach won't stop yelling, and the crowd is on top of him, it's a fucking microwave in here. And then Manny sets a screen for Nassir, and there's a hole in the defense, and Nassir is flying through the seam. Hands slip off his icy feathers that shine angelically under the gymnasium lights, an angel in shorts and a jersey, black and green and white, and the crowd is all White, every single last face is White and screaming, and—

Look! Greg! I'm laying it up now, and there's red, look: there's crimson shooting across yellow, the key is yellow cake and there's a bubbling of raspberry frosting, and my stomach burns, and my nose is the sun, and I can't breathe. Where are you?

An eruption of screams from all directions. Nassir had a clear lane to the basket until an elbow hit him flush in the nose, popped it loose, and transformed his nose into a blood faucet. Blood splashed across the yellow paint. And no foul was called. The painfully White referees gestured to Coach Day and RMAC with arms and shoulders up like "Didn't see anything," and they yelled over the roar of the crowd to play on. "PLAY ON!" The Hood River guard who decked Nassir is at the other end of the court with the ball, about to shoot a three-pointer. And that's where you can find Greg.

Here I am.

Greg bullrushes the offender and smashes him against the far wall. He stands over him, wanting murder, and the offender pleads for mercy.

The crowd has been set loose. They wanted violence, screamed for it, and received it. They storm the court. RMAC is at a ref's throat, squeezing his pink larynx, taking the life out of his bulging White face. All of Hood River's eyes are trained on RMAC and the referee at center court—their hate and fear of the Black man confirmed. "See! See what they are! ANIMALS!"

Greg tries to punch the Hood River guard. He wants to smash his face in. "Stop blocking your face! Allow your judgment!"

From somewhere deep in the stands, Jasmine yells, "No, honey! No! Please, stop!"

Nassir coughs out the blood pooling in the well below his tongue. Jasmine and Mr. Peterson are suddenly at his side. Mr. Peterson holds Nassir's head up and wipes blood off his face. Nassir looks up and sees Greg push through the crowd with Marcel the Supplier and Manny and Andre the Captain and Ben Jones the Double Outsider in tow—

We are all superheroes, we just don't know it yet, Greg.

A wave of violence rolls through the gym.

"Where's my dad?" Nassir asks Mr. Peterson. "Where is he? You know where he is." Blood bubbles and bursts from his left nostril.

The father or uncle or large friend of the kid whom Greg intentionally fouled and re-fouled again and again is trying to get to Greg, all elbows and fists. But RMAC knocks him to the ground. RMAC wheels around to Greg and pushes him, hard, a deep sadness in his eyes, "You didn't have to do this!"

And look, here's Naya now, bent down and crying next to Nassir. She uses her pom-poms to clean his face, smearing the blood into his light brown skin. Her eyes try to focus, try to find a singular point, but her eyes are just like the rest of the teams'. Open. Seeing what needs to be seen.

Jerseys are ripped.

The wheels of the bus melt in the fire.

Veins pump on necks.

Fists are hurled.

Final score irrelevant.

The foul, the attempted punches, the melee, goes viral.

The wheels slow. The bus coughs up black smoke.

Nassir opens his mouth and sticks out his tongue and looks up into the searing lights. He claws at his tongue, trying to find the coin, trying to find his payment.

Where is my coin? Greg! Where's my coin?

20
Further Down

The spectacled White woman finished her testimony and took her seat. Monty *slowly* raised his hand. He was the only Black person in the secret meeting of fifteen or so people, so he modified his movements as much as possible to not trip their genetic alarms. Gilliam, the only person who responded to Monty's post about the DC incident, and who Monty turned out to half-know from the church his wife infrequently attended, took the White woman's place at the center of the group and nodded towards Monty.

"You're telling me that two weeks after the towers fell, they were still finding traces of thermite?" Monty asked.

"That's right. And where, or what, is thermite used for?" Gilliam asked the group.

"To burn metal," The Group responded in chorus.

"How... how is that possible?"

It wasn't that Monty couldn't believe it, if true, but more so that *if* the things The Group believed back then were true, then what? Then what would Monty have to do, or, willfully *not* do?

"Thermite?"

"Thermite," Gilliam affirmed.

The Group believed in looking for foundational truths and, once found, once those undeniable facts were unearthed, parsed out from the rubble of half-truths and lies and side-mouthed ideas that the MEDIA and POLITICAL APPARATUS (typically spoken of in The Group meetings with that type of all-caps emphasis) wanted people to believe, The Group encouraged its members to then works backward towards Ultimate Answers.

Monty couldn't decide if he trusted Gilliam. Gilliam made it clear that he believed God placed him in the men and women of The Group's lives to shepherd them towards their own Ultimate Answers, and that part of being a seeker is to seek real, foundational truths.

Gilliam had (and still has) a nervous energy that the stooped-shouldered men and women of The Group gravitated towards like mosquitoes to their electric death. He had answers. He had plans.

"Thermite, Monty. Traces of thermite throughout the ruins."

"I mean."

"Three buildings, complete free fall, Monty."

"Sure, but, I mean the planes and all."

And Monty felt his stomach digest itself. *They're looking at me*, Monty thought, all those shadowy faces, their eyes and head-tilts that say he, Monty, the lone Black man in the room, out of everyone here, should believe the conspiracies, should believe the thermite hypothesis and his own tale about the leg in the back of the black town car—because, in fact, it was Gilliam who had answers about the leg; it was Gilliam who told Monty that the leg belonged to a man named Heath Flowers, a man who was in Building Seven just before it collapsed on its own, the lone witness to the non-plane-aided collapse of the previously structurally sound building; and it was Gilliam that told Monty that in The Group Monty could seek out the right questions to ask. Questions that, for him, for Monty, a Black man in

America, could/would lead him to answers he needed to live a truthful and fully aware life. That's what he thought they were thinking about him during that first, of many, meetings of The Group that Monty attended. The first meeting was the first and last innocent meeting. Before things spiraled towards that inevitable American end.

21
Down by the River

"We are all orphans," Naya says.

"But I have parents," Nassir says.

"We all have parents."

"…"

"We're all alone, inside."

She isn't trying to scare him, she's just a high schooler after all. What does she know? Even as she says the words, she's not sure she believes them. Just winged ideas taking flight.

"What do you mean? I'm right here, with you, holding your hand," Nassir says.

"If I let go and walked away, then you'd be alone, just like that. Poof."

"But I could find you."

"Imagine if everyone just walked away from you. Imagine your world was suddenly completely, like, empty. The rooms were hollow echoes, the hallways nothing but footsteps to nowhere. Imagine if you were all alone."

"But I'm not, you're here."

"The mind is a construct of needs. What if it didn't need you?"

"… Stop."

"I'm not saying anything."

Two summers ago, Naya was visiting a cousin in Brooklyn. Experiencing life on the East Coast. Life in the boroughs.

Her cousin wanted to show her the roof of their building.

"What if your mind turned its back on you? Just turned around and walked away. Then what would you have?" Naya asks.

The Columbia River is black and blue, like a wet bruise. She stares at the river. Nassir watches her stare at the river. Her cousin walked her to the edge of the roof, and said, "Look how beautiful the city is from the edge of the roof."

"Why would my mind ever do that?" Nassir asks.

"Do what?"

"Turn its back on me."

"Your dad's did."

"…"

"What if there was nothing on the other side?" Naya asks.

"I love you, Naya, you know that, right?"

"I know you do, Nassir. Let's walk along the river some more, I like feeling the cold against my skin."

"Did I tell you about the dream I had?"

"Why did you steal the car?"

The smell of skunk floats towards them from a buoyed house down the river. Nassir sees a pregnant woman walk away from a man standing in the dimly lit doorway. He can't make out faces.

"Why not?" Nassir asks.

"What was lockup like?"

"It wasn't like anything."

"…"

"The counselor kept walking past the window and looking at me, and then he'd make a note and keep walking."

"…"

"What if it was just… black."

Nassir looks at the night sky; purple-gray clouds sweep in from the east. A plane drops its wheels and screams by overheard.

"We were being chased down an empty hallway," Nassir says.

"Me and you?"

"Greg and I."

"Your dad scares me. Last time I saw him he was wandering the streets holding onto his butt like he was about to shit his pants or something. Nassir, did you hear me?"

"When did you see him?"

"I don't know. I can't tell when it was or if I was imagining it."

"There was nothing but terrible yelling in my dream. No, not yelling, like, a sound like a rocket blasting off, nothing but white noise."

"What if you turned around and you fell down a hole that never ended, like, you just kept falling?"

The sand along the river's edge is coarse. They both keep their shoes on as they slip down the embankment towards the push and pull of the river's ebb.

22
11:35 pm, NBC, Monday–Friday

"Who's our first guest, Jimmy?"

Tyrell knows he could record it, but he likes to watch his *Late Night with Jimmy Fallon* live. He likes to be surprised. He doesn't even read the little info box to see who that night's guests will be.

"Who is it, Jimmy? Is she one of your favs?"

Tyrell is at the opposite end of the room from the TV, from where Jimmy is, looking in the mirror. Tyrell practices smiling like Jimmy. The wide-mouthed, loose smile. That almost-shy smile. The I-can-do-no-wrong smile.

"The Roots, everyone! The greatest band on late night!"

Tyrell watches how Jimmy takes his seat and settles in behind the desk. He wants a desk like Jimmy's to settle into. Actually, he ordered a replica, but when it was delivered there was a garish scratch along the front panel. Tyrell screamed at the delivery man, chastising him for not taking his job seriously. How was Tyrell supposed to transition from a dance/workout/talk show to a legitimate talk show if there was a scratch on the very desk that would make it possible? Needless to say, as his landline phone rings, Tyrell does not have to get up from behind a desk to answer it.

"Hello, you've reached Tyrell Jones."

"Tyrell?"

"Yes?"

"I can't, well, I can't believe this is your number… an."

"Of course it is, sister. Tell me, what's your name? What can I do for you?"

Tyrell watches Jimmy Fallon moving backward in the mirror's reflection. This is Tyrell's favorite part of a call, the wait for a request, a plea for help—the feeling of being wanted and needed that accompanies the crack in the caller's voice at the moment of breakdown.

"Jasmine. Jasmine Peter—I mean, Booker, you may remember the email I sent?"

"Jasmine… Jasmine…" Of course, he immediately remembers her email, but what's the harm in adding a little drama to the scene? "If I recall, you're the lovely lady with carpal tunnel?"

"Pregnancy-induced carpal tunnel. But you, well, I guess I should say *because* of you, it's gone. Healed."

"Yes! That's correct! My viewers were delighted to hear and to share in the good news. So, tell me, Miss Jasmine, what can I do for you?" Tyrell fixes a smile like Jimmy's in the mirror.

There's a long silence on the other end. Tyrell can hear Jasmine take a deep breath. A door seems to close and then the ambient noise on the other end, the hum and churn of a dishwasher, the patter of rain against a window, falls away.

"It's my husband. He, no, maybe it's my son, I don't know? And then it's my daughter sometimes. Sometimes I think no one understands me. Sometimes I think they all look at me and think I'm failing them, every time I talk to them. An. And."

"Tell me about your husband."

"He's my third husband, you may have heard of him."

"Does he watch the show and call in, too?"

"He doesn't. But one of the older women who dances

behind you, I forget her name? Shirley? Cheryl? The one with the scars on her head. The older, Black lady. The one with the permanent smile? She was a customer—or I guess he'd want me to call her a *patient*—of my husband's."

Jimmy, wearing a big blonde wig, sings and dances on stage. Jimmy laughs with the Roots. Butterflies flutter in Tyrell's stomach. *This is what I want*, he thinks. He wants to dance in front of a band. Only, his band will be White.

"Mr. Jones?"

"Yes, sorry. I do know about him. Quite a bit of controversy around what he's doing, according to Carly."

"Carly, that's it."

"Carly says, she's told me in our one-on-one counseling sessions, that, although the science behind the procedure is valid, their techniques are, how'd she put it, somewhat unproven?"

"You offer one-on-one counseling?"

The butterflies exuberantly flap their iridescent wings at the sound of the undeniable verification of this caller's need, this Jasmine Booker or Peterson, or whatever she said at the beginning of the call who he, Tyrell Jones, has healed of carpal tunnel syndrome.

"Of course I do, Jasmine."

And Jimmy Fallon is up and clapping and standing at the side of the stage, just off the end of that big, beautiful, flawless, dark brown wooden desk, and he claps and smiles and waits for the guest to come out from behind those luxurious blue curtains, and wouldn't you know it, of course, the guest turns *left* instead of *right* and heads for the band instead of to the waiting Jimmy, and the guest, the Billy Crystal or the Eddie Murphy or the Denzel Washington or the Ellen DeGeneres or the Will Ferrell or the Presidential Candidate Who Wants to be Funny and get More White votes feigns ignorance, turns back to Jimmy and walks towards him like *Oops!* and, as Jimmy claps, Tyrell watches Jimmy in the reflection of the mirror behind the flawless, dark brown skin of his own face, and Jimmy is clapping and hugging and awkwardly dancing with the guest, and Jimmy's ushering the guest to their seat and he's standing again and clapping again as the guest almost sits but then stands at the last second and everyone laughs, and Tyrell's nearly in tears, and he says to Jasmine, says to her with the love and passion he knows she needs to hear from him, he says, "Of course I offer one-on-one counseling, Jasmine."

23
February 2017

Greg [If I make fifteen jumpers in a row from just beyond where the three-point line would be, I'll allow myself to go inside. Look, my mother's peering through the curtains again. Twelve. If I make fifteen jumpers in a row, thirteen, tomorrow I'll get a call from UCSB telling me not to worry about the fight at Hood River, telling me that they understand, telling me that, fourteen, that I was in the right. If I make] misses [fifteen in a row, one, the warmth of *achievement* will radiate from inside me and, two, melt away the cold. Look, Father Figure 3.0's now peering out at me, too. How do I look to them? I look, three, clearly in control. He wants to be my dad. She wants him to be my dad. She wishes he were my dad. Four. Dad, will you be at my next game? Will I see you cheering for me? Dad, five, if I make fifteen in a row from just beyond six where the three-point line would seven be will you be eight there at nine my next game? Ten. Will you tell me, *Well* eleven *done*? Look, here comes Three-point-oh].

Father Figure 3.0 catches the ball as it falls through the net. Greg is nearly hyperventilating. A few minutes ago, he tossed his shirt next to the icy grass. That's when Jasmine called her husband and asked him to go check on Greg. Out shooting hoops on the street in the cold. Eyes ablaze. His breath turns into ice and shatters against the ground. [Pass me the ball or I will evaporate.]

"Ball, please."

Father Figure 3.0 passes him the ball. Greg catches and shoots [twelve].

"Come inside, your mom's worried about you."

". . ."

"Just come inside, Greg. For your mom."

". . ."

Greg snatches the ball from Father Figure 3.0's hands and sprints back to his spot, turns, fires, the ball leaving a trail of sweat behind it [thirteen] as it leaves his frozen hands.

Greg [If I make fifteen shots in a row from just behind where the three-point line would be, then my father will be at the next game and watch me play and redeem myself and the UCSB Coach will call me and] misses.

"Okay, there, now can we go inside?" Father Figure 3.0 says, watching the ball carom off the rim and bounce away down the street—in and out of the circles of streetlights.

Greg hears nothing but his frenzied breathing as he runs after the ball [If I make fifteen in a row my mother will stop looking at me from the window].

[One.]

24
When Jasmine Became a Hazel

Seven years after Jasmine and Matheson's wedding, Jasmine initialed next to the red Xs littered throughout the divorce papers. The divorce proceedings were, much like their marriage, one-sided. Matheson was granted custody of Shasta for weekends, vacations and summers. Jasmine was responsible for stressful school mornings and tense homework nights—until Trench showed up and then Shasta moved, full-time, to Matheson's home in the West Hills.

Jasmine had never heard of Postpartum Depression, where the Mother goes out of her way to eliminate the very thing that parted from her. She was assured by the psychologist Matheson paid for, before the divorce, that it was a common condition. Jasmine watched her baby sleep in the days and months after Shasta was born, convinced she had no right to raise the baby. She'd fail the baby. She'd accidentally kill the baby. Drop the baby from her arms in the grocery store parking lot when transferring the baby from the cart to the car seat. There are millions of ways a baby can die, and Jasmine imagined them all. She even felt herself planning them. She hated the baby for making her feel that way. Hated herself for hating the baby. For thinking of it as *the baby* and not *my daughter, Shasta.* Matheson found Jasmine standing over the crib, crying, in the middle of the night, two weeks after they brought Shasta home. Just standing there crying. Sure, they'd talked about abortion, just as an idea, a thought, a possibility, because Matheson's job had changed just as they found out Jasmine was pregnant. But it was just an idea, a thing, it was there and then gone in the next second. Two years later and Shasta still cried through the night. And then Jasmine left Shasta in the bathtub. Just left her there. Jasmine heard the phone ring in the living room and she got up, Shasta's eyes probably watched her walk away, and Jasmine answered the phone and didn't come back. Shasta was barely able to hold herself up. She coughed and sucked in water. Jasmine doesn't know if she imagined Shasta sitting in the warm water, laughing and smiling. Imagined her little girl with bubbles caught in her hair and on her nose. But Jasmine heard the phone ring and she kissed Shasta on the cheek and left to answer the phone. She just got up and left Shasta, who probably tried to push herself up with her little hands and little fingers and slipped and called out "Mommy, mommy," and the bubbles probably got in her eyes, and then when one hand wiped the bubbles away the other slipped on the bottom of the tub. And Shasta cried. Shasta splashed and coughed and Matheson ran in and scooped her out of the water. Shasta wailed and clung to Matheson's neck. Jasmine came back and stood in the doorway and Matheson screamed at her. She said she was sorry, that she forgot, that she somehow just forgot, and Jasmine sobbed. She still wonders if Shasta remembers being left in the tub. Remembers her mother forgetting her. Do you ever forget being forgotten?

Soon after the divorce, Jasmine found herself attending church again. Time was murky, post-divorce. The way time undulates, slips by, after a traumatic event. Days melted. Calendar pages evaporated. Jasmine and Shasta were living in a small two-bedroom house in North Portland. Matheson offered to continue to pay the mortgage on the condo, but

Jasmine declined, sold the place, and bought a small house near Overlook Park with brown shingles and moss that crept up the northern wall. It was cute and symbolized a fresh start. She made new friends and had them over for dinner. They talked about things women were supposedly supposed to talk about. Jasmine deflected questions about her past. She enjoyed the idle conversation, the meaningless details. Those women loved details. She learned how to talk details with the ladies and finish thoughts with *and*. But like: *an*. School pick-up times and warped Tupperware lids and dentist visits and cavities and JC Penny's and which mall was safer (which was code for *which mall had fewer Black people*) and the husbands in the garages and the husbands at the golf courses and the husbands in beds, and everything was said simply, factually, but monumentally, and the sentences all ended with and. Trailed off like that, like: my husband is a real bore in bed, and. But *an*. No d, if you're part of the club. And then another lady would pick up the trail and push the thought, the detail, into its proper place: humble but hard-won holiness, *an*. A lady who cackled when she laughed asked Shasta if she attended church. This lady was the last to leave the Tupperware party, was halfway out the door, holding an empty salad bowl in her hands, and said, "You should check out a Church, an." Church with a capital "C." Her eyes moved to Shasta, who was in the kitchen, drawing. There was Shasta to think about.

The following Sunday, Jasmine helped Shasta fasten the small metallic buckles on her shiny black shoes. She straightened out Shasta's frilly pink dress. They stood in front of the mirror and smiled because they were both so pretty.

"We're so pretty, aren't we, Shasta?" Jasmine's smile turned to a soft frown.

"Mommy, where're we going?"

"We're going to church."

"Do we go to church?"

"I used to. It'll be fun."

There was a small church with a white steeple not far from their new little home. Jasmine helped Shasta up the stairs and, when she looked up from her daughter to the front door, he was there waiting for her—not God. No, far from God. It was Anthony, the future father of Greg. He smiled and held the door open for Jasmine and Shasta. He had piercing blue eyes. A hard smile. But a gleam in his eyes made Jasmine's heart stir. That's not right, his eyes didn't pierce, they boiled. Jasmine thanked Anthony for opening the door and six months later they were married. It was that simple. Because everything was a blur. Because Jasmine traveled in blurs. Because decisions were made alone and on the fly. Decisions made in the never-ending crush of the now.

A month after they were married they were in bed, chest to chest. Her toes played against his shins, their mouths only a breath away from each other.

Jasmine inspected his face, "How are your eyes so blue?"

"Don't ever leave me, okay?" Anthony, instead, asked.

"I won't."

"Don't ever leave me, please. Okay?"

"I promise."

Rather than ask him why she would leave him, and what in *his* past led to that fear/question, she told him, for the first time, about how she left Idaho and drove to the Oregon Coast.

"Why'd you want to go to the beach?" Anthony asked. "What beach?"

"The coast. Lincoln City."

"Why?"

"Because I hated the lake. Hated where I was from. And

I told myself I wouldn't stop until I saw the rolling waves of the Pacific. I didn't even know what that meant, what it meant to stand on the beach and look out across the waves, across the blue-green. And you know how the world just drops off at the end? where you can't see the water anymore? it just slopes down and out of sight? I didn't even know what that felt like."

"What did it feel like?"

"When I first got there, to Lincoln City, I parked and got out of my car and it was raining, but the rain clouds were low and they seemed to kind of blow up against the rocky cliffs behind me. The dark blue sky opened up at the shoreline. The rain blew sideways, diagonally maybe, and the sun was shining, but only way out over the ocean in small thin slats. The edge of the ocean drops away and the Earth curves out of sight. I'd never seen it in person. I was eighteen. The lake just lapped. It just moved back and forth. When you look across the lake you see the other side. It's just the other side. I had to see the ocean. The Pacific. The waves. Rain and dark thunder clouds and sun breaks. The edge of the world. I had to see it to know I was here."

"I love you, Jasmine."

"Your eyes scare me."

"Don't ever leave me."

"I promise."

They bought a house in North Portland. Way out therein St. Johns. Anthony worked for the city. He did city jobs in city garages and repaired and maintained city vehicles. He became the man he saw other men being. When Anthony held Greg in his arms at the hospital, Jasmine in bed next to him holding Shasta's sleeping head to her chest, he looked into Greg's eyes and Jasmine made him promise that he'd never hurt Greg. Anthony promised he'd be a better father than his own had been. That's the way it goes: we learn from the past: we improve on the past: we make the future better. It's the way the world has supposedly always worked. But soon their life would be:

Killingsworth St. Portland Ave. Lombard Ave. Sumner St. Interstate Ave. Names on green street signs perched atop metal poles that leaned like trees braced against a heavy wind. Streets that led to steel bridges that disappeared inside gaping mouths of mountains made of evergreen forests. Streets that led around corners to bars where White and Black men with orange vests sat alone, together. Streets that drove by Black faces and White faces. Motels called Mo's and Tropicana and The Palms with hookers and pools with dry basins that were painted yellow. Where dogs barked. Where children rode bicycles without helmets. Where police cars drove slowly and Black people got the unblinking eye of the law. Streets that would later be forsaken and forgotten and moved on from and thought of as the past, only the past, and that was only in the past, and let us move on from *those* streets. Let us not ruminate on the past. Streets where Anthony and Jasmine tried to build a family but opossums were everywhere: two in a garbage can, another on the roof, another in the garage. The pale and hairless tails. And when the flashlight hit their marble eyes they flashed red and Jasmine screamed from behind Anthony, clawed at his back, and told him to "Just fucking do something about it." "Your son found it, Anthony!" "Imagine what could've happened!" she screamed. Streets where trees grew tall and green. Where Anthony chased the opossum with a bat. Jasmine said, "There's an opossum in the garage, Anthony." She said, "Do something about it!" Streets where Anthony chased the opossum to the front of the house, bat held high above his head, and where he beat the skull of the opossum into the cement of the sidewalk right in front of their lawn. Where he left the opossum to rot. One eyeball oozed from its smashed head. Anthony's chest heaved. Sweat on his brow. He looked back at the house with a look that said, *Are you happy now?* only to see Greg and Shasta in the front window watching him, the bat and the dead opossum next to his feet. And then Jasmine's hand on their son's neck in that loving, protective way, as she ushered Greg and Shasta from the window.

25
February 2017

"Hey, listen, there's going to be a party after the game." "Are we invited?" "Yes." "Should we go?" "I think so." "I don't feel okay." "What'd you mean?" "I don't know." "Is it the drugs?" "It's the drugs." "That's what I just asked." "I couldn't hear you, because of the wind tunnel in my ears." "It was supposed to make things clear." "Too clear." "Yeah, too clear." "You'll be okay by the party." "You think?" "You'll sweat it out during the game." "Did you take one, too?" "Yes."

Foot toeing the center of the free throw line. Look closer: there's a nail at the very center of the charity stripe. It, the nail, is covered in paint. The ridge of the nail sucks at the paint. The nail is gravity. The paint is black. See the outline: reach down and touch it with your finger: trace the edge of the nail: the slight bump. Ignore the yelling from the referee. Right foot at the nail. Left foot shoulder-width apart from your right foot and placed slightly behind your right. Are you balanced? You must be balanced. Shoulders square to the hoop. Dribble the ball once on the right side of your body; push the ball with your right hand to the floor ahead of your right foot. Just one bounce. Bring the ball up in one fluid motion, fingers spread wide and fingering the grooves, fingers holding the ball away from the flat warmth of your palm. Your left hand stays on the left side of the ball as a guide. Your left elbow is not flared out to the side but tucked next to your body. Your right arm rises, elbow bent at an angle just past ninety degrees, your wrist bent back on itself, fingers holding the ball half an inch from your palm. You bend your knees slightly, rise onto your toes, and in one fluid motion (it must be fluid, fluidity is key, fluidity shows professionalism, fluidity will make them love you) you catapult your forearm forward, the ball moving up directly in front of your face, elbow straight and economical because there can be no wasted movements. At the precipice of the catapult motion, your wrist flicks the ball towards the center of the back of the rim, and your middle finger and index finger of the right hand are last to touch the sacramental leather. The left hand is left alone, plank straight, just above and to the left of your eyes. Your follow-through is of utmost importance; as important as your shoulders being square to the hoop; as important as your left and right arm/hand coordination; as important as ignoring Nassir trying to ignore Monty, who's here at the game. The follow-through is the ultimate judge. The hand flicks at the wrist: loose, elegant. The ball whisks off the tips of your fingers, and the wrist bows before the back center of the rim. The elbow/arm is fully extended and stays in the air as a telepathic guide, wrist worshiping the rim. The ball, if released correctly, will rotate evenly. Its seams will spin backward at an even speed as its trajectory rises and falls towards the orange halo. No wobble. There can be no wobble or sideways rotation. And at the exact moment of release, of ball leaving body, of ball traveling toward the rim, through the chilly ozone of the gymnasium, through the circumferential eyes of the home crowd in the stands tracking the flight of the ball, the path of your supplicatory request, you will be judged on the sincerity of your worship by the outcome of your free throw attempt. Empty yourself of all thought and concern and stress and love and need and want and desire and ambition and insecurity and feel nothing but the back of the rim and the ball and the bend of your knees and the flick of the wrist and never take your eyes off the back of the rim no matter what incidental thoughts flash across your mind. God is the rim. God is all. The rim is a greedy lover. And when the fans roar, when the fans exhaust their lungs in a celebratory scream as you make both free throw attempts to win the game versus David Douglas during the sludge of the late-season schedule and you are surrounded by teammates and the coaches are shaking hands and your teammates' mouths are agape and ecstatic and they're patting you on the back and hugging you and you're looking through their loving arms and faces and hairs and the black and bulbous but then beady and glowing eyes of Nassir and searching out your mother and your third figure of a father at the top of the stands who aren't looking at you or the spastic scene you have caused, created, given life to, but instead are accepting hands and hugs like diplomats who've brokered a nuclear peace pact between two warring nations and you want nothing else but for them to see you in the middle of your team being exalted as a Glowing Golden God and for them to stop accepting credit, jointly, for your life when the *real* partner to your mother in the whole life-creating act isn't up there. And your chest explodes because he, your father, isn't there. But you are a God who tamed the God of the Rim. That's the key. You toed the center of the free throw line and emptied yourself of everything, save a solitary focus on the back of the rim, and you prayed to the God of the Rim to make them see you for who you are. No one will remember all the shots you missed. They will remember this moment you elevated yourself above all else.

The moment in time you scored thirty-one points and hit the game-winning free throws. The moment you became a God. A moment that, by definition, was momentary.

The front yard of Jenny Owendale's mom's house is fenced in by eight-foot-high plywood boards. The tops of the unpainted, untreated boards are uneven; some are spiky, some blunt, others with rounded or scooped-out tops. It looks halfway artistic. Maybe it's symbolic. Bass thumps from within the house. Maybe that's symbolic, too. Blue and white lights are strung across the front yard from the limbs of the pine trees that reach up to an inky sky. There's a light misting type of rain in the air. Tiny raindrops flutter past the blue and white lights.

Ben Jones the Double Outsider leans against the front gate, holding a can of beer in one hand and his cell phone in the other. He simultaneously tries to text, keep his beer upright, and wipe rain from the face of his phone.

"Here they are."

"At your service." Nassir curtsies.

"You okay, Ben?" Greg asks.

Greg and Nassir stagger towards the entrance like Rosencrantz and Guildenstern. They slump against the fence.

"What's Shasta say about my dad?" Ben peers into Greg's swelling and pulsing eyes.

"I haven't heard her say much, Ben."

"The Double Outsider," Ben corrects.

Nassir whips his body forward to peek inside the open gate. "The party's packed. I'm not sure I can..." Nassir tries to find words for his mouth to regurgitate, but his chest interrupts him with a heave. "Naya's here."

"Nassir?"

"Nassir, your dad is here." "I can't see him, not right now, RMAC." "Nassir, you okay?" "Did he tell you to ask me that." "He didn't say anything, he's just there—but his neck looks bad." "I can't talk to him, it's all too illuminated inside me right now." "Nassir, you fucking doing drugs?" "I forgot you're an adult; I shouldnt've said that thing about the illumination." "Do you need a ride after the game?" "No, Gregory and I are going to a party where everyone will want us to be bigger and better versions of ourselves. I'll have to put the mask on. How's this look, RMAC? Does this face make me look harmless?"

Jenny Owendale is barely wearing clothes. Greg and Nassir wobble into the living room. There's a keg against the far wall, next to a couch full of their teammates. There's a hallway off the main room leading to other rooms that are most likely full of kids doing things that Greg's never done, and that Shane the Youth Pastor tried to make him and Nassir promise, with the aid of a ring, to never do before they're wed. Jenny Owendale aims a glistening smile at Greg as she saunters up to him, a beer for him in her perfect hand. Naya is beside her and locked onto Nassir.

The beer missile is cold and slippery in Greg's clammy hands. Naya takes a long drag from a joint and, with a mouth full of swirling smoke, presses her noir-lipsticked lips against Nassir's and pushes the smoke into his mouth. He exhales through his nose. Greg is in awe.

"Do you like Miller Lite?" Jenny Owendale asks.

"Of course," Greg lies.

"It's what my mom bought for the party." Jenny is a nuclear bomb. Greg vanishes in her blast.

"She sounds cool."

Stomachs full of burning suns. The lights are perfect, the music is suitably loud, and the speakers are just as suitably suited to this kind of teenage hormonal explosion with their crackling, tinny, reverb. Seconds ago, Jenny Owendale's drunk mom slipped out of one of those rooms down the hallway, where Greg briefly thought he spotted the shaggy head of someone he vaguely recognized in connection to Shasta, and the drunk mother in question turned the music up even louder, just as Greg and Nassir entered and people yelped and whooped, and the drunk mother asked how everyone was doing and, "Is the music loud enough for y'all," and everyone wondered where her husband slash Jenny's father is and Jenny's drunk mother, still holding court, isn't wearing a ring, and she has a fake tan that is the exact same hue as the White man in the White House that the Whites at Greg's church, at every Church, voted for, and Jenny's drunk mother is also wearing the same shade of orange bikini top that her daughter is wearing—that's showing through her basically see-through top—and so Greg tries to hold the beer harder and harder as Jenny grabs him by the forearm, causing waves of magma to surge through his body, as she leads him to the kitchen and away from his teammates, Andre the Captain and Marcel the Supplier and Manny, who are the center of attention on the overflowingly-peopled couch.

Nassir's stomach is on the floor, biting at the shoelaces of Marcel's seriously tattered Jordans. His head rolls around in the palm of his right hand. He raises his hand to his eyes, surveys his mind. Marcel's booming laughter fills the living room.

"My hair is on fire," Nassir says, touching the top of his head.

"Do you love me?" Naya asks.

"Marcel the Supplier, is it okay for me to drink and now also smoke *whilst* on the pill?"

"Answer me, Nassir."

"He said, *whilst*! Jenny, I like your friends! He's so eloquent, this one!" Jenny Owendale's drunk mother cries and turns the music up even louder, blistering eardrums.

Marcel the Supplier stands and shrugs off an underclasswoman with incredibly curly hair. She laughs and falls back onto the couch, swallowed and forgotten inside the twisting teenage mass. Marcel walks over to Nassir and takes his right hand, unknowingly crushing Nassir's mind. Nassir lets out a gasp. He feels at his head with his left hand, fearing that his mind is still in there somewhere.

"The trifecta's never been attempted. You're on your own."

"I see. I can see that very clearly now." Nassir reopens his eyes after a long blink and there, in his right palm, is his mind, again, rolling around like a tiny translucent globe.

"Do you love me, Nassir?" Naya asks again.

"Tell me what you see," Marcel says.

A glass breaks in the kitchen. Jenny Owendale's voice carries over the music, "It's okay, Greg."

In between the first and second quarters, Shane the Youth Pastor scrambled down to the bottom of the bleachers, just behind the Riverview bench, and leaned over the railing, his blocky head moving into place between Greg and Nassir. The cheerleaders were making a pyramid at center court. Pom-poms flashed. Nassir poured sweat. Greg was ice cold. "Nassir, Monty asked me to get a message to you." Sweat dripped off the end of Nassir's nose. Greg said, "Shane, now's not a good time, we're watching the cheerleaders." Nassir said, "They're performing the famed Ziggurat maneuver." Shane said, "I get that, I do, but Monty said it was important. He said to tell you, Nassir, that he can't ever go back to ignoring truth with a capital T, no matter what that means for him or your family." Sweat poured from Nassir's forehead, down the bridge of his nose, and he caught the drops in his cupped hands. "Look," Greg said, "they've almost completed the pyramid." "Ziggurat," Nassir corrected. "Somewhere inside that Ziggurat," Greg said, "is the answer." Shane asked, "Do you want me to tell Monty something?" Nassir slowly tore his eyes from the completed Ziggurat as Naya, the final piece, raised her arms triumphantly, which brought the crowd to their feet. Nassir's eyes grasped onto Shane's bubbling face and Nassir opened his mouth and evaporated Shane with an illuminating light that burst forth from his burning stomach.

The ceiling in the kitchen is only six-and-a-half feet high. Six feet, six inches. "Is the, uh, Jenny, the uh, is the ceiling like, low... er, in here?"

Jenny Owendale spins to Greg, making her hair do that thing that only she can make it do, and looks up at the ceiling, "It's an addition."

Greg nods, or rolls his head around, or drops it on the ground and picks it back up. He raises both hands to the ceiling, places his palms flat against the beveled burgundy wood. The ceiling presses back down on him. First, his lower lumbar collapses. Then, his vertebrae pop one-by-one down his spine. His arms fail, head crushed against his right shoulder as the ceiling forces itself further down.

"Greg, hello?"

"Yea?" He pulls his arms back down, lets his limbs hang unnaturally at his side.

"I said, Mr. Brian is here."

"What? Who?"

"Your brother-in-law! Why the hell's that creeper here? He always looks at my knees. At my fucking knees!"

Jenny Owendale pulls Greg by his hand, their fingers interlock, again sending rivulets of sizzling liquid through his veins, and then she grabs him by the jaw and forces Greg to look around the corner of the poorly constructed kitchen wall: "There, look, that's him. Right?" At the front door where, unless Greg's eyes deceive him, Brian fills the doorway with concern.

"My name is Brian Harris, mam."

"*Mam*, who're you callin' mam, honey?"

"Brian!?"

"Greg, there you are. Excuse me, just, I, I'd like to talk to Greg. Oh, hey, Jenny."

"My eyes are up here, Mr. Brian."

"Don't you look at my daughter that way!"

"I don't know which way you are talking about, *mam*."

"There you go again with that mam bullshit. Go on away, Mr. Harrison—"

"Harris."

"We're just having a fun little harmless party here."

"Harmless? Look in the corner, Mrs. Owendale."

"MISS."

"*Miss* Owendale, I'm sorry."

"You don't need to apologize about my petite ex-husband. You'll see Mr. Harrisburg, you'll see what it's like being married."

"I'm sure I will, but I just need to get to Nassir over there, it looks like he's thrown up on himself."

"Nassir!"

"Here we go, Greg, on three, help me get him up."

"Where do I put my hands?"

"Under his knees!"

"I can't, my hands are orbs of fire!"

"Come on, Greg! Focus!"

"Greg, where're you going?"

"Jenny, I'll call you later. Can I call you?"

"If the ceiling doesn't crash down on me, you can. Without you here I don't know who will hold it up for me."

"How'd you know we were here, Brian?"

"It doesn't matter."

"Nassir!"

"Naya, there you are, get some paper towels or something and meet us outside, please."

"Okay, Mr. H."

"Where should we put him down, Brian? Brian, how'd you know we were here?"

"Shasta told me you might be here, so I looked at Jenny Owendale's pictures online and saw you and Nassir in the background."

"You love Jenny, don't you? You love her knees."

"Greg! Here, let's put him down."

"Don't worry, Brian. I won't tell Shasta."

"There's nothing to not tell her."

"We all know you want to fuck Jenny."

"How dare you."

"It's true, Mr. H. I know you want to fuck me."

"Jenny… please, get your knees out of my face."

"I'm sorry, Brian. It's a new me I'm trying out."

"Well, I don't like it, Greg."

"I don't want to put Nassir down here, I want to put him in the sky."

"Here you go, Mr. H. It's all I could find."

"Do you like this song, huh, Mr. Harrington!? I've turned it up as loud as I can."

"Miss Owendale, not now. Go inside! There, just like that, wipe his face off, turn his head to the side."

"Jefferson's Airplane!"

"Don't cry, Naya, he'll be okay. Fuck's sake, Greg. What the fuck are you doing here?"

"…"

"It's called, White Rabbit!"

Brian and Greg stuff Nassir into the backseat of Brian's car. Miss Owendale strides confidently to the gate, looks down and sees Ben Jones the Double Outsider passed out against the fence. Brian's car squeals away.

Gerald slinks up to her side and slips his arm around her waist.

"There goes the father of my baby."

"What?"

26
Shasta's New House

There's a crib in the baby's room now. Earlier in the day, Greg and Jasmine came over to Shasta's house and they *oohed* and *ahhed* about the baby blue walls Brian had painted. Well, Greg didn't ooh nor did he ahh. Jasmine held onto Greg like he might fall off a bridge if she let go of his arm. Before Brian left for work in the morning, he told Shasta that the counselors and teachers were now on "high alert" at school regarding Nassir and Greg. Shasta said, "Well, Brian, let me know how I can help, I guess." She said, "How's Jenny Owendale handling everything?" He said, "Shasta, don't."

Greg and Jasmine have gone back home. Shasta dresses in the mirror for her shift at Lucy's Cafe, as Brian undresses from his own day of work. She turns to the side to assess the roundness of her belly. She says, "You think Jenny would still be skinny if she were pregnant?"

Greg looked at the baby blue paint on the walls and told Shasta that his counselor, Mrs. Schuster, said he should avoid stress. He ran his fingers along the wall and Jasmine watched him with a look on her face like he'd already sunk to the bottom of the ocean. Shasta asked, "How's Nassir?" Greg stared into the blue of the wall and said, "That's what everyone wants to know, isn't it?" Their mom said, "Nassir's going to be staying with us for a while. It's been decided that it might be best." "Oh," Shasta said. "One big party," Greg said. "Greg…," Jasmine said.

"I wouldn't have looked at her profile," Brian says, "unless you asked me to."

"You just found her profile *so fast*." Shasta buttons her shirt and irons the wrinkles out of the black button-up with her palms. At work, her customers will wish her pregnancy well and tell her that she's going to be a great mom and that everything will work out with her and Brian and that she will grow to love him and that everything is going to be fine and that her baby won't be autistic and that she won't have P.P.D. like her mom did with her, but not with Greg for some unnamable reason, and that if the baby *is* autistic and she decides to give it up for adoption because she doesn't know how she could handle it, the autistic thing, she would still be a great person. This is what she wants the customers to tell her.

"I need you to believe me, honey," Brian says.

"Okay. I believe you."

Greg ran his hands along the just-dried baby blue paint in the baby's room and said, "We all need to stop being so stressed, don't we?" He considered the specks of paint on his fingers. "Maybe that's the answer. But, maybe not stressing about anything, not fighting for change will just keep the status quo. Which is cool for us, our family. But, Nassir said Fanon said violence is… is… Shit. I forgot. Don't tell him I forgot." And when Shasta asked if he and Nassir would be suspended, he said, "For what?" Jasmine said she loves both of them and she's sure God will work it all out. It felt like an unconscious tic, like she was batting away a fly, and Shasta, for the first time in her life, felt empathy for Jasmine.

Brian has big, dopey eyes. He's sitting on the edge of the bed. He wants Shasta to comfort him. Her baby will have no lips because Brian's lips are so thin. She hasn't thought about Gerald in a couple of weeks, but she thinks about him now as she surveys Brian's mouth. That's a lie. Gerald called her about Greg and Brian being at the Owendale's house (which led to her telling Brian), but when Shasta asked Gerald why *he* was there, he didn't answer. Gerald started to say that she was the married one, but stopped. And when Shasta told Brian that he should go get the idiots from the Owendale's house, he acted completely and totally flabbergasted and surprised that they were there, like he hadn't *already* known they were because he secretly follows Jenny Owendale on every social media platform possible.

"I have to go. Have a good night." She kisses him on the cheek and leaves for work.

When Jasmine excused herself from the baby blue baby room to use the bathroom, Shasta waited to hear the bathroom door close and then she shut the bedroom door and whispered to Greg, "You doing okay?" She tried to convey that she could be trusted, because she, too, had done things. "You can talk to me."

"I'm doing great. Just trying to empty myself. Find God's will for my life. What college to go to, and all that. You know? It's becoming clearer, I think." Greg sat on a tiny kid-sized chair, knees up to his chin. "Can't believe I'm going to be an uncle. A half-uncle."

"You don't need to say those things to me about God and his will. Just because Nassir is kind of…"

"Kind of what?"

Shasta picked at some painter's tape around the edges of the door frame. "Going down the drain, you know, it doesn't mean you have to as well." The toilet flushed. "What are you taking, Greg? What's the team been taking? You have to be careful, you know? Sometimes you don't know what's really in those pills. Trust me."

Greg raised his eyes to her and they held each other's gaze. A sink turned on. The sounds of hands being washed. "Ask your boyfriend what it is."

"…"

"It's supposed to make things clear. Maybe it's what you were taking when you moved to your dad's, you know? Right before Trench hit Mom? Fantastic timing."

"That's not fair."

"Must've been nice. Living in the hills like you did."

"Fuck you, Greg."

As dinner service slows to a walk and all the servers come out of the weeds, Shasta thinks about Gerald's lips: his thick, kissable lips. Thinks about how chaotically controllable he is. Shasta watches from the back server station as a guest spills her glass of white wine across the table. Shasta sips her sparkling water.

When Jasmine's footsteps closed in on the baby's room, Shasta and Greg watched and waited for her to push the door open. Jasmine came in, gave them a hopeful smile, and dried her hands subconsciously on the back of her pants.

"Everything okay?"

"It's great, Mom. Thanks for coming by," Shasta said, eyes glistening.

27

The Vice Principal's Office

The Vice Principal, the Athletic Director, and the flowery, immaculately-saloned counselor, Mrs. Schuster, are seated across the table from Nassir and Greg. Both the boys are wearing one of Greg's button-up shirts. Mrs. Schuster has a loving, but concerned smile plastered to her face. The others, well, do not. The stage is set for what will surely be a very serious meeting about, as Greg and Nassir were informed before entering the room, their "academic and athletic fates."

"Boys, thanks for being on time," the Vice Principal begins. "…"

"Mrs. Schuster told us, Nassir, that you're staying with the Petersons now? Is that correct?"

"I'm not a Peterson, I'd like the record to show. My name is Greg *Hazel.*"

"Of course," says the Vice Principal, already on the verge of seething.

"You're absolutely correct. I'm staying with Mr. Peterson, Jasmine Booker, and Gregory Hazel," Nassir says. "Note that I did not speak that sentence with an Oxford comma." Nassir winks at Mrs. Schuster. She frowns. He tilts his head, and gives her the "Denzel Look."

Mrs. Schuster clears her throat and straightens up a bit before saying, "I talked to both of your mothers, and it's just temporary, but seeing as. Well. We all just agree it might be better for you, well, *both of you*, frankly, to have a little more supervision. With Mr. Peterson there as well as your mother, Greg, we think it'll be the best-case scenario for the rest of the school year."

"Rob, our massive assistant coach, told me I could stay with him for a while."

"Hmm…" Mrs. Schuster clearly doesn't like this option. "Let's just stick with the plan, Nassir. It's what we think is best for you."

"Hasn't Mr. Peterson helped out enough?" Nassir asks. "I asked him, last night, if I could have one of those make-happy things he gave my dad. You know, with the dial on it. I asked if I could have one, you were there, Greg, you heard me—"

"I was and did."

"—I told him, in his language, well, in *your* language," Nassir lets his eyes briefly settle on each of the White adults' noses, "that if he just gave me one of those dials, I could turn it up and be happy. Just like my dad. Just like the other Black people in Riverview he's helped. What if I was able to turn up my Whiteness? It'd be like the movie *White Chicks* but without the White-face."

"Nassir," the Vice Principal searches for the right words. "Sometimes we just have to face hard facts in life. And, well, unfortunately, you're being forced to do that at an earlier age than is ideal."

"Are you talking about Trayvon Martin?" Nassir asks. "And the perpetual violence against men and children who look like me?"

"Oh, Nassir…" Mrs. Schuster is nearly epileptic with concern.

Greg starts to say something, but Nassir has more:

"I've been reading some interesting books about America recently—"

"In your history class?" the Vice Principal asks, his voice full of surprising hope.

"No, sir. At home. And these books, this new way of looking at America, and the Trayvons and the Alton Sterlings, have made it very clear to me that without the quintessentially American anti-Black violence there wouldn't be an America at all. I'm paraphrasing, obviously."

"Obviously," Greg says, grinning sarcastically at the adults.

The Vice Principal turns tomato red with anger. The way certain indignant White men do when their "America" is questioned. Mrs. Schuster mutters German words to herself, something she's known to do when times get tough.

"Let's not dance around this bullshit anymore, okay?" The Athletic Director straightens up, firing a perturbed look at the Vice Principal. "Here's the deal, men. You two have been allowed to skate by all goddamn year. You realize that? I have gone to bat for you two, behind the scenes here, me and Mrs. Schuster, because we believed that you two would figure your fucking shit out. But here we are, okay, almost done with the season and we can't just keep overlooking the absences and this whole ordeal at Jenny Owendale's house."

"If I may," Nassir begins.

"You may not!" the Athletic Director shouts, slamming his fist on the table. "You certainly may not! I got Mr. Harris coming into *my office* telling me I have to do something about you two to send a message. Mr. Harris! Your brother-in-law, Greg. That sniveling piece of shit."

"Hey," says the Vice Principal, trying to calm the Athletic Director.

"What a narc," Nassir says.

"Can't believe it," Greg concurs. "Actually. I can."

"True."

"You just don't get it, do you? We're suspending both of you for the next game."

"And there's only four games left," the Vice Principal states, a sad quiver in his throat.

"For what?" Greg asks.

"For what? We should've suspended you a long time ago! You know how much flak I've taken for not suspending *you* in particular after the disaster at Hood River?!"

"It'd be a shame to miss the playoffs, boys. We're so close," the Vice Principal says with the tone people use that's meant for shaming.

Nassir laughs sardonically.

"Mr. Chissler?"

"Nassir, just, come on," Greg whispers.

"Tell me, esteemed White leaders who've been selected to lead us young men into our bright and burning futures, for WHOM exactly would it be a shame for for US to miss the playoffs?"

"Nassir…"

Nassir gives Greg a dark look, before transforming his face into the Denzel Look. The look that says, *Tell me I'm wrong. Tell me you know better than me.*

"Don't you want to go to college, Nassir?" Mrs. Schuster bursts out. "I'm sorry."

"She's right. Don't you want a future beyond high school?" the Vice Principal adds. "Or what, you want to end up like all the other Riverview *thugs* out there on the corners?"

"Oh boy…" Greg shakes his head in disbelief at *thugs*.

"I want a bright and burning future."

Mrs. Schuster chokes on a sob.

"Don't be sad, Mrs. Schuster," Nassir says. "Greg's youth pastor says God is watching over us."

"He sure is, honey."

The Athletic Director clears his throat and flexes his hands, trying to find the right temperament to convey his thoughts. "Listen. Sorry 'bout what I just said. But come on. What are the scouts going to think, Greg? If not UCSB, then it's George Fox, right? Or, any other of a handful of schools that'd be happy to have you. Even you, Nassir. We all know you're smart. Really smart."

"That's very kind of you," Nassir says, eyes washing across the synod's faces.

"We'll take our punishment, okay?" Greg says.

"Well, there was never really an option, but I'm glad to hear it," the Athletic Director says with a smirk, his face regaining its peachy-red hue.

Greg and Nassir are up out of their seats and just about to exit when Nassir turns back around, "Who did you vote for? All of you?"

The trio of White administrators shift in their seats.

"That's not relevant, Mr. Chissler," the Vice Principal says imperialistically.

"I think my mom voted for Trump. I know she thinks she loves me—just as I'm sure you all think you very much want the best for us—but outside my thoughts, all I can do is sift through reality. Unlike my mom. She and Phil, her new boo, want me to embrace my White side, as if that'll help me *ascend* to some higher level of being. Phil told me that half of me ain't bad, ain't ruined. To use his words. He's an idiot, of course. But he's White, so he's got that going for him. I mean, look, we all know I could act as White as I possibly could, whatever that means, but I'll never escape the black hole of Blackness in America's eyes. But, what do I know? I'm only in high school."

Nassir walks out. Greg takes a deep breath and smiles at

the administrators—who all have that deer-caught-in-the-headlights look.

"Pretty crazy that I'm the one in honors and not Nassir, right? I don't even know what *ascend* means."

28

The Make-Happy Surgery

Monty wants to stand. He's been sitting, waiting for so long. He *would* stand if he could, except for the gigantic chair and surgery apparatus he finds himself strapped to. Monty was skeptical when Jasmine first approached him about the new possibilities at the hands of her new husband, Mr. Peterson. She told him to look at the videos that Mr. Peterson had shown her. "You can see for yourself, Monty. Let him show you, an. I just," she said, "I just don't want you to be in any more pain." By pain, she meant, he assumed, the perceived delusional state of his life since he'd begun questioning things. Finding answers to those things. Then, never being able to get past the answers to those things.

It turns out that the videos were just as miraculous as Jasmine promised. There was a boy whose body was, without his choosing, twisted, gnarled in on itself, and was becoming more and more so, slowly, daily, from the time he was born until at the age of seven his organs were on the verge of having the very life squeezed out of them—unless man intervened. In the video, the boy could only crawl, feebly, and push his left foot against the ground and use his curled arms (his forearms stuck against his chest) in a bastardized version of the Army Crawl. The brain surgeon, who had intervened in the absence of God's ability to right the boy's body, narrated the video. He recited details of the boy's case, like how long he would live if nothing was improved (not long). And then it was six months later and the boy's head was shaved and scarred, much like what Monty's head would soon look like (minus the youth and the still-innocent smile), and the boy was walking. Upright. On his feet. *Walking.* He walked down the hospital hallway, swinging his arms. He dragged his left leg a little bit, twisted his hip to get the right leg forward, but, all in all, all things considered, he was up and walking. A few nurses stood in doorways along the hallway and held their hands over their mouths.

Jasmine wasn't trying to be the guilt-stricken White lady with the bleeding heart, she assured Monty when she showed up at the Chissler's doorstep one rain-drenched night a couple of months before the surgery. This was after Monty lost his job, but before they had to move out of the house they lived in for well over a decade. She had just married Mr. Peterson, and he made the surgery sound like a no-brainer (bad pun intended). And Monty. Monty had seemingly lost his mind by spending too much time with his deep web community, researching conspiracies, looking for answers to questions that no one should ever ask. Jasmine saw a problem and thought she had a solution. Monty hugged her, at the end of their talk, and he choked on his tears. "There's things I want to forget, Jasmine, and I can't."

It started with the dead leg dangling from the black Towncar. The Group led him to 911 conspiracies. 911 conspiracies led him to Heath Flowers, the only man known to be in Building Seven—and who was the presumed owner of the dangling leg. The only man, a Black man by the way, who gave a televised interview following Seven's collapse and told the truth (as The Group saw it). An interview that'd been disappeared by the powers that be. The Group and Gilliam had recovered the interview for Monty. And while Monty thought The Group had it wrong about Building

Seven, the "discovery" of Heath Flowers led Monty to look further into his past, looking for more lies, and looked into his wife's past, and when he found out that her family owned slaves in Alabama, and that his family line could be traced back to Alabama, to the very same county his wife's line hailed from, he shuttled back and forth through time and became unsure if God was playing a trick on him—this whole life, a cruel game he was just a pawn in. But not just him, all Black men and women, a pawn in White America's rigged game. A game that could only end one way in their minds. He searched for a reason. For a cause to all of it. He wanted a narrative. Gilliam and The Group encouraged Monty to press on, go farther, and let his new knowledge and new truths redirect his life. This was before The Group became a delirious QAnon group with visions of child sex trafficking that Portland FBI agents would watch and track online. And so, Monty fractured. Not so much because of his wife's family's possible enslavement of his family members, but because it felt like he had dug a hole that could never be filled. What was he supposed to tell Nassir? What, if any, was his responsibility to his ancestors? He broke. He couldn't find any causality to explain the pain, and he broke.

Jasmine only suggested the surgery because she truly did think it would help. Help Monty keep his family intact. Monty cried and cried. He called Mr. Peterson the next day. And now—

Monty tries to stand, but his head is firmly locked in place. Mr. Peterson hovers above him. The surgeon has his hands raised straight up in the air, arms bent at the elbows, waiting for a nurse to slide on the gloves. Monty wants to talk, but a tube runs down his throat. He wants to scream, *Stop! I changed my mind!* But he's gagged and immobile. Finally on the verge of a forced freedom.

The video of the boy who used to Army Crawl was followed by a video of a man with Alzheimer's. When the dial was turned, the man's face lit up as his brain was flooded with long-lost memories. "The problem is," Monty said to Mr. Peterson during a second consultation meeting (or was it the first?), "I'm not trying to remember things, I'm trying to forget them."

Gas pumps into the mask secured around Monty's face. His eyes slowly shut.

"There he goes," the nurse says.

The drill revs to life and Mr. Peterson guides the spinning drill bit into his head. The sound of the drill entering Monty's skull is as sickening as one would expect it to be.

29
Jasmine's Secret Phone Call

Jasmine didn't want to, but as soon as she had a moment alone in the bedroom she called Greg's biological father. "Your son was suspended, did he tell you? Your son needs you, did he tell you?" She said, "Fine, don't come to the game, don't be there."

"I have to work, Jasmine. Child support. Remember that whole thing?"

"Sometimes I wish you never left, Anthony."

"What's that?"

Jasmine said forget it and asked again if he'd be there, for Greg's last home game. "It'd mean the world to Greg, even if he doesn't say it… I have to go, I hear my husband yelling at Nassir."

PART THREE

30
Four Games Left

There's a new starting five. The names are scrawled across the whiteboard. Ben Jones the Double Outsider in place of Greg. One of the nameless bench players is in Nassir's spot. Greg and Nassir weren't even allowed to dress for the game. They're seated in the locker room, both wearing Greg's game-day clothes. Coach Day refuses to look at them. Rob the Massive Assistant Coach can only shake his head—his disappointment rendering him mute.

Riverview needs to win at least two of the remaining four games left on the schedule to have a reasonable chance of securing a playoff berth—a feat that hasn't been done in well over twenty years. Greg feels like he should wash his teammates' feet. His hair isn't long enough, though, for feet washing. Surveying his teammates, Greg can see how it, the game will turn out. "Coach," Greg says half-audibly, "can I say something?"

Nassir nudges Greg and whispers, "Just say it, Gregory. We're running out of time."

"Coach, if I may, I've seen the future."

Andre the Captain giggles.

"I say we let him speak, Coach," Manny says.

"What the fuck's happening here?" Coach Day sighs. "These two jeopardize your no *our* entire season and all you want is to hear the supposed future from this bug-eyed, White motherfucker?"

"I can feel the love, Coach. But you're right, because we, my best friend and new roommate, have put the team's collective hopes and dreams at risk. So I'd like to share the vision that God has entrusted me with about our immediate and post-immediate future."

"Go ahead, boy," Rob the Massive Assistant Coach grumbles.

"Preach, Pastor Hazel!" Nassir shrieks.

"Everyone up, everyone in a line. The light is perfect in here. It's almost dream-like. Bright halos circling your perfect heads. This is what God is telling me: There is nothing to fear. There is nothing to fear beyond these doors, beyond this life, because there will be nothing but bright and blinding and infinitely warm light when we open the last door of life and step into the void. So stand and face me and grope at your halos; look into the fluorescent lights and imagine the buzzing as the blessings of God falling heavy upon our souls.

"We will win this game. *You* will win this game. It is clear. This was all, ultimately, meant to happen. Ben Jones the Double Outsider, you are starting in my place. You will graduate high school and move away and never look back. You'll find a boy and you *will* fall for that boy and you *will* call him your boyfriend with no space between boy and friend and when you're ready you *will* bring him back to Riverview and introduce him to your father at Lucy's Cafe and my sister *will* be your server and your father *will* say things like, 'If this is what makes you happy it makes me happy,' but it'll be years, Ben, *years* until you'll feel comfortable inside and outside of your skin. You'll no longer be The Double-Outsider once you leave this place. You will only have one thing to be on the outside of."

The players' heads glow against the darkness. Their bodies undulate. It's beautiful. Even the hardly-ever-mentioned

     SUICIDE RUNNERS

bench players are beautiful at this moment. Momentarily heroic.

"Some of you will go on to community college. One of you will die of an enlarged heart, leaving behind a wife and two kids at the age of thirty-two. Another will die, mysteriously, of a choking accident. Doubts will be cast upon the cause of death. You were so funny, you the choker, you were so smart, you the choker, but alas, you'll choke and you'll die. Some of you will never step foot inside this high school again. Others will never touch a basketball again. One of you is destined to be homeless within two years. One of you joins the Marines or the Army or the Navy, after a few years of listlessness, and you'll be deployed to an oil-rich country and lose two legs and two arms and be saved by your loving comrades, but you'll forever wish from that day forward that you would've died out there on the sandy battlefield. One of you will work the same job for thirty years. Thirty fucking years at one desk. One of you will rob ten houses and be put in jail and be released and your mother will still love you. Two of us will meet in a bar in ten years and yell over beers and through tears burning the corners of our eyes that this was the best moment of our lives. One of you will walk into work one day and tell your boss that you killed your girlfriend in a flat, monotone voice, and everything will make sense about who you are, now, in this moment. Some of you will have kids. Others will have kids you don't want and they will grow up keenly aware of the fact that you don't want them. We will all fall short of the glory of God because the game is rigged. We are preordained to fall short of the glory of God."

One by one they file out of the locker room after receiving their blessing. The only two left are Greg and Nassir.

"I think that went well," Greg says.

Riverview, minus Nassir and Greg, lost by fifteen.

"You didn't say anything."

Three games left and two wins are needed to prevent a communal implosion of Biblical proportions.

"What do you mean I didn't say anything?"

"You just sat there. Coach asked if you had anything to say for yourself, speaking to you but meaning me and you, and you raised your head and smiled."

"And?"

"And that's all."

The future is bright and the halos are gold, Greg thinks he says.

31
Portland Public Access

"You're live in," and a cough.

"You are," and another cough.

"You are live in three, two," and another cough.

"What's the problem, Angel? Huh? Got something stuck in your throat? Got a tickle? A scratch? Huh? Just do the fucking countdown please, and stop saying live like you're living. It's L-I-V-E, like we are just barely uh-live, okay?"

"It's Angel, the *g* said like an *h*. We are uh-LIVE in three, two, and."

Jasmine is awash in a pool of light, drowning in her nerves. She can see her image on the monitor next to Camera A. Dark shadows hang from her eyebrows. She moves her head from left to right, but it only makes it worse. If she tilts her head down, her whole face ends up covered in a half-circle of gloom. Her forehead ablaze like a lake of burning sulfur.

Tyrell takes his seat next to Jasmine. Angel (with an h) moves behind the camera, slipping into the shadows. Jasmine squeezes her hands and the previously carpal-tunneled tendons whisper back to her loose and juicy. Tyrell pats her on the knee. His smile is infectious. She blushes and wonders if it might remedy the extreme paleness of her face on the monitor. Her mother would pinch her cheeks until it hurt before she walked on stage when she was young.

"Welcome to Dancing with Tyrell Jones, I'm your host, Tyrell Jones. We are going to try something a little different tonight. Now, don't be scared, I can hear your grumbles through the television, ladies."

Jasmine imagines the Bible Study Ladies standing in their living rooms, dressed in their home-workout outfits, water bottles on coffee tables, bangs pushed to the side; imagines them seeing Jasmine on the screen instead of the customary group of saggy-boned extras who stand awkwardly behind Tyrell and wait for instructions on how to dance and stretch. Jasmine can hear Judy scoffing at the sight of her.

"Jasmine Peterson is my guest, my inaugural talk show episode guest. This will be a night to remember. Jasmine's been an avid watcher, even a caller, of the show. Isn't that right?"

"It is, yes," Jasmine says. She doesn't know whether to smile at Tyrell or to the camera, where Tyrell is aiming his lighthouse-like grin.

"Jasmine here's dealt with carpal tunnel syndrome for, for how long was it again, Jazz?"

"About twenty-six years."

"And, when did it begin?"

Jasmine shifts uncomfortably and then sees her reflected self doing the same thing in Camera A's monitor a half-second later. "It started during the pregnancy of my first child."

Tyrell rubs her knee again, reassuringly, "What kind of treatments were attempted?"

"Everything. Anything. All the drugs the doctors could prescribe. All the braces. An ex even got me into acupuncture for a while. Another ex told me to try yoga. I've tried everything."

Tyrell beams into the camera, again. Again, Jasmine is unsure if she should follow suit. She can make out the silhouette of Angel (with an h) behind the camera giving Tyrell a thumbs up… or is it the middle finger?

"And what, finally, after twenty-six long years, in your own words: 'cured' your pregnancy-induced carpal tunnel?"

"You did, Tyrell."

Tyrell is all smiles. His hand again lands on her knee.

"And, Jasmine, you told me beforehand that there may be something you'd like to read. Is that still the case?"

Jasmine pulls out a piece of folded paper from her purse. She turns it over in her hands. Tears well in her eyes. "I'm not sure, I guess."

Tyrell signals to the Camera B operator to get a close-up of Jasmine and her tears. The money shot. *Eat your heart out, Jim Spagg,* Tyrell thinks. *I'm the new king of Portland Public Access.*

Jasmine's face fills the TV screen in her living room, where Greg and Nassir are watching the show.

"What's she doing?" Greg asks, sprawled across the floor.

"Drinking the Kool-aid."

"Don't be afraid, Jasmine. The only way to heal is to reflect," Tyrell says and, both in real life and in TV life, leans toward her confidentially. "What do you have there?"

Jasmine composes herself, "A letter."

"To whom?"

"To my son."

"Oh, God. Please, God, no." Greg sits up.

"Imagine the ratings," Nassir jokes.

"I don't know," Jasmine says, faltering.

"Just try, Jasmine."

Camera A is a two-shot, poorly framing Tyrell and Jasmine. Camera B is tight on Jasmine's face. Eyebrows to chin. Her eyes sparkle. Jasmine unfolds the paper, hesitates.

"Go on, Jasmine."

Jasmine clears her throat, "Dear Greg…"

Nassir rubs Greg's shoulders, "This is exciting."

"I didn't mean to make it worse. I promise. When you're

older, you'll understand. I was a single mom of two. I'm not apologizing, I'm explaining. You need to know. I need you to know. Everything got so much worse after I met Christopher Trench. So much worse."

"And who is this Christopher *Trench*, Jasmine?" Again with the hand on her knee/thigh.

"How many men will I have to kill, do you think, Nassir?"

"As many as it takes, Greg." Nassir aims the controller at the screen and cranks the volume to maximal levels.

"Trench was a boyfriend."

"I see. Please, continue."

"When you're older you'll understand, honey. I promise. I hope. I hope you'll understand. I know it was bad. I know he was terrible. But look in my eyes and know I'm telling the truth. You'll understand when you're older, when things start to fall apart, when God stops talking to you, stops listening to your prayers, then you'll start to understand, you'll start, *then*, to understand."

Mr. Peterson walks into the living room, "Hey, can you turn that down I'm…" but sees what's on the TV. "What the hell's she doing?"

"Go back to your room, Three-point-oh," Greg says.

"Don't you dare talk to me like that."

"Mr. Peterson," Nassir says, "back to your room."

"There's no one here to protect you."

Neither Greg nor Nassir move their eyes from the constantly changing picture of Jasmine and Tyrell Jones: close-up, two-shot, close-up, two-shot.

"You have to believe me, I didn't know he'd change so much. So fast. I was a single mom. Can you forgive me? I know I can't ask that of you yet. When you're older. Hopefully, when you're older you'll forgive me. I met Christopher Trench two months after your father left me. Left us. Remember that too, Honey, remember that *he* left *us*. Not just me. Not just you. He left us. Me, you and Shasta. He left us in that house in St. Johns with no way to pay for it. His family said we could move into their basement, into his uncle's basement."

"And Shasta is?" Tyrell asks, face smiling.

"My daughter."

"Why is she doing this?" Mr. Peterson takes a step closer, and both Greg and Nassir turn to him, eyes full of murder.

"She's clarifying backstory, Mr. Peterson!"

"She's gotta explain how she ended up with you, Three-point-zero. Everyone's been wondering."

"They had a utility room in the basement that they could turn into a bedroom, they said. There was a shower and a toilet and a sink—the same sink they used to wash mud off their shoes—and we could stay down there until we landed on our feet, they said. I couldn't imagine being that close to his family. Not like that. Not down there. There weren't any windows down there, Greg. Did you know that? Did you know there weren't any windows down there? It was like a prison. I got on my knees and prayed, just like the ladies at church always told me to do. That was the best they could do for us, your grandfather said. He said he didn't know where Anthony went off to. Just poof. That's when I met Christopher Trench. And that's when Shasta left. Right after I met him. Do you see? You see why I fell into Trench? I was scared."

"What were you scared of, Jasmine?"

Jasmine looks at Tyrell like, *That's what I'm about to say.* The cameras re-focus.

Blood pools below the headless body of Mr. Peterson. Nassir holds the bloody sword. Greg sits placidly in front of the TV.

"There's a lot of blood, Gregory!"

"There can only be one!"

"I was scared they'd take you away from me. Scared that if we lived in the basement, Matheson would take Shasta. And then what? Then who'd I have? You'll understand later what it's like. You'll understand why I did what I did, and you'll forgive me. You will. No matter how much you hate or hated me. You'll understand. I met Trench and he was a sweet talker and he owned a few dry cleaners in Riverview, and, well, I didn't see what my other choice was. Trench. What a terrible last name. He had big ideas. Broad shoulders. I was reeling. I was still looking out the window of the N. Portland house the last day we lived there, hoping Anthony would walk back up the steps. Say he was sorry. Ask me, us, to take him back. I know you wanted him to come back, too. You did, even though he hurt you like he did. You don't have to admit that now, it's fine, honey. I'm just trying to explain what I was doing. Trying to get you to understand that I love you and that I did it for you. I did. If I didn't marry Trench, they would've taken you away. Shasta told Matheson that Anthony had beaten you and that I watched. I'm sorry, Honey. I'm sorry I just watched. It was just the one time, I know. He didn't mean it, I know. I didn't have a place for us to stay. Matheson called and told me he would let you live with them for the time being until I could get back on my feet. So I met Christopher Trench—if I keep saying the name, the full name, the whole, disgusting, four-syllable name, there will be no power left in his name. Not over you. Not over me. And I saw an escape. I saw a way to keep you and Shasta with me. I needed you more than you needed me, but I couldn't tell you that, not back then, not when you were so young. I couldn't let you know that I got so much strength from you and Shasta. I know how much you hated Christopher Trench always said, 'Whatd'ya say.' And I know how much you hate that you have to see him sometimes in the locker room.”

“Wow. Quite a bit to process here, Jasmine. Should we do some stretching maybe? Clear the bad energy out of the air?” Tyrell asks.

“Please, just let me go on.”

“Nassir! Where’d the head go?” Greg screams.

“I think it rolled down the stairs!”

“Ah. So it did. The trail of blood leads the way.”

“I tried to tell Trench to stop swimming at the high school. But he wouldn’t. He still does. And you still see him there. I’m sorry. But listen, I’m so proud of you, honey. I hope you’ll be able to understand one day when you’re older, when you’re laying at the bottom of the lake looking up into the starry sky and straining to hear God’s whisper—I hope *then* that you’ll forgive me. I hope then that you’ll love me. When you came home from Nassir’s house that summer, eighth grade. When you came home and I had a black eye and my arm was cut and bleeding and the coffee table was broken, the one with glass inlay, I was so scared. And you hugged me, Greg. And you told me it was okay. And I felt so weak. I’m your mother, Greg. I want to be your rock. I want to be there for you. I want to show you how strong I can be. And I’m learning how. Learning to be that woman. But when I told you that I fell, when I told you that he didn’t hit me, when I told you it was just an accident and the church ladies were on their way and Nassir’s mother and Monty came over and stayed all night and watched the road and. He did hit me. He did push me down. Let me say it simply: Christopher Trench was a bad man.”

“Look, Nassir, look what I’ve done.”

“Oh, Gregory, Mr. Peterson’s severed head fits perfectly on top of the mantel. He has risen indeed!”

"Are his innards suitable decorations, strewn about as they are?"

"You've never done anything so right, my brother."

"I'm learning how to be an accomplice, Nassir."

"I don't think you're ready yet. Ready for what it means."

Nassir turns the volume on the TV up even higher.

"Shasta was right to want to leave before it all happened. She was so right. I just couldn't see it. Don't blame her for leaving us, Greg. Don't hold it against her anymore. I don't. I was too blinded by my fear, by my loneliness, to see it before. Before I was lying on the ground looking up at him. I told him to leave. I screamed and yelled and kicked and he pushed me down onto the coffee table and I picked up a shard of glass and threatened him. I asked Nassir's parents to stay with me that night. We played Hearts. I had to get the locks changed the next day. I had to change the code on the garage door. I had to unhook the light fixture first, on the garage door motor thing, and then in a panel inside that I had to manually change the code. We talked about marriage. I can't believe it. We talked about me becoming a Trench. That's why I didn't take Mr. Peterson's name, officially. I'm tired of changing for someone else. I'm just Jasmine now."

Mr. Peterson peeks his head (which, contrary to popular hope, is still intact and not bleeding out) around the wall and lets out a guffaw.

"I can still hear you, Three-point-oh."

"Quite a revelation for you, Mr. Peterson. All of our dirty laundry being aired out on television."

"No one's watching," Mr. Peterson says, like a petulant child.

"That's what I fear," Nassir responds.

Greg says, "God is watching."

And Greg and Nassir cock their heads to the ceiling and

from their clenched fists they shoot rays of light to heaven. The ceiling crumbles around them. They dance in its vacuous splendor.

Jasmine folds the paper and closes her eyes, trying to keep tears from escaping. The close shot is magnificent. Tyrell looks at the monitor and sees a twinkling, single tear roll down her cheek.

"That was beautiful, Jasmine."

32
Three Games Left

Greg's phone rang last night. He didn't even know it was capable of ringing. No one *calls* Greg. The call came from an 805 number: Santa Barbara, CA. Greg almost shit himself, but he was able to regain control over his sphincter in time to answer. An assistant coach for the UCSB basketball team was on the other end. He wasted no time informing Greg UCSB wouldn't be extending a scholarship offer. "You can walk on if you want to," the assistant coach said. "But there'll be no promises." When Greg asked if it was because of the blowups on the court, the fighting, the stuff that made it online, and now the suspension, too, the assistant coach said, flatly, "Well, you're a borderline talent, to begin with, to be honest, so yea, none of that shit helped your case." Greg imagined he could hear the ocean, the waves, and the sounds of a hundred Jenny Owendales in bikinis outside the assistant coach's office.

When Greg told Jasmine the news, she said, "Well, okay, I guess God closed that door. So, now we'll look for a window. You know how they say in church." She drew in a deep breath. "It'll work out," she said, "annnnnnnnn." Ever since her semi-public confession on *Dancing With Tyrell Jones* (semi-public because Mr. Peterson was right, after all, only Judy and the Bible Study Ladies had been watching [even in the quick-to-shame world of Riverview High School, Greg hadn't heard nary a peep about it]), the space between Greg and Jasmine has been fraught with unsure words. Greg cried later that night, after Jasmine's televised apology, alone in his room. Nassir stood outside his bedroom door and whispered over and over, "There there, there there, there there." Greg didn't know he needed an apology. Didn't know a parent could apologize. Maybe the maternal side of a parental unit is the only one allowed to apologize? Greg and Jasmine hugged when she returned home from the community access studio. She brushed off Father Figure 3.0's look of embarrassment and headed straight for Greg. Greg held her tight and whispered, "I'll make things right." A chill ran through her body. Nassir stood beside them and opened his long arms, mockingly, inviting Mr. Peterson in for a big ol' hug.

Now it's the middle of the night and Greg has to pee. With his hand on the doorknob, eyes half-open, Greg remembers that Nassir's in the living room where he's been sleeping on the couch until, as Jasmine said, "Things just, well, figure themselves out." Greg tip-toes towards the living room. He peeks around the corner and tries to spy the couch Nassir's been calling his Home 3.0. "Now I've got a Three-point-oh, too."

They both agreed that they should stop taking the pill that promised Clarity and a Clear Conscious. Marcel the Supplier said the dude he got it from called it *Three-Cubed* (this unnamed *dude*, Greg was pretty sure, was Shasta's ex-boyfriend, Gerald). A side-effect was deep sleep. A side-effect of cold-turkeying Three-Cubed is unrelentingly fitful sleep.

"Gregory. I'm over here."

Greg jumps, startled, and finds Nassir sitting upright in a chair across from the couch. "Can't sleep?"

"I am imagining what it'd be like to call that couch my home for the rest of my life."

"The couch?"

"Yes."

"It'd be a pretty small life."

"The smallest."

" … "

" … "

"I didn't get a scholarship to UCSB."

" … "

" … "

Greg staggers back to the bathroom. He pees. He flushes.

When he's back in bed, after saying goodnight to Nassir and not hearing a reply, he pulls the covers up to his chin and wonders if his mom will, at some point, need to marry a fourth man. She's just like everyone else, he thinks, even though she holds the title of "Greg's Mother." She is weak and frail, or strong and confused, and she's looking for love. Looking for her own paradise filled with her own Jenny Owendales, or, in her case, Ryan Reynolds. He thinks at some point in the future the two of them will get along great, just like she wants. "Because life's too fucking short," she said. "Sorry. It's just too short, Greg."

Greg can see it out there, beyond college, beyond the pestering about the George Fox application's extended deadline that's fast approaching, "Since you didn't, you know, honey, get a scholarship to UCSB." Out there beyond her nightly worried looks. Just before Greg falls asleep he wonders if God listens to her prayers. And then the airplanes do their red-eye rumble thing in the sleeping sky. There must be sleep because the next day is the next game. And so on. And so *he* becomes *we*, just like team sports demand.

We are told we must win this game. "This is a must-win situation," they tell us. The coaches repeat it to us, as if the more they say it the more the words will become more than just words. We are in the furthest stall to the right, in the boys' locker room inside the bowels of the gymnasium. We hear yelling and laughing and someone is saying he finger-banged a cheerleader last night behind the Wendy's on 122nd. Everything echoes. Bang-bang-bang-bang… We are on the toilet. Key-scratched messages litter the metal walls around us. We used to dream of playing in the NBA. We used to dream of being drafted in the NBA Lottery. The older Black man, the usher, the omnipresent slender figure in the Green Room who's on every camera during every draft, would walk up to us with a smile that says, *Welcome to the club son(s), everything will now be different and glorious*, and he'd hand us the snap-back hat of the team who drafted us—the Blazers, the Hawks, the Mavericks—and we'd put the hat on, snug it tight twice like the draftees always do. And our mother is there. And our biological father, too. Look, they're sitting on opposite sides of the round table with the red phone in the middle. And the commentators talk about wing-span and shuttle times and verticals and our collegiate stats and but all that matters is that our parents are sitting at the same table for the first time since only God-knows-when. And in the dream, when the phone rings, just before we are drafted, our parents look at each other and their lips turn up towards their cheeks, something resembling a smile, *yes*, an authentic smile, and she forgives him for everything, for the yelling, for the failures, for the bruises on our bodies from the it-was-just-the-one-time that we choose not to remember, and they'd be right there, our parents, celestial *and* earthbound, seated across the round table with all the world watching, and their eyes would meet and melt, across the ringing red phone that we'd answer and say, "Hello, yessir, we can't wait. We'll do our best to make you proud," like all the young men do when they answer the call that says everything paid

     SUICIDE RUNNERS

off: all the hard work, all the endless hours in the gym, the escaping to the gym, escaping to the hoop on the street, to the park, to anywhere, the getting the 1000s of shots up, the required Basketball Rosaries, the every day, the every fucking day, the trying to shoot with our eyes closed under the streetlights, our fingers icy, our noses running, rain tethered to swinging clouds, and the voice on the phone in the dream says, "Congratulations son(s), you are a now member of the Timberwolves, Warriors, Bucks. This is who you are now, it all wasn't pointless." And everyone cries, everyone hugs, slaps hands and bro-hugs. And our father is so proud of us, we haven't seen him like this in years, and look, everyone, look! Even our mother cries joyful tears, not sad tears, not the usual hands and fingers buried in and tearing at her hair tears, the tears after Trench, the tears in her room, the tears above empty dinner plates, the tears of wakeless mornings, the tears of "I'm sorry I can't do it anymore," and here comes the slender man with the natty suit winding his way through the tables towards us in the Green Room, and he gives us the hat—the Sixers the Suns the Clippers—and now we're on stage and shaking hands with the Commissioner and look it says NBA DRAFT behind us in blue and red and white.

We have five minutes for this: for the runny, nervous shit we must take (leave?) before every game. Nassir waits for us. Nassir stands at the sink. Nassir complains about the smell. Nassir has broken out. Zits have exploded across his forehead. Nassir complains about the smell of our shits and picks at his new zits and a few underclassmen materialize in and out of the stall next to us, zipping and unzipping at the urinal. Nassir complains that his head has ignited. We can hear the groan of the gym floor above us. We know that our team is about to take the floor. We hear the stands filling with anxious Black and White Riverview fans. We hear the band warming up. Nassir says that he thinks it's the anti-depressants that our mom suggested he resume taking that have caused the acne outbreak. We don't ask if they're working. We feel old. We feel like old men. We want to do it all over again. We're eighteen. We want to be ten. No, four? Five? We want to be six again and at the beach with our dad, climbing onto the barnacled remains of Peter Iredale as it reaches out from its sandy grave. We want to be six again with our dad's hand on our back telling us to watch out for the rust and to pull ourselves up. We want to die. We stopped taking Three-Cubed and, as predicted, we remember that we wanted to die. We can see Nassir through the space between the door and the stall. And maybe that's the only way we can truly see him? In the space between. The here before the now. No past, no future, only this space between. His shoes are untied. Marcel the Supplier's Jordans. They're ripping at the seams because Nassir wears them all the time, not just for practice and games. We tell him that he doesn't have to wait, that it's his fault he's standing there smelling this, our shitty nerves in the toilet. He says, "You're right, Gregory, this is my fault. But I'm here, waiting for you, just in case Trench is swimming in the pool. Just in case I need to be *your* accomplice." We thank him. We see him in the space between. We pray for a win, but the ceiling is right there and is made of cement.

We are here. In the gym. On the floor. The stands are full. We take a deep breath and Andre the Captain and Marcel the Supplier and Ben Jones the Double Outsider and Nassir and Manny and The Bench, whose faces and names no one will remember in twenty years, are huddled outside the green double doors of the gym. They ask Nassir to pray because he's the smartest. He knows the best words. So everyone puts their hands in the middle. All the colors of the world, right here in Riverview. Sweaty, clammy, hands, all of us. And Nassir says, "Our Lord in Heaven, hallowed be thy name. Thy kingdom come, thy will be done. For it is said, 'Black people and Non-Black people do not exist in the same universe or paradigm of violence any more than fish and birds exist in the same region of the world.' Amen." And we all scream AMEN at the top of our lungs and we burst through the green double doors and Nassir laughs, pushing us from behind, and we're all dressed alike, we're all in green and white and black warmups that say *Broncos* across the butt, and we hear the fans cheering, and the legs of our warmup pants are only buttoned at the very top and bottom because that's what the seniors did all those years ago when we thought they were cool, and we thought they were God's only true sons, and we thought that we would be granted eternal happiness when we too could button our warmups just like them when we were on varsity. We see the band director, the old White man with gray hair and a sweaty face and droopy brown pants, conducting the sins out of the band. And the tall, skinny, White kid with the oboe, who everyone thinks is the smartest kid in the whole school because he already got into Yale or Harvard or Brown, blows his purified heart out. We and our army, our gang, our murderous crew, are circling the gaping White faces of the Century High School Boys Basketball Team. We are all boys. We know they are from Beaverton and we know they are mostly rich and we know they are all White and we know they are looking at our teammates as we circle their half of the court, dribbling and staring them down, "Putting the fucking fear of God in their cracker-ass hearts," like Andre the Capitan said before we exploded onto the floor. They know we know we need this win. This is a must-kill situation. Fuck peaceful protests. Fuck turning the other cheek. We know these fuckers are looking at our Brown and Black teammates and demanding a peaceful protest from *them* and are watching the way Marcel bounces when he runs, the way they think Manny drips with swagger, the way Ben runs upright, the way we and Nassir and Andre are obviously the lead dogs, the way Nassir is already sweating through his jersey, the way they think we are all useless druggies, and we know they are looking at our Black team, because a team's racial makeup is like the 3/5th compromise compromised by all those God-fearing White fathers of yore, and they are thinking to themselves something like *Fuck these n-words*, but they're saying it, we know they're fucking saying the n-word to themselves as they bend their knees and flick their wrists and try to ignore us and our team of marauders as they push their floppy blonde and brown hairs out of their faces because the new White President made it okay to publicly hate our Black and Brown teammates again. We want to kill the Century players. We stand in the layup line and wipe the bottoms of our shoes with our hands and we want to kill them. We lick our hands, then wipe our shoes, and we still want to kill them. We squeak our shoes on the floor. We make our shoes sticky. We do this religiously. Andre the Capitan tells their center, right before the referee tosses the ball in the air, that he's going to fucking kill him. "I'm going to fucking kill you, you hear me?" Their center looks away. We saw him look away. We used to dream of playing in the NBA and being drafted in the lottery, interviewing with the ESPN reporter immediately after shaking the Commish's hand and trying not to cry during the interview but getting choked up when the reporter asks how proud of us our family must be, how our mother must be so excited, and we'd have to look away, to hide our big, fat, embarrassing tears. And the band plays. And the oboe player's playing *Rapper's Delight*, and everyone loves it because the oboist is tall and skinny and White and going to an Ivy League school and *he's* playing *Rapper's Delight*, and it's all so culturally- and racially-ironic, and he's playing a fucking oboe, and no one knows what the fuck a fucking oboe is! "WHAT'S A FUCKING OBOE?" we scream. We see Nassir's White mom in the stands with her new White boyfriend, her savior, Phil, her correction to normalcy, and she looks like she'd rather be anywhere else but here because maybe Monty will show up and demand everyone's attention and scratch at the wire trying to escape from his neck. We see our mother and *your* Father Figure 3.0, and our mother waves and tries to smile, and your Father Figure 3.0 talks to an elderly person, selling them volts and drills and electrodes. We see Brian hover awkwardly around the teachers, whispering, pointing at us and Nassir. We see Shasta coming back from the bathroom, holding her belly. We see Ben the Double Outsider's father. We know that he doesn't know Ben is gay. And Gilliam's here. Gilliam is all smiles and reflecting glasses. We see Shane the Youth Pastor, the half-virgin, and we see he brought a couple of kids with him from the youth group. We see them and we know we should try, with everything we've emptied inside of us, to not cuss out there on the floor tonight. But we will. We see the Bronco flag and we hear the beat of the bass drum in our chest and we fear the whistle and we don't make eye contact with Coach Day because he's the one who said, "It's a must-kill situation tonight." So we put our arm around Rob the Massive Assistant Coach's towering, expansive, safe, loving shoulders. Coach Day is going over the game plan but no one cares, neither we nor our teammates care one fucking bit how desperately Coach Day and the Synod of Riverview and the PTA and the Boosters and the White people at our White church who voted for a return to Whiteness want this win, this kill, this bloodletting sacrifice. They want to watch the blood run from Century's throat. They want to hear their gurgles because it will bring meaning to the meaningless boredom of their everyday lives. See, they not only want us to win the game, they want us to humiliate every player and coach on Century. They want us to bury them. We and our multicultural team are *allowed* to do this for them. This and only this. And then go back to dribbling a basketball and shutting up, they tell Nassir. We win. And we hate that they are happy.

33
The Ultrasound

The ultrasound monitor's display is black and white. Were it in color, Shasta might not be as hesitant to look at the screen. She's never gotten used to it, the ghostly grayish-white face of her baby with its body smushed against the screen. It doesn't feel real yet, this *thing* inside her. The first ultrasound was easier to stomach, even if she was surprised by the wand needing to be "inserted" into her vagina to see the baby that, at that point, at twenty weeks, even though Brian vehemently disagreed, definitely did still look like an alien.

Brian squeezes her hand as the image on the screen rotates. The nurse moves the wand around the ever-widening circumference of her belly. Her huge, belly-button-protruding belly. She smiles because that's what she's supposed to do, isn't it? Smile? Inside this cramped room, she should smile as she strains her neck to see. "Can we pull the monitor a little closer? It's, yeah, there you go, thanks."

If Brian hadn't mentioned Jenny Owendale, *again*, last night in the middle of getting ready for bed—toothbrush jamming in and out of his mouth, saliva- and toothpaste-foam sloshing all over the place—maybe Shasta would be genuinely excited that the nurse said something about the baby looking healthy. A healthy little boy. "Jenny Owendale," Brian said last night, "gave a presentation in class and— what's that? Oh, no, not in my class…"

"A healthy baby boy, only one more month to go," the nurse says.

If Shasta could be one hundred percent certain that Brian wasn't thinking of Jenny Owendale when they had extremely uncomfortable sex the last time, like two months ago, then maybe the smile she's faking wouldn't need to be so painfully fake. Why is this room so small? It's the insurance provider's fault. They should have, like Shasta wanted, gone to the doctor that her father, Matheson, suggested. "Who can afford that?" Brian had asked, insulted even by the idea. "My dad can." And when Brian kept talking about Jenny Owendale and her presentation and how she had posed the question regarding the legal status of the refugees at the border, and if they were in fact *refugees* in the classic sense, Shasta asked Brian if he'd rather call Greg to discuss Jenny Owendale. Brian stopped brushing, toothbrush dangling just above the sink. Starting at each other in the mirror seemed to be the only thing left to do.

"You'll need to stay off your feet as much as possible in the near future," the nurse says.

If Gerald used a condom the last time they had sex, as she'd asked him to do but didn't necessarily insist, then maybe the strain her fake smile is putting on her face, coupled with the way she keeps flexing her hands subconsciously to ward off pregnancy-induced carpal tunnel, tripled with the acrid smell of the gel, wouldn't all be aiding the nausea that's bubbling up in her stomach somewhere behind the alien's globed head. But, then, wasn't she already pregnant when she and Gerald had sex the last time? Wasn't that the whole point?

"Let me just wipe this off here… and, there you go," the nurse says.

Shasta pushed Gerald off of her after he came inside her, back when they had sex after she was pretty sure she was *probably* already pregnant. After she watched the way his eyes tightened at the moment of release. After she almost started to cry right in the middle of the act, right when she pulled his face closer to her face and buried his mouth and nose into the mattress next to the crook of her shoulder. After he said, "I can't breathe."

"We advise first-time parents to, at this time, start getting a plan together for when the baby comes. The bag. The route to the hospital. You know. The fun stuff."

"I have plans in place, don't you worry," Brian, the exuberant father-to-be says. "Plan A, B and C.

"Do you have any ideas for names?" the nurse asks.

Brian squeezes Shasta's hand and smiles that big, new-daddy smile. He rattles off a few that they're trying out. Shasta lets herself lilt.

34
The Waffle Debacle

Mr. Peterson (aka Father Figure 3.0) is on the phone, in the kitchen, trying to convert a warm lead from the church into a sale. Another gray morning outside. He hears a rustling in the living room. "Excuse me one second." He covers the mic with his hand and concentrates on listening. He doesn't hear anything, so he turns back to—

"Boo."

"Fuck!" Mr. Peterson yelps as he finds Nassir suddenly next to the refrigerator, shirtless, cadaverous, rubbing the sleep out of his eyes.

"Nassir. G'morning." Mr. Peterson looks down at the phone cradled in his hands like, *Uh, do you mind?*

"I pissed the couch, Mr. Peterson."

"You what?"

"Kidding. Just kidding. Where's Gregory and Miss Booker?"

Mr. Peterson takes the name *Booker* like a dagger to his kidney. "They're visiting George Fox, remember? Coach Murgle invited them down."

"Ah, yes. Murgle. An unfortunate name. Kind of like Peterson. Pee-terson. Pee. Full circle, Mr. Pee-terson. Right back to pissing." Nassir appears to instantly forget Mr. Peterson exists and opens the refrigerator door.

"Sorry 'bout that," Mr. Peterson says, returning to his phone call while warily eyeing Nassir. "We've had a house guest the last few weeks and, well… uh huh, that's right. Gloria's son. Yep, we're just doing our part. Amen's right. Anyway, where was I?"

Nassir pulls a box of frozen waffles from the freezer and rips it open, followed by an insanely loud attempt to tear open the plastic bag inside the box. "These things, am I right?"

"Excuse me." Mr. Peterson again covers the phone and turns to see Nassir now holding a bag of frozen waffles up for inspection.

"Indestructible. No secondhand shit here. These bags do what they're designed to do. You know? Fulfill their promise to the paying customer. *You* know what I mean, you're a salesman. These waffles will, once I'm able to get this fucking bag open, be frozen. As promised." Nassir makes a big show of trying to pull the bag open. His muscles strain, sinewy tendons rising to the surface of his skin.

"Nassir."

"All…most…there!" POP! Frozen waffles explode from the bag, skidding across the linoleum floor like waffle pucks.

"I'm going to have to call you back, uh huh, I really am sorry." Mr. Peterson ends the call and looks at the frozen waffles puddling on the floor. "Jeeze, Nassir."

After a long, tense, awkward, boiling silence, Nassir says, "Shouldn't we be doing something… constructive?"

"What?"

"No no no, your line is, 'What did you have in mind?… A short, blunt human pyramid?'"

Confused and disgusted, Mr. Peterson shakes his head and bends down to grab one of the waffles, but Nassir kicks it away. The waffle slides past Mr. Peterson's fingers. Mr. Peterson jumps up and pushes Nassir against the refrigerator, his forearm pressing Nassir's body to the cold door. "You think you're pretty clever, don't you!" Mr. Peterson is a good six inches shorter than Nassir, so he has to look way up to meet Nassir's eyes. "Let me fill you in on a little truth about life."

"Yes, speak your truths to me! *Whitemansplain* the fuck out of me!"

"Monty was gone long before the surgery. Jasmine thought he was savable, but she was wrong, and I knew it from the very first moment he came into the office babbling on and on about his half-baked conspiracies and all this shit about slavery and, I mean, give me a fucking break. It's 2017, okay? It's not your poor mom's fault, not her people's fault—that was *centuries* ago! You can't blame anyone but your goddamn self. Get it?" Mr. Peterson pushes his forearm hard against Nassir's chest as he releases him. Tears sting the corners of Nassir's eyes. "He drove himself crazy wanting to forget all of it. And your mother, Nassir. She was scared of him, okay? She felt vulnerable, even. She told me and Jasmine."

Nassir massages the spot on his chest where Mr. Peterson's elbow had been.

"That makes sense, her being afraid of him. Her capacity for anti-Black violence is part and parcel of her White womanness; it's embedded in her ontology. I know you don't know what that means, but trust me, someone way smarter than you and I combined said it. Anyway, my dad going, in your words, *crazy*, is good for you, isn't it? Both from a business side of things and from a humanity side of things." Mr. Peterson is dumbfounded by confusion and rage. "Without expendable Black men like my dad, how would you know you were human? He's the cat to your dog. *Get it?*"

"Do me a favor, Nassir. Can you do me just one favor?"

"For you, Mr. Peterson? Anything. Should I bow, too? Or, better yet, stand in a dark corner? Would that connect you back to the plantation days like a bolt of lightning, *sir?*"

Mr. Peterson's eyes burn bright and fluorescent. "Do whatever you want with your life, but don't drag Greg down with you as you go. If it were up to me, you'd be out on the street just like Monty. You hear me?"

Nassir tries to make his face do the Denzel Look, but nothing happens.

35
Two Games Left

Greg leans in and feels the heat of his opponent's body as both players work to gain leverage for the rebound. The opponent jumps. Greg waits. When the opponent reaches the apex of his ascension, Greg undercuts him. He thrusts his hips under the player's knees and the opponent lands head-first onto the court. The crowd gasps. Greg stands over him and blinks. Nothing more. The other team pushes past Greg, cursing and yelling at him. The referee blows the whistle. Again and again. Greg looks for Nassir. All the emotion of the season boiled down to a single, monotonous, hum.

"We have to finish the game," Nassir says. Nassir screams. "Then what?"

Greg looks up at the scoreboard: 35-27. It doesn't matter which team is ahead. The sweat on his forehead is cold. He wipes it away with his forearm. Things are shouted by Coach Day, whose drunk words ring hollow against the rafters.

The referees decide it was a common foul, no technical. The opponent is helped off the court. He looks at Greg and says, "Fuck you."

Greg smiles. He searches the stands and finds the George Fox scout scribbling new scriptures into his notepad.

Near the end of the game, the win is easily in hand. Playoff hopes can stay alive for one more game. The starters have been pulled. They sit five in a row on the bench, victorious and effervescent. The bench players, The Forgettables, run hard and play like their lives are on the line. The theater of the crowd is rich and alluring. Nassir, still consuming the normal Three-Cubed dosage as suggested by Marcel the Supplier—"Just until the end of the season, Nassir. We need you lucid for these games."—is at one with the audience. He elbows Greg, causing him to spill the water he's chugging down the front of his jersey. The audience roars with agitated excitement as attention is directed to, "Look."

Monty and Gilliam are engaged in a heated argument at the precipice of the gymnasium. The band rises to their feet, swaying and playing triumphantly. Each time they lean to their right they temporarily block Nassir and Greg's view of Gilliam and Monty. Monty grabs Gilliam by the collar and yells in his face. He jams a finger into Gilliam's chest. Security scrambles up the bleachers, headed for Monty.

"The White guy believes the new President is going to save sex-trafficked children. My dad just believes there's too much reality he can't accept."

"Your dad is heroic."

"To be heroic, Greg, you need a story arc. And we aren't allowed narratives."

Monty keeps pushing Gilliam. But Monty stumbles and grabs his neck, heading towards the exit. Even from the bench, Nassir and Greg can see how infected and painful Monty's neck looks. Nassir stands up. It's more like he stands at attention. The rest of the starters raise their eyes to their comrade. Coach Day and RMAC peel attention away from the waning moments of the game to watch Nassir. Marcel the Supplier whispers to Andre the Captain, "He's seeing clearly now."

Just before Monty is wrenched violently from the scene by security, he manages to grab onto a railing and look down at Nassir. Nassir salutes him. Monty smiles. Or cries? It's hard to tell. And the crowd cheers as someone makes an inconsequential layup. Jenny Owendale, Naya, and the rest of the cheer squad flutter.

36
Monty

Monty sits. He's not sure where he's sitting. Actually, he's not even sure how long he's been sitting wherever he's sitting. He wishes he was on a bluff. Overlooking a river. Or on the beach, listening to the wind. He wishes he was in South Carolina. Wishes he was wading into the Atlantic. He remembers this: he remembers reading a poem, no, seeing a poem performed by a young Black woman in N. Portland. He's crying. He remembers taking his son to the performance. He remembers the auditorium's beautiful brown wood. He remembers faces in the water. The poet began quiet, then yelled, then ended quietly. She stomped. She screamed. She said she had a dream about the Atlantic, about the faces of her ancestors in the waves. He tries to turn the dial up, but nothing happens. He remembers Nassir's face, his rapt attention, the way he leaned forward. He remembers the ride home, when Nassir asked about the poet, about her ancestors in the waves, and asked, "Do we have ancestors in the waves?" The pavement is cold under his thin jeans. He didn't think it'd end up here, like this, in the dark of night, in a dark place, back when he sent the first message asking for any information on the dead leg. But here he is. He remembers telling Nassir that they did have ancestors from the South. From South Carolina, or was it Alabama? Was that where the poet's ancestors were from? He remembers seeing a poster in a museum in N. Portland, in Albina, in the Red Line District, that simply said, "Pour one out for those who jumped into the waves." He didn't tell Nassir what he had found, not then, not in the car on the way home. He didn't want to ruin the moment of pure Black pride that the poet had ignited inside of Nassir. Didn't want to remind him of his White mom. He can hear the whistle screeching. He must be near the gymnasium. Near his son. On the other side of the wall. He told Nassir, eventually, about his White mother's White ancestors. The slave owners. The possible ownership of his ancestors. In response, Nassir joked, because it was all he could do, "Hey, if it worked out for Thomas Jefferson's kids…" He remembers that. He's weeping now. He turns the dial again. He feels something. But it doesn't feel right. He cranks it back down, then back up. He wants to feel something. He wants to feel heroic. He wants to save his son. He wants to forget his past. He wants to not care. He wants to forget The Group and that Gilliam had whispered to him about a man named Q, making him realize how hopeless his journey toward truth was turning out to be. He wants to wade into the ocean's cold love. He wants to go back. Go in. Go down. He tries to stand up, but he feels a warm rush of blood to his chest. It's too much to handle, he remembers.

37

The First Quarter of the Final Game
of the Regular Season

The song begins. The crowd hears the haunting wind chimes. A creepy reverb inhabits the near silence. Then more wind chimes, this time with a little touch of bass added underneath. And then the voice. That voice.

It was a dark night, pitch black, May 20th, 19…
  Approximately 11:30 p.m., a Black child was born
   Upon his arrival and rapid growth
    Being exposed to the many casualties of the streets
     He has now realized what must be done

The crowd grumbles. The enraged Athletic Director shouts and shouts and shouts, directing someone to "Go change the fucking song!" The door to the sound system is frantically yanked at, but it's locked. The seniors planned that, too. And now it's too late, because—

…He must bring the ruckus to all you mother fuckers…

…He must bring the ruckus to ALL YOU MOTHER FUCKERS…

…He must bring THE RUCKUS TO ALL YOU MOTHER FUCKERS…

HE MUST BRING THE RUCKUS TO ALL YOU MOTHER FUCKERS!

Riverview takes the floor like blood-thirsty harbingers of the Lord Almighty's wrath. Except, unlike the alabaster angels in the Bible, the players come in all different degrees of melanin. They agreed on Busta Rhymes the night before at Andre the Captain's house, after a search into the catacombs of hip hop's past. The first track of Busta's first album, *The Coming*. Andre's parents hovered around the seniors with juice, pasta, and his mother's warm and loving hands on their shoulders. They sensed that something was happening, or would happen. "It'll be an invocation of the Holy Redeemer, Busta-Bust, to lead us into the playoffs," Nassir said after the votes were cast.

The five seniors dribble in unison as they hum to the beat of the song that thumps to life after *The Coming* came and went. They circle the opposing team. The cheerleaders are a shimmering mess of emotions and leg kicks. Naya is tossed into the air. She spins, twirls and lands in the cradled arms of her squad just before what would, surely, be a final impact. An event horizon. Jenny Owendale whips her hair counter-clockwise, rewinding time. See Naya zip back up and careen again toward the ground. Again. Again. The cheerleaders are the buffer between the players and those teetering on the verge of hysteria in the crowd. The Whites and Blacks. The never-ending origin story. The swaying mass. The soon-to-be hurtling throng of clappers and screamers. Feel it. The air pulses. Everyone's breath is hot and spastic. Open your mouth and try to laugh it off. Feel it. The trees outside petition God for rain. Hands smack the backboard as layup lines form and uncoil.

Riverview vs Hood River. Again and again and again. It's been played and replayed throughout time. It'll be played throughout the future. Good vs Evil. White vs Black. Black if not all White. Black if two drops. Black if brown paper

     SUICIDE RUNNERS

bag. Black if urban. Black if slang. Black if sagging. Black if thug. Black if welfare. Black if White says Black is Black.

And the one who elbowed Nassir in the nose the last time they played Hood River, the one who broke blood like it was bread, the slim, White one, is the object of Riverview's concentrated, seething wrath. He's become the Hood River Villain. Andre the Captain cocks the ball behind his head and dunks it with two hands. The rim rattles. Teeth rattle. The gym rattles. The Earth rattles. The clock counts down the minutes before the first eight-minute quarter commences. Say your goodbyes, because there will be no going back.

But, there's a problem. A secret slowly whispers through the crowd with the potential power to derail the game. The game that Riverview, and its fans, need to win. A secret so terrible that both sides of the home crowd, the White *and* Black sides, are unsure what to do about it. A secret they cannot willfully ignore.

In contrast, the audience chooses to ignore the truth about Greg Hazel. The truth is that his violent outbursts on the court, which went viral, not only hurt the reputation of Riverview's basketball team but hurt Greg's chances at a basketball scholarship. The audience chooses to ignore this truth because Greg, being White—let's just be frank about it—holds the infinite-benefit-of-the-doubt trump card in his back pocket of which all above-average-looking White teenage boys are owners.

The audience also chooses to ignore Coach Day's grain-distilled demons slurring his lucidity and the pre-tip-off injunction that the (unfortunately for Riverview) all-White referees felt necessary to have at midcourt with Rob the Massive Assistant Coach. Out where everyone could plainly see them, in the safety of the public. "Just now, listen, just now listen, Robert," his birth name being said like *Boy,* "we just can't have anymore crazy stuff like the last time you two teams played. And you, well, you know."

The crowd can just as easily ignore the accusing eyes of the White away fans watching Marcel the Supplier, Andre the Captain, Ben the Double Outsider, Manny and et al huddle together under the basket as the horn sounds, forming an impromptu persons-of-color only gathering that's nerve-wracking because they can't hear a word being said between the melanin-rich players.

But, the home crowd cannot ignore the shocking news of Nassir's father's death. Monty Chissler. RIP. They all knew it was coming, his death, but now? An important player's father dying right before tip-off of the biggest game in decades? In one silent, unified moment, as Jenny Owendale sings the national anthem at half-court (Greg checks to see if Brian is watching and, yes, Brian is watching Jenny closely), the home crowd agrees to do that thing where they don't get word to the only person present that the news would truly affect. Devastate. Destroy. Unhinge. Nassir is out there, wedged between Andre the Captain and Greg the Disgrace, his head bowed, waiting, just like the rest of the crowd, for Jenny Owendale to NOT try and hit the high note at the end of the anthem.

It's for own his good, isn't it? They know what's best for Nassir, don't they? How would he control himself if he were to find out Monty died of a heart attack? If he were to know Monty died in the parking lot of the gymnasium? In a dark corner near the emergency exit. The evidence of a small electrical fire that had burned through his pocket. Burned right through the fabric. The make-happy device Mr. Peterson gave him, inserted into him, napalmed Monty from device to brain. Nassir can't know that, can he? Can't know *that* before what's possibly the last organized basketball game of his life, unless some low-rent college in the boonies of Oregon takes pity on Nassir and throws him a scholarship because everyone knows Nassir's mother and her new boyfriend won't be of any help post-graduation. Even the White Riverview fans can acknowledge *that* as truth. So, just before tip-off, the home crowd collectively agrees that it would be what Monty would want for Nassir. For him to play. Play for them. The home crowd. Play, Nassir. Play. Win. He's starting. Nassir is. Because he finally ran a twenty-three-second suicide. And thanks to his suicide, the home crowd can cheer for him.

Andre the Captain wins the tip-off. Nassir is running free. He makes a steal. He dribbles up the sideline, crosses over the defender, pulls up for three, and, "Look," the home crowd shouts, "the ball went through the net and we are all standing and cheering, and if only the cops would agree to stay where they are, up there around the edges of the halo track, behind the drum section and its thumping, insistent bass, like we, like the principal, like the history teacher, Brian, all pleaded that they just wait, to just please fucking wait, officers, Monty's already dead isn't he? we aren't hiding anything, we aren't doing anything wrong, we just want to take this one night for Nassir, for the Chisslers, in memory of Monty, for the good of all, for the good of, look, see, look, look, just, we aren't asking for much, but Andre just set a back-screen for Marcel at the three-point line and Nassir throws an alley-oop to Marcel who catches it with two hands and dunks it on the Hood River Villain's head and Marcel's knees do that thing where they intentionally but just unintentionally-looking-enough swing into the HRV's face and then the back of his head when he, the HRV, ducks and covers, and Marcel lets go of the rim and it snaps back up with a crack and he lands on two feet and he stares at the Hood River bench and flexes both arms, fists balled in front of the black and white striped waistband of his shorts, and yes, he screams, we all scream, and see! had we interrupted the game with news of Monty's predictable demise, everyone would've been robbed of this fantastic, eternal moment that's now being topped off by the White kid with the samurai bandana and the Bronco flag running up the sideline with the flag flying high and rippling behind him, and he whips it back and forth and, yes, we implore you, play that fucking song, Oboe Kid! play it so that when we remember this moment we won't remember Monty's death or Nassir's unknowing laughter out there on the court, but instead we'll remember the cheerleaders and their flashing ruffle of ecstasy and that, because of Monty's death, this was just another night we were reminded that we, the White part of the crowd, are Human."

38
When Jasmine Became a Quasi-Peterson

A handful of years ago, Jasmine was listening to the news on the radio about the upheaval in Algeria, which raised serious concerns about an impending mass influx of refugees into Europe, when the story was interrupted by a commercial for: "Early-onset Alzheimer's? Dementia? Depression? Are you, or someone you know struggling with any of these, and many other previously believed to be incurable afflictions? Have you tried everything? Has your doctor prescribed every pill under the sun? Well, look no further, Deep Brain Stimulation is—"

Greg and Nassir were in the living room doing homework (Nassir helping Greg with his honors classes that Nassir wasn't even in), and Nassir said, "The long-lasting blessing of the colonizers strikes again!" At the time, Jasmine didn't know what that meant but she looked it up later and learned all about the French colonizing Algeria. Anyway, the point of the matter is that she called the number listed after the advertisement for Deep Brain Stimulation. Two days later, she was sitting in a consultation room at the clinic where, unbeknownst to her, Mr. Peterson had recently been hired as a D.B.S surgical technician, and she asked questions hoping to find answers for Monty Chissler. Mr. Peterson told Jasmine it was just an electrical problem in Monty's brain. For her, it was something like love at first sight. Only *something* like it because, post-Trench, she wasn't sure she should try to find love again. Mr. Peterson asked Jasmine out to dinner that same night. They were married eight months later by a city official in the courthouse downtown.

39
The Second Quarter

Freestylers in lanes one and two. Backstrokers in lane three. Breaststrokers in lane four. Timed laps in lanes five through eight. The Man Named Trench is in lane one. Plowing through the water. Goggles sucked tight to his face. His graying hair clipped even tighter to his scalp. Blue and red lights dance across the ceiling above the pool. The chlorine is nauseating. Trench somersaults underwater, pushing off the far end, headed back to complete a lap. His head crests above the water, looking to his right, he gets a glimpse of the ambulance outside, in the parking lot, before he dips back under the water. A missile. He's been crawling to us since the beginning. Aimed at finality.

The police officers moved into position between the first and second quarters. Moved in that half-robotic way they do. Chests stuck on inhale. One of the White officers could barely twist his neck when he looked left and right. Their walkie-talkies chirped. In unison, they turned the volume down. They posed with their hands on their hips, their fingers looped into their belts in that practiced way they think communicates unquestionable authority. Communicates do not resist. Communicates do not run. Do not breathe. Do not wear your hoodie in public. Do not walk past a house where a White woman lives. Do not *be*, Nassir. And the Black section of the home crowd hopes that these blue soldiers, this trigger-happy breed, are equipped with toy guns.

Greg elbows Nassir, "Look. Are any of them the ones who showed up on Christmas?"

"They're all the same."

The referee blows the whistle. Hands the ball to Nassir. The crowd claps nervously. Claps in that encouraging way. Claps to build a floor underneath Nassir.

"I know it's a reductive thing to say," Nassir continues. "Because, obviously, the Black officer up there, and the Latina, too, they've had different life experiences than the White guy with the stiff neck. But. They've been lactified, indoctrinated. Their identities have become cucks to their own colonized histories."

The referee counts the seconds, "One, two, three, four." Just before he reaches five, Nassir passes the ball to Greg from under their basket.

"I don't know if I know what you mean, Nassir." Greg dribbles up the court. "But whatever happens, I'm with you."

"I need an accomplice, Greg, not just a best friend."

Nassir sets a screen for Greg. Greg hesitates and then makes two quick dribbles, forcing his defender to chase him over the screen. When Nassir's defender slides in front of Greg, he drops a pocket pass to Nassir.

"But even then," Nassir says, eyeing the police, jab-stepping, "it's *me* they want."

Greg sets a screen for Andre the Captain, who flares to the corner. Nassir throws a perfect skip pass over the heads of two defenders. Andre catches the ball. The crowd anticipates greatness.

"Do I look like Tamir, Greg?"

"No."

"Do I look like Trayvon?"

"No."

The police are moving down the bleachers. Closer to the

court. The blue and red lights behind them, spinning against the windows, are now so violently bright that it's hard for anyone to continue ignoring them.

"Your story is going to be different!" Greg yells across the court to Nassir, as Andre drives to the paint and is fouled.

"The last thing my dad said to me was, 'We aren't allowed a narrative, Nassir. We have to have agency first. Agency precedes narrative.' I told him I didn't know what he was talking about, but I said it sounded right. Sounded like a terrible truth."

"When?"

"I saw him a week ago when I went to the motel to visit my mom. But she wasn't there. Her White boyfriend told me she was somewhere else. And then I saw my dad on the way back to your house."

"How'd he look?"

"Inverted."

Riverview is up by four. Coach Day paces in front of the bench. Paces to keep his blood flowing. To keep from tottering. Rob the Massive Assistant Coach stands, sits, cringes, yells and glares at the ref.

Andre the Captain shoots the first of his two free-throws. He is going to Oregon State next year on a full basketball scholarship. His brothers and sisters are in the stands with his parents. They cheer and scream as he makes both free throws. They cheer because his form is perfect and practiced. They cheer like everything depends on it. On him hearing their cheers.

Greg sees Shane the Youth Pastor step in front of the White police officer, stopping him from making it down to the Riverview bench. Gilliam is next to Shane. And Gilliam points to Nassir. The tension splits atoms.

Nassir and Greg are at the top of the trapping 2-1-2 zone, screaming "Dog! Dog! Dog! Dog!" at the Hood River Villain.

40
When Doves Cry

Shasta watches from the safety of the server station as the hostess guides Mr. and Mrs. Meyers, Shasta's elderly regulars, into her section. She tried to get the night off to go to Greg's game, but no one was available to cover her shift. Shasta makes her way to the table. She feels enormous. She's a little past eight months now. But she feels like the whole galaxy is inside of her. Like she's going to give birth to every known planet in the entire fucking—

"Welcome back, Mr. and Mrs. Meyers, it's so good to see you two again."

Mr. Meyers has deteriorated with age. He is an opera of infinitesimally small sounds. Tiny, constant, grumbles and grunts, lip-smacks and sticky tongue-clicks.

"Oh, Shasta, why do they still have you working?" Mrs. Meyers says. "You have to be so close?"

Mr. Meyers murmurs his choral backup of blinks and mouth tremors.

"Just a little less than a month, they say."

"You're just beautiful." Mrs. Meyers reaches out her thin hand and squeezes Shasta's. There's a hint of jealousy there. A hint of regret. A hint of, *Look at my husband, decaying in his seat. Listen to my husband, Shasta, can you hear death approaching?*

"Ah shit... oh my god—"

"I guess he'll take the Bordeaux again and I'll have, you know, Shasta, I guess tonight I'll have—"

But, S.O.S. because water is cascading down Shasta's legs. Fluid breaking, darkening her gray work pants. She looks down in disbelief. In seconds, the restaurant swirls about Shasta and her puddle. And Mrs. Meyers knows that look. Mrs. Meyers is crying, she's so happy. Mr. Meyers fumbles his hands and says, "Oh… oh… oh!"

Out in the parking lot, Mr. Jones ushers Shasta to his car and helps her into the passenger seat. "Are you comfortable? Do you need anything? Water? For the drive?" Mr. Jones is sweating from the brow. He's already consumed two three-fingered Scotches. He wasn't planning on an emergency journey to the hospital.

"I'll be fine, I just, I guess I need to get to the hospital?"

"That you do." Mr. Jones shuts her door and runs around to the driver's side. Shasta's fellow servers run outside and laugh and cry and wave and they sing *When Doves Cry* in perfect harmony. The chef barges through the door just in time to hit the sensual high notes. Mr. Jones, just before he dips into the car, yells out, "A round of drinks on me!"

Inside the car, he looks at Shasta, "Shasta. This may be as close as I'll ever get to a son or daughter of my own ever having a baby. Ever having to do this for a son or daughter. As you probably know, my son is gay. And that's a beautiful thing, but, as you know—"

"Mr. Jones, please!"

"Right."

The ignition turns over. The engine roars. Yellow lights are sped through. Red lights are completely ignored. This is how we all come into the world. This is the only way. Shasta tries to concentrate on doing the *hee-hee-whose* thing, but she can't help but notice the beads of perspiration rolling down Mr. Jones's nose.

"Are you—hee-hee-whose—okay?"

"I'm fine. Was it just me, or were the staff singing *When Doves Cry* as we left?"

"Mr. Jones."

"You're right. We're almost there. That's the question, isn't it though: Who will your child end up being like?"

"Hee-hee-whose. Hee-hee-whose."

"You're right. Hold on!"

Brian got the call during halftime and now *it*, fatherhood, the moment it has all led up to, is at last happening—a month early. A month early? So what, right? So the baby will spend some time in the NICU? Who cares! It'll all work out, won't it? Shasta's not Black, she's White! And it's Black women who are 40% more likely to die during birth, right? Brian's woke, as the kids say, he gets it.

When Shasta called, she was *hurtling towards the hospital.* Her words. She asked if Brian would call Matheson for her. And Jasmine, too.

"Yes, honey," Brian accidentally screamed, "I'd do anything for you, you know that! You should never question that. Someday, before you know it, we'll be celebrating our fiftieth anniversary with our kids and grandchildren—and what is that, the fiftieth? is it the Golden Anniversary? I'll get you bricks of gold, Shasta! I will! Wait. Who is singing *When Doves Cry*? Why is Mr. Jones signing *When Doves Cry*?"

"I don't know why! But we're almost there, I can see the sign in the distance. Providence! Are you almost here, babe?"

Mr. Jones *is* crying. He's just so fucking happy and incredibly drunk and the cross on top of Providence Hospital is a sign, isn't it? Literally and metaphorically, Mr. Jones screams.

"LITERALLY AND METAPHORICALLY!"

Shasta starts to cry.

"Shasta, listen to me: Love your son. Promise me, Shasta."

"I'm having a girl."

"If you don't love your son, I'll have to fire you!" They buh-bump over a speed bump into the ER's parking lot and Shasta's head knocks against the ceiling of the car. "I can sing Prince, you know?" Mr Jones continues. "I can love Prince *and* his music. So why not my son? Shasta! Love your son! Shasta, listen, Prince changed his name to a man-slash-woman sign and guess what?" Shasta barrels out of the car and runs towards the sliding doors of the ER. Well, she's more like waddle-running really, but who cares. "That's right! I still loved him!" Mr. Jones yells to her through the open passenger-side window. "I still loved Prince, no matter what!"

Whoosh, whoosh. The sliding doors open and close and Mr. Jones watches until he can't see Shasta anymore. He rests his head against the headrest of his seat.

"Mr. Matheson, this is Brian."

"Go ahead."

"Shasta went into labor!"

"Tell her that when she was young I used to watch her play in the backyard, and when she picked the taraxacums and blew the fluffed seeds into the wind and giggled, tell her that I smiled, and that I have no regrets."

"What's a taraxacum, sir?"

"Mrs. Peterson—"

"It's Booker, you know that, but call me Jasmine, Brian."

"Jasmine, she's here! She's early, but Shasta wants you there, can you make it?"

"She was so embarrassed by my public apology. In the end, it wasn't all that public, now was it, an. No, AND!"

"Is she going to be like you, Jasmine?"

"Does that worry you? My counselor, Tyrell, told me the past is best left unsaid."

"That sounds like terrible advice, Mrs. Booker."

"It's Peter—no. You're right. It's Booker. *Miss Booker*. I've always been a Booker."

The truth is: The baby girl who is crowning, who makes Brian faint with her bloody and alien-like entrance into the world, who forces Matheson to burst into the room and drag his son-in-law out into the gleaming hallway, who makes Shasta realize that anything from this point on will never be as painful and as beautiful and as hateful and as filled with love as this thirty-eight hour moment has been, could be Gerald's baby.

She watches Matheson drag her husband out of the room. They are replaced at her side by her rippling mother. And now Jasmine's hand is on her forehead, and then a cool washcloth is next and it feels like an ocean of violets in bloom. Jasmine kisses her on the cheek and whispers in her ear that she's doing great and that she is so proud of her. Shasta reaches out and grabs Jasmine's hand and now this will be the only memory that matters.

41
The 3ʳᵈ Quarter

1. I am dreaming. 2. This has been a dream. 3. Those seated and sweating around me are only alive in my dream. 4. I think and I speak and I talk in threes because our brains are supposedly wired to think in threes, to respond to threes, because of the Holy Trinity. 5. Because of the three days White Jesus spent inside the tomb. 6. I hear Naya's voice calling to me. 7. Where is she? 8. She is banging on the rock they rolled into place. 9. She is raising me out of my slumber. 10. We are up by eight and have two quarters left to play and Naya bangs on the locker room door and calls into my dream, "Nassir, Nassir, I need to see Nassir." 11. I am dreaming. 12. It is only a dream. 13. Greg shakes me and pulls the nails from my palms.

14. I shake Nassir. 15. He is staring into a flaming nothing. 16. Coach has stopped talking, stopped cursing. 17. He doesn't even seem mad. 18. He whirls around to the whiteboard and draws lines and circles and more lines through those circles and he wants everything to be impossibly linear. 19. I shake Nassir harder. 20. I say, "Nassir, Nassir, Naya needs to see you." 21. It is my stepfather's fault. 22. It is Trench's fault 23. And I can hear him, swimming in the pool.

24. I am standing in the hallway outside the locker room and my dream teammates are clumped together just inside

the doorway, watching me and Naya. 25. Naya is crying. 26. I am dreaming that she is crying. 27. I reach out my hand and wipe her tears away and they are boiling hot. 28. She holds my hand next to her dream face. 29. She tells me that my dad has died. 30. "Monty is dead, Nassir." 31. "Do you hear me?" 32. "Nassir, your dad is dead." 33. "He had a heart attack." 34. "His heart failed him." 35. But I am dreaming. 36. But this is a dream. 37. Her words, the letters, are red.

38. I am standing next to Nassir and Naya, and Nassir tries to wipe the tears from her face but they burn his fingers. 39. Coach can't, he won't decide if he needs to say something to Nassir's face. 40. I tell Coach it's my fault. 41. Coach says, "We need to go back out there, boys." 42. I tell him that it is the Father's fault. 43. Coach says, "You don't have to come out if you don't want to, Nassir." 44. "It's just a game, Nassir."

45. It is a dream.

46. The horn sounds and Riverview files back onto the floor. 47. The home crowd stands, waiting. 48. The Hood River team forgoes their huddle, also waiting, also watching the slow-moving line of Riverview players. 49. The home crowd now knows that they forgot to *not* tell the cheerleaders. 50. They forgot to keep the news of Monty's death from Naya. 51. The band director calls out *Louie, Louie*, feeling duty-bound to break the silence, and he thrusts his arms up and then crashes them down, but the Oboe Player screams out for everyone to, instead, follow his lead as he plays the first few somber notes of *Just a Closer Walk with Thee*. 52. The First Chair Clarinet stands, joined by the Trumpets and the Brass section, all rising onto the balls of their feet, their tippy toes,

and they blow in, they lay into the cavern of the gymnasium the slow dirge of a funeral march. 53. The Riverview second-liners sway onto the court, step by slow step. 54. The entire band stands up and the Drums and the Sax are now blowing and drumming and the low, slow, mournful notes lay there for everyone to hear, over and over. 55. It can no longer be ignored. 56. Someone from the crowd lets out a wail. 57. A spirit washes over them. 58. Andre the Captain's mother wails. 59. The police, not trained for empathy, for tears, recede into the dark of the night.

60. I am dreaming. 62. I am marching, swaying, slow and low and in line and it must be a dream. 63. Coach grabs me by the shoulders and mouths the words, Are you sure you want to play? but all I can hear is the snare drum. 64. I am dreaming and I say, "Yes." 65. The whistle blows and the referee calls both teams back onto the floor. 66. The Drummer goes solo and picks up the expiring beat as the Oboe player calls out "A-FLAT!" and my march quickens.

67. I pass the ball to Nassir and someone in the stands dances in their row and slaps a tambourine. 68. An entire section of Tambouriners materializes. 69. People send their screams to the heavens. 70. And people are singing *Down by the River They Walk*. 71. Down by the river we will all go. 72. A woman faints into a man's arm. 73. Another. 74. Another. 75. Shane the Youth Pastor places his hand on the foreheads of men and women and heals them. 76. But I can hear Trench, in the pool. I can hear him coming for me and Nassir. 77. Shane spins in time to the music, letting the love of the savior flow through his right hand, and women and men fall into the arms of those behind them, Black and White alike. 78. They are emptying themselves of all that God can

count. 79. The music dies down. 80. We are suddenly and inexplicably down by five.

81. I am dreaming. 82. This is all a dream. 83. Naya told me that my father died and I told Greg that it was his fault and he explained to me that, if he's been reading the books I've given him correctly, it was all of the White fathers' fault, and maybe even Thee Father's fault. 84. Where is my dad? 85. Where is my mom? 86. Has she forsaken the White half of me?

87. I tell Andre and Marcel and Manny and Nassir, as we walk back to the bench, down by five, that if we lose this game we won't have to play any more games, that we can finally rest. 88. They laugh, they say they can never rest. 89. Eyes explode. 90. Mouths eject lips.

91. I am here.

92. Where are you?

93. I am dreaming.

42
The 4ᵗʰ Quarter

Manny performed twenty textbook pushups at center court during the third intermission. He jumped up after the twentieth and implored the crowd to give way to the screaming inside them. "Fill us!" he yelled. He was extremely Clear and of Clean Conscious.

Eight minutes. Greg knows this should be the most exciting eight minutes of his life. Forget the best friend whose face looks like it is falling off his skull. Forget that his mom had to run out at halftime to be with Shasta. Forget that Trench is in the building. That Greg can FEEL him in the building. Forget it all. Basketball is supposed to grant freedom. Salvation. It's supposed to feel like flying through the air on a cloudless day with nothing in sight except a slowly setting sun and all the hues of all the pinkish colors.

Minute 1: dribble dribble dribble dribble, pass, pass, screen, jump for rebound, swing elbows, run back on defense, squat, slide slide slide slide, wave arms and hands, yell defense defense defense, ball ball ball, box out, sprint down sideline, catch ball, dribble dribble, jump, duck under basket, pat backboard on other side, two points, down three, run back on defense, turn and backpedal, look to sideline, cheerleaders, Jenny Owendale pops her gum, POP POP POP POP, neck snaps to the right, ringing in ear, didn't see screen being set, cuss at floor, cuss at teammate for not calling screen, cuss at everything, crowd groans, run back on offense, catch ball, pass pass pass pass, ringing in ears, catch ball, throw bounce pass, ref blows whistle.

Minute 2: Coach Day is furious. "A fucking bounce pass! We're down by five and you throw a fucking bounce pass?!" Coach Day is epileptic with anger. An older White man in the crowd stands up and yells, "If you don't win, I will go home and be forced to hate my life for the next week!"

Minute 3: Down three. Nassir needs to be at the block for the play to begin, but he's listless, he's crying, he's burning up, he's sweating through his tears. The ball is stolen from Marcel the Supplier by the Hood River Villain who sprints towards the other basket, his dribbles long and exaggerated, and only Ben Jones, the Self-Advertised Double Outsider, is close enough to do anything about it. RMAC jumps up and yells, "GET HIM GET HIM GET HIM!" The crowd stomps their feet and implores Ben Jones to run faster, to foul him harder. The seconds drip by. Legs become catatonic. Bodies give into rigor mortis. From the three-point line, elbowing anyone close enough to injure, Greg watches Ben Jones jump with the HRV and violently slam his arms down onto the HRV's shoulders. This is what the home crowd wanted. The Double Outsider is called for an intentional foul. Andre and Marcel pull Ben Jones up off the floor victoriously. "Of course it's fucking intentional, you stupid fucking idiots!" Greg screams into the huddle of referees. And another whistle, this time a technical foul. Hands making a T and then a finger pointing at Greg. The home crowd groans. Coach Murgle, the George Fox coach, smiles. Jenny Owendale POPS her gum in the momentary silence.

Minute 4: The Hood River Villain steps to the free throw line. He was awarded four shots: two for the Obviously Intentional Foul, plus another two for the technical against Greg, and then Hood River will be given possession following the free throws. The gym quakes. Fans hammer their feet into the plastic boards of the bleachers. Both teams clump together on either side of him, just behind the three-point line. Greg will walk on. No, that's not right. He won't walk on. He won't even go to UCSB because it's ludicrously expensive, and Father Figure 3.0 said, "It's not like your dad's going to help pay." Nassir's hands grip the fabric of his shorts. He is playing the game but his brain is a sprinkler, stuck trying to ke-ke-ke-ke back to Monty. Andre says to Ben Jones, "You're riding with us tonight." The party is at Jenny Owendale's house, as always, and Ben is now, finally, part of the crew. Bump bump bump clang. The crowd goes wild. The HRV only makes one out of four and his coach can't even look at the kid because he is an utterly disgusting useless fuck.

Minute 5: I blacked out. I tried to block It out, blot out my dead dad, and I blacked out instead. When I came to I had the ball in my hands and was already midway through the motions I go through to shoot a jumper. I had jab-stepped and pump-faked and was already raising my arms above my head with the ball in my hands and my stomach plummeted into a sinkhole. "This is basketball," I said to myself. "This matters."

Minute 6: Dear Dad,
 This is your son, Greg. Tell me, am I making you proud?

Minute 6:30: *Nassir, come in, can you hear me?*
  Greg, you're coming in loud and clear.

Minute 7: Andre the Captain scores seven straight points. The home crowd slaps their hands together in unison. Andre is at the line shooting a free throw. He makes the free throw and now Riverview is up by one and the world rights itself on its axis. All that was upside down is now right-side up and makes perfect sense. Hood River calls a timeout and everyone knows that a play will be called for the Hood River Villain. If he wins the game for Hood River, every Riverview fan of every color will rush the floor and tear him limb from limb. This is basketball, Greg keeps telling himself, as he and his brothers huddle around Coach Day. This is only basketball. Greg looks for his father in the stands, as Coach Day yells deliriously and draws deliriously and screams even more deliriously. Nassir nods his head feverishly. The whistle is blown and all the players' guts tell them that they are supposed to run a suicide. Nassir convulses, knowing he'll never again make a 23. How many more whistles? How many more suicides? Coach Day says, "Let's do this for Monty." And everyone nods and Nassir melts into a puddle and evaporates and someone should cry. Hood River passes the ball in underneath their own basket. Greg and Nassir trap and press the guard the whole way up. Every fiber of every muscle inside their bodies wants to quit. Wants more oxygen. Wants time to tick faster. Wants the end, now. Wants to run away. Wants to escape the moment they might see Trench. Escape Monty's death. The guard moves the ball past half-court and Riverview drops into a man-to-man defense, denying every pass. The HRV gets the ball at the top of the key. Andre hand-checks him. As the minute ticks down, the HRV makes a move to his right and Andre lets him past, expecting Marcel the Supplier and Ben Jones the Double outsider to close down the lane to the basket, but they are not there and

Minute 8: the HRV jumps off his left leg and uses his right hand to swoop towards the basket. Hearts and minds shatter inside the Riverview fans and nothing will ever stop the bleeding if the shot goes in. The ball goes through the hoop. The ball is quickly passed to Greg, who sprints up the court, dribbling with his left hand the whole way. A timeout is called once he crosses half-court. There's time for one last possession. Time collapses on itself. There was never a before. There was always only now. The crowd is silent, except for the grumbles and whispers regarding who should get the ball and where and how and when. All eyes are on Coach Day. Nassir can't hold his head up. He contemplates the floor and the shoes gathered around his own. Marcel's Jordans liquefy around his feet. Andre the Captain wants the ball. Marcel the Supplier wants Andre to have the ball. Greg can feel every blood vessel pop inside each vein. Everyone's jerseys are soaked through. The play is called for Andre. A double-screen on the baseline for Ben Jones the Double Outsider as a second option. Manny is so high that he honestly believes Ben will make the shot if the ball goes to him. Manny whispers to Ben, his arm around Ben's shoulders, "Ben, listen to me, Ben the Double Outsider, don't think about anything. It's how I get through life." And Ben knows that Manny is correct. The whistle blows and suicides laugh at the players. The crowd is spastic. The parents of the players bite their fingers off. Andre has the ball and the minute never ends. Marcel sets a decoy screen and slips out to the right side before cutting through the key. Andre uses the half-step he gets on his defender and crashes to the left. The audience can't breathe but screams instead. Greg and Nassir are shoulder to shoulder, covering their nuts, as Ben Jones the Double Outsider runs the baseline to the right, rubbing his man off the double-screen, popping wide open just past the three-point line at the same moment Andre is double-teamed. The clock ticks down to three seconds, and if the world ended right now no one would notice. White Jesus himself could be allowing sinners and people of all colors and immigrants from brown countries into Heaven, free of charge, regardless of what they believe or who they voted for, and not one White person inside the gymnasium would give two aborted fucks about it. Andre jumps, and the defender's hands are all over him. Greg watches Andre think about the shot, but he catches sight of Ben at the last moment and fires a pass to The Double Outsider. Ben's hands envelop the ball. The crowd holds their breath. Ben does exactly what Manny told him to do. He thinks about absolutely nothing. He feels free. Empty of thought. He finds The Zone. The Zone finds him. The ball goes through the bottom of the net. The horn erupts. The crowd piles on top of Ben. Andre and Manny sprint towards the heap of euphoria. The kid with the samurai bandana and the flag rips it left and right. The Oboe leads the band in a frenzied version of some deep-cut Tupac song that only he knows. Greg and Nassir are accosted by Naya and Jenny Owendale and the rest of the cheerleaders. Greg grabs Jenny Owendale by the hands and asks her to heal him. Asks her to find his father and ask him if he's proud of Greg. Jenny Owendale blows the biggest bubble Greg's ever seen with her gum, it pops all over her face. Marcel levitates, floats, feet on the heads of revelers, and says, "My job here is done. We are CLEAR and finally of CLEAN CONSCIOUS." Rob the Massive Assistant Coach has Nassir and Greg in a double-headlock, loving them with all his might. The team huddles together amid the frenzy inside a bubble of happiness that can never be popped as Andre and Marcel shout about destiny and how this is the team of destiny that will put Riverview on the map. The team that will never be forgotten. Nassir and Greg hold on to the men around them. Someone says, "This is for your dad, Nassir." And that's the fucking worst.

After the game, long after everyone else made their way to the party, Greg and Nassir are still in the locker room, slowly putting their costumes back on.

"When do you think the funeral will be?" Greg asks.

"I don't know."

"Want to go to the party tonight?"

"Yes. Congratulations, by the way."

"For what?"

"You're an uncle."

"Oh. Right. Thanks."

What do you say to a best friend whose dad just died of a heart attack, right outside of the gymnasium, during the last regular season game of the season? Do you say, *I can't imagine.* Or, should it be a question: *I can't imagine?* Do you pat him on the shoulder? Hug him? Do you say, *You can stay with us as long as you need, since your mom has gone AWOL.* Or, do you say, *Once we graduate we'll get our own place, together, then we'll go to the same school next fall, the same college, be roommates, like the movies, like best friends do, and we will leave all this behind.*

Greg doesn't say anything. They just sit there and listen to each other breathe. They hope they both breathe forever.

But they hear a door creak open, somewhere in the recesses of the locker room. The hollow echo of footsteps. A man's voice asking but not really asking another man, "Whatd'ya say."

Greg knows that voice. Knows that meaningless phrase.

Nassir notices Greg's attention focused on a point in the middle distance.

"What?"

"It's him."

"Who?"

"Trench."

The man who left his mom with a black eye. Left the house with a broken coffee table. Glass shattered on the carpet. Left Greg and Nassir with bloody fingers from picking glass out of the depths of the thick fabric.

Like the whistle in Coach Day's mouth, like suicides, Trench's voice induces rage. A rage that connects. That fills. That makes sense. Suddenly, Greg is up, moving with purpose through the locker room toward the entrance to the pool. Nassir is right beside him. They round a corner and see Trench, with a towel wrapped around his waist, fresh from the pool. Trench, the man who left Jasmine sprawled on the floor. Trench rubs the water out of his silver hair.

Greg runs toward Trench, past the green lockers, the black walls, the white lights flickering through his eyes, and all Greg can see is a beautiful, deep red. Nassir doesn't have a look on his face. Nassir is blank. Is gone, already. But Greg can't see that, because the red is so pure and smooth. Greg yells, "Hey, Trench!" and he is flying, light as a goddamn feather, happy and free, toward the body of Trench. Trench turns—

And Greg's fists pound the man into the floor. Nassir's fists are next. After a few meaty blows, Trench's head gets wedged between the corner of the lockers and the cement. Can you hear his tooth crack? His jaw dislocate? A barrage of fists. Blood and chlorine fill the air. Someone behind them screams for help.

There is no feeling here. No desire. No thought. Only emptiness. Complete emptiness. Maybe this is Kenosis? Maybe this is what White Pastor was talking about all along? Maybe this is The Zone? Greg and Nassir are synced up, their bodies acting as one. Their knuckles thudding against Trench's bloody flesh. One thought killed after the next. See how Trench's eye swells shut? See his nose twist? He tries to block the punches, but Greg swats his hands away, grabs Trench by the wrist with his left hand, pins his arm above his head, and continues to punch with his right hand. Nassir is crying.

Nassir, are you okay?

I don't think so.

A rush of energy behind them, people screaming for help, saying they should call the police. Trench coughs, spits up blood. Greg hits him again.

"Stop, Greg! He's not moving anymore."

43

Heavy, quick breaths echo off the cement walls as Greg and Nassir run from the locker room to the back exit. They don't have a plan. Except to run to Jenny Owendale's party. Escape across the baseball diamond, through the cold outfield, under the bleachers. Adrenaline blocks out everything but their need to get away. A heavy fog suffocates the night sky.

Down Shaver Street, past the line of cars waiting at the four-way stop, past the Hood River bus. Greg and Nassir bang on the bus's yellow hull and flip off the defeated faces in the dark windows with their blood-caked middle fingers. They keep running. Windows slide down and just run. Windows slide down and "Fuck you motherfuckers!" Cars honking. But no sirens yet. They heard the cries for help as they left the locker room, but no sirens yet.

After a few blocks, they come to a stop. They look both ways. No one has followed them. Sagging power lines buzz overhead. Nassir slowly wraps his jersey around the swelling fist of his right hand. Greg watches. What to say? The streetlights above them are yellow. A luminescent mist. They don't make eye contact. How could they?

"My dad was right, you know."

"About what?"

"My mom's family owned my dad's family, as slaves, back when this all started."

Nassir tightens the jersey around the mountains of his knuckles. He rears back and punches through the driver-side window of the Niemann's Mustang. Glass crunches against the pavement. They just stand there, in front of the broken window. Greg tries to find the words, to remember something. "It's like the book you gave me at the beginning of the season says. Maybe Monty, in the end, felt like he needed to be liberated *from* the world. Like that was his only choice."

"Greg. You read the book?"

Lights come on inside the Niemann's house.

And sirens wail in the distance.

And the reality of the moment washes over them like a tidal wave. A White boy and a Black boy just beat up a White man. Just broke into a car. And the White boy knows he put the Black boy in greater danger than he was already in. Put the Black boy in greater danger than the White boy will ever be in. Again, there are no words. So, instead, here's the perfect plan:

The perfect plan is to drive to Jenny Owendale's house where everyone knows there will be enough alcohol to erase memories. To erase the present. The whole team will be there, erasing. They will be heroes for the night. Right after the final buzzer sounded, amidst the chaos of the win, Jenny Owendale told Greg that she hoped he would be there tonight. "You will lose your virginity to Jenny Owendale," she said. "Isn't that hot?" And Naya told Nassir that she would meet him there, too, and Nassir said, "And then where will we go?"

The perfect plan is that they will park the Mustang down the street from Jenny Owendale's house and walk in like everything is normal. And sure, their hands are a mess, but there's a sink in the house that they can use to wash them.

And sure, maybe the party will come to an awkward halt when they first enter, cold drinks pausing midway to teenage mouths, and maybe reality will cease being ignored and will rush back, front and center, for an incredibly painful cluster of moments, but once the blood on Greg and Nassir's hands are replaced by beer and the perfect waists of Jenny Owendale and Naya, then reality will be pushed so far into the darkness it may never see the light again. That's the plan. It's such a good plan.

Nassir, in the driver's seat now, asks, "You know how to hot-wire a car?"

"No. Fuck. No. I don't."

"Me neither."

Nassir, come in, this is Greg.

Hey, Greg. I think we're in trouble now. I can hear sirens. Police. They're coming for me.

For us, Nassir. For us.

Right.

Nassir rips some wires out from underneath the steering wheel panel. He touches them together. Like they do in the movies. Like best friends do in the movies. They wait for the sparks that will light up the night.

"Fuck. Fuck. Fuck."

The Niemann's front door opens.

Greg sees Mr. Niemann on the front porch, "Let's go."

And they are running, racing towards the past, running even faster than Coach Day's suicides required. Sprinting, sweating, laughing. Blue and red lights ignite the fog behind them.

But look up as you run, just for a second, look up and see how the dark trees pierce the fog. Look up and feel the breeze. Their legs charge through time, together. They are a wave. There is no stopping them.

Run and feel Riverview slip away at the edge of your vision. Run and don't look back. There will be a funeral and the tears will be set free for the man with four holes in his head. There will be time to remember, but now's the time to run. All you can do is run and feel the cold night against your face. The wet sting of the mist. All you can do is run until your shoes fall apart. Run until you never have to speak of this again.

If you run fast enough, everything will be a blur.

Everything will be okay.

ACKNOWLEDGEMENTS

This book would not exist without the love and support of many people throughout the last ten years. First and foremost, my wife and also my partner in bringing this book to life, Krystle May Statler. Without your encouragement, I may never have "finished" it (for the umpteenth time). And, without your artistry and mastery, it quite literally would not be a book in physical form.

To all the writers from that long-lost defunct grad writing program at Otis College of Art and Design, I am forever grateful for your feedback and your thoughtfulness during the early, chaotic stages of the manuscript. A special thanks to Brittany Williams, George Fekaris, Halley Sutton and Justin Wilson for all the laughs, love, drinks and life we lived. And to the teachers, Peter Gadol, Paul Vangelisti, Guy Bennett and Marisa Matarazzo, thank you for giving your time and effort to this project and believing in me when, frankly, you probably shouldn't have.

To Marisa Silver, if I were to create a pie chart of all those people who have helped me in the writing of this book, your portion of the pie would be the biggest and boldest. Your mentorship alone was worth the infinity of loans I saddled myself with while at Otis. Thank you for helping me become a better writer.

To Jesse Taylor and the rest of my Parkrose High School Basketball teammates of the late 1990s, I hope you found love and a good life outside the icy confines of the gym and our coach's maniacal whistle. And to Ron Spratlen, thank you for teaching me how to play and love basketball.

To Jon Veles, Jill Blankenship, Galen Gilbert, JJ Bailey and Bryce Van Kooten—we did it. Right? Those nights in Jon's living room pitching terrible procedural ideas will forever be some of my favorite times in Los Angeles. Here's one: a time-traveling, alcoholic, one-eyed detective solves crimes by jumping into the bodies of bartenders in different eras. Sell it. You're welcome.

To my mom, thank you for never giving up on art. For the past five decades, you have been the best unknown artist in the Pacific Northwest. Thank you for your truly unconditional love and support. And to Del, thank you for always being there for me. Your presence in my life, from Sumner Street to adulthood, has always helped fill the gaps.

To my dad, thank you for being the best father I could have wished for. And to Connie, your unwavering love and kindness will never be forgotten.

To all my sisters, thank you for putting up with me and for sharing your family's lives with me.

In some way or another, each of you mentioned here has helped shape and form the words on the pages of this book. Thank you.

ABOUT THE AUTHOR

Kevin Thomas was born and raised in Portland, Oregon, where he and his wife, Krystle May Statler, currently live. He received an MFA from Otis College of Art & Design where he was awarded the First Book Fellowship for an early draft of *Suicide Runners.* This is his debut novel.